S0-ABB-707

WORM IN THE BUD

Recent Titles by Judith Cook

BLOOD ON THE BORDERS
DEATH OF A LADY'S MAID
KILL THE WITCH
MURDER AT THE ROSE
SCHOOL OF THE NIGHT

DEAD RINGER *

* *available from Severn House*

WORM IN THE BUD

Judith Cook

This first world edition published in Great Britain 2003 by
SEVERN HOUSE PUBLISHERS LTD of
9–15 High Street, Sutton, Surrey SM1 1DF.
This first world edition published in the USA 2004 by
SEVERN HOUSE PUBLISHERS INC of
595 Madison Avenue, New York, N.Y. 10022.

British Library Cataloguing in Publication Data

Cook, Judith, 1933-
Worm in the bud
1. Ex-police officers - England - Fiction
2. Murder - Investigation - England - Cotswold Hills - Fiction
3. Detective and mystery stories
I. Title
823.9'14 [F]

ISBN 0-7278-6013-5

Typeset by Palimpsest Book Production Ltd.,
Polmont, Stirlingshire, Scotland.
Printed and bound in Great Britain by
MPG Books Ltd., Bodmin, Cornwall.

Acknowledgements

My thanks to all those people who contacted me, eventually too many to be listed by name, following my request for information on the Meon Hill murder published in the *Stratford Herald*. Responses ranged from solicitors and ex-police officers to those who, as children, were living nearby at the time. The Meon Hill murder is one of those true mysteries which continues to seize the imagination. I am sincerely grateful to you all. Also to the staff of the Stratford Record Office and the *Stratford Herald*.

Author's Note

On the 14th February 1945 the body of a man was found at the top of Meon Hill, near Stratford-upon-Avon in Warwickshire. A billhook had been driven through his chest and a hayfork through his throat. He had also been hit on the back of the head. Almost from the beginning it was suggested that this was some kind of a ritual sacrifice or witchcraft killing, a legend which has grown massively over the years. The case has never been solved. The facts of the murder, as detailed in this book, are accurate. The surmise is fictional.

While all other places named really exist, there is no such village as Lower Horton on the 'back road' between Stratford and Cheltenham.

Epigraph

Duke: And what's her history?

Viola: A blank, my lord. She never told her love,
But let concealment, like a worm i' the bud,
Feed on her damask cheek: . . .

Twelfth Night Act II, Sc. 4

Prologue

It was the week before Christmas and the rain had been falling steadily all evening as it had for the last two days. The young girl, huddled for shelter against the high stone wall, had been without trade since the previous night. The road running along beside the Millbay docks in Plymouth was regularly used by the downmarket whores, the slightly classier girls working the clubs and pubs of the city's red light district centred on Union Street. The residents of the houses sandwiched in between Union Street and the docks endlessly complained about the women who stood brazenly every few yards along the Millbay road each evening, and in summertime long before it was dark, but to no effect. That part of Plymouth had served that kind of purpose for a good two hundred years or more and as well as men from the country coming to the city for a night out, there was also trade from the naval base and the dockyard close by as well as from a marine barracks not far away.

From early evening a steady stream of vehicles had been travelling up the dock road, throwing waves of water up on to the pavement, but these weren't drivers cruising round looking for paid sex. Schools had broken up and the cars and camper vans belonged to second-home owners or those in search of a Christmas break, steadily making their way to the overnight ferry to Brittany. Eventually the flow ceased and there was a lull before the sound of the siren signalled that the ferry was leaving port. Almost at the same time the rain finally stopped. The girl on the pavement considered her options. It was late, after midnight and a weekday with few people about because of the rain. She would pack it in for the night before she got pneumonia. At which point she saw the lights of a large car coming slowly along the road. Several women stepped out towards the edge of the pavement to flag it down but it continued on its way, then, as it came nearer to her, it slowed to a stop, the engine still running.

The driver wound down his window. 'How much?' he enquired.

She told him. He leaned out to take a better look at her. He saw a small, bone-thin girl. Her dyed red hair clung to her head in rats' tails, the mascara was running down on to her cheeks. Her thin top and brief leopard-spotted skirt were soaked and her thigh-high boots, made of white plastic, grubby and scuffed. She was shivering and had trouble keeping her teeth from chattering and there were goose pimples on her skinny arms. He wondered how old she was. She looked about fourteen, though in actual fact she was nearly twenty. He looked her up and down again: unattractive, no flesh on her, wet through and grubby . . . .

But she was cheap and available and the punter was in a hurry. 'Hop in,' he said.

One

Across the road from his crime bookshop in Bristol, Keith Berry was having coffee with his friend and old colleague, John Latymer. The two men had known each other and worked together for several years when both had been with the West Midlands police. Both had, for different reasons, taken early retirement.

'So you reckon it really is as bad as that? Tess still hasn't come round?'

Latymer sighed. 'I've done my best, Keith, I really have. I've gone over why we got involved in that business in Scotland again and again but I still can't get her to understand what drove me – us – on to pursue it as we did. Now she's given me what amounts to an ultimatum: if I'm not prepared to move to Somerset then she'll go without me.'

'Somerset! Why Somerset? I thought she liked it here.'

'So that she'll be nearer to her daughter who's having her first baby.'

John'd had great hopes of this second marriage. His first had failed in part because of his work, yet another casualty of the high rate of divorce among police officers working all hours God sends. But then both he and his first wife had been very young at the time, she'd wanted children, he hadn't felt ready. The break-up had been pretty devastating at the time, but he'd understood why she'd been driven to finding solace elsewhere, and the last he'd heard of her she was long married with a family. But his relationship with Tess had been quite different. He was older and, he trusted, wiser and she'd been married before and had two children but both were now grown up and apparently living independent lives of their own. When he and Tess met, she'd just decided to give up teaching for much the same reason he'd left the police force: too much bureaucracy, too much paperwork and rapidly diminishing job satisfaction.

From the start this had given them a good deal in common. They got on well, enjoyed each other's company and, after several months of commuting between each other's homes, had bought a house together in a pleasant village near Chepstow and decided to marry. Almost at once Tess had thrown herself enthusiastically into various local activities and acquired a circle of acquaintances, if not friends, the result of which had been a great deal of entertaining and being entertained. It was then he'd felt the first stirrings of doubt. Most of the old villagers had long been priced out of the area and a succession of evenings spent with retired businessmen, bank managers, estate agents and the middle-aged living off investments, left him depressed and restless. He needed something to do, and Tess had been both pleased and understanding when he'd found himself a summer job acting as a tour manager shepherding Americans around the country for Becketts Literary Tours.

But when his last season's tour had included murder, drug running and eventually the involvement of the security services, Tess had been neither pleased nor understanding. Once she'd realized what was going on she'd continually begged him to stop. This wasn't what she'd married him for. For heaven's sake, he'd given up being a policeman, hadn't he? Surely he wasn't proposing to become some kind of private detective? But he'd doggedly gone on to the end even though he felt increasingly that the rift between them was widening. Afterwards he'd done his level best to patch things up with little success. He frankly envied Berry whose wife, Kate, was so much more sympathetic; a point he made to his friend again.

'Whatever I say, she simply doesn't believe I won't get involved in something again. What are you smiling at?'

'Sorry. It's just that . . . it *was* good, wasn't it? The hunt, the old adrenalin rush . . .' He stopped, then changed tack. 'So what do you intend to do? I take it you'll be off again soon?'

'Yes, but on a far more limited itinerary. The effects of 9/11 haven't gone away, there's so much uncertainty, which means that the number of tours has been drastically reduced. A lot of Americans are simply not prepared to risk coming over here any more. So not only are there less tours, we no longer go as far afield. My first two are relatively close to home. They start in London, go on to Oxford and from there to Stratford-upon-Avon, and that's it.' He grimaced. 'From what I recall of a similar tour I did last year, "literary" in Oxford equates almost entirely with detective fiction. Those that read Dorothy Sayers want to see Shrewsbury College, in spite of the fact that she told them it doesn't exist, and the exact spot on the river where Lord Peter Wimsey and Harriet Vane made love in a punt after she'd accepted his proposal at the end of *Gaudy Night.* Then they all want to be taken round "Morse's Oxford" and are quite miffed when they discover the tour doesn't include a trip round the headquarters of Thames Valley Police and they have to make do with the Bodleian Library.

'Stratford's easier, though, there's so much laid on for them that doesn't involve me. They go on a coach trip with a Blue Tour guide who takes them round all the obvious places: Anne Hathaway's cottage, the birthplace, Hall's Croft, Shakespeare's grave and so on. There's a couple of optional talks in the Shakespeare Centre and theatre seats for several plays. There's also a spare day which they can spend shopping, visiting Warwick Castle, or both. I'm really only there to make sure the hotel bookings are OK and see to any emergencies. There are always some, I can't remember a tour when someone didn't manage to leave their luggage behind somewhere.'

'When is this?'

'The first one's next week, the second two weeks later, designed to take in Shakespeare's Birthday celebrations on the 23rd. That party has an extra day added on for it.'

Berry reached into his pocket and took out his small diary. '23rd April . . . let's see. Yes, I thought so. That's when I'm in Stratford at a book fair. Weekend of the 20th, going on until the 24th. So we could meet up, have a chat and a few beers.' He looked at his watch. 'I'd better get back. I've a dealer coming in to look at some second-hand books.'

'I'm sorry to have dragged you out,' said Latymer, 'and bored you with my problems.'

'I'm not bored, I just feel sorry things have turned out as they have. Have you decided what you're going to do?'

Latymer stood up. 'Tess is in Somerset now making the rounds of estate agents. She wants me to go down there with her to look at houses in the gap between the tours. Either way it's going to mean selling the house. If we split up there'll be a reasonable amount each since there's no mortgage, sufficient I suppose for me to buy a flat. God, I thought I'd done with living in flats! Well, I've still not made up my mind. I suppose I'll have to see how it goes.'

Getting away from home helped, but he was feeling little better when he guided his flock into their Stratford hotel a week later, thankful that although he'd been so preoccupied with more pressing matters, everything seemed to have gone well. Before leaving, he and Tess had sat down 'to talk it through' yet again. He still couldn't understand her desire to move to Somerset even if her daughter was expecting a baby. 'It's not as if you're all that far away,' he remonstrated. 'You can be in Taunton within an hour or so of leaving here. And don't you think Diana and her husband might actually prefer not to have you looking over their shoulders all the time?'

Tess could hardly contain herself. 'Diana says she's depending on me being there, not just for when the baby's born, but afterwards. I've even said I'd be prepared to help if she wanted to go back to work. She didn't work so hard to get a good degree to let it go to waste. As for Peter, he seems more than happy.' Latymer said nothing. 'If you'd had children of your own you'd understand.'

There was no answer to that. The upshot had been that he'd at least agreed to go down to Somerset with her for a few days at the end of the first tour, but as he left for London to pick up the Becketts' tourists, he was feeling increasingly that the move would mark the end of their marriage. But what if some miracle happened and he did persuade her to stay together where they were? In the small hours of the morning when everything seems bleak, he'd looked at the prospect of what life would be like: more awful social evenings, nothing more demanding than Becketts tours, watching every word in case it triggered a row.

On the morning of the first day in Stratford, he waved his flock off in the special bus organized to take them round the various places of interest, promising he would be waiting for them when they returned at the end of the afternoon. It was a pleasant, sunny day, if somewhat chilly. Most unusually, knowing he would have time to himself, he'd driven to Stratford and left his car in the tour hotel, then gone up to London by train. Now he got out the road map to help him decide where to go. The Evesham valley was pleasant but the best time to see it was later when the orchards were in full bloom. He looked at his watch. It was only half past ten. He'd have a walk round the town, take in that excellent second-hand bookshop he'd noticed when he was here last, then . . . He looked at the map again . . . Go to Welford for lunch. Legend had it that Shakespeare had taken his last drink at The Bell in Welford in the company of his old friends Ben Jonson and Michael Drayton, catching the chill that killed him from walking or riding home in the rain. He must remember to tell his party the story when he saw them again in the evening.

The afternoon was clouding over as he left the pub after an excellent lunch. He'd realized that it was the first place after Stratford where it was possible to cross the River Avon by road, and so he decided to drive over to the other side then go where the fancy took him. The road on to which he turned, which ran along the edge of the Cotswolds, would eventually lead him circuitously on to Cheltenham, but he didn't want to go that far. He negotiated a series of bends, noticing as he did so a signpost to Lower Quinton. The name rang a faint bell but he couldn't recall why. He drove on a few miles further until he reached the outskirts of a village which he learned from the sign was Lower Horton. A brown notice pointing left informed him that it boasted an interesting fourteenth-century church.

He'd time to spare, so why not? He turned off into the winding lane leading down to the church, parked on the green opposite, then went into the churchyard through a pretty lych gate. In spite of being off the beaten track, the path up to the church looked well-used. The building itself was small and plain and he was wondering what made it so special when he glanced up at the roof. All round the edge, above the gutters, was a riot of stone carvings: heads of all kinds, men, women and children, sad and happy, comical and grim, no doubt based on the local people of the time, as well as mythical beasts such as dragons and unicorns, alongside hares, birds, fish, even an eel. He walked round enchanted until he again reached the front door to discover that the stone posts each side of it were also elaborately carved, the one on the left depicting the Green Man, that throwback to an older faith so often found in old churches. This one was emerging grinning from a mass of fruit-bearing greenery. He tried the door and was surprised to find it open, so many churches were locked these days.

The inside was plain, the walls simply whitewashed. A notice informed him that morning services were held every fourth Sunday and gave a telephone number for the churchwarden. There was a smell of damp. He picked up a leaflet which informed him that the font dated back to 1108, a gift from the local baron whose tomb was on the right side of the chancel. The church's main claim to fame, it continued, was the carved heads. He went outside, blinking in the sunlight. Old graveyards always interested him. His father, a keen amateur historian, had always dragged the family to any church or castle of interest when they were out for the day. 'You'll find the history of a place written in the old graveyards', had been his perennial comment, while his children had rolled their eyes and mouthed 'not again!' But the old man had been right.

The grass around the graves close to the church had been perfunctorily cut but even so early in the year, brambles and ground elder grew thick in the oldest part. A splash of colour caught his eye and he went over to see what it was, the brambles catching at his trousers, and discovered it came from bunches of daffodils and freesias placed in a stoneware pot in front of a small gravestone. He bent lower down and saw that the lettering had recently been cleaned up and that the writing, though faint, was now legible. The inscription was very brief: 'Elizabeth Bidford, aged seventeen. And child. Our trust is in the Lord from whom cometh all our help'. The date was 1830. And child? A stillbirth? Did Elizabeth Bidford die in childbirth? It made Latymer think of the poor girl in Hardy's *Far From the Madding Crowd.* What was her name? Fanny Robin, that was it. That was what was chalked on her coffin: 'Fanny Robin. And child'. He straightened up, noticing as he did so that about a square foot of the earth immediately in front of the stone looked as if it had been disturbed, then stamped back into place. Perhaps whoever had brought the flowers had also pulled up some docks and brambles.

As he went back towards the path down from the church, he saw that a woman was coming up the other way. As she came nearer he realized from her dress that this was the vicar, a pleasant-looking woman probably in her forties. She smiled as she came up to him. 'I take it you've admired our roof.'

'It's wonderful. I've never seen anything like it.'

'It's what helps keep us going. Visitors almost always put something in the box. We're merged with three other parishes you see and this is the smallest church of the lot.'

He told her he was surprised to find it unlocked. 'I was holding a wedding rehearsal here this morning but our churchwarden's very good. He lives in that cottage over there. He has the key and when he's in he keeps the church open during the day. It's locked up securely, of course, when it gets dark. But you'd be surprised how many people do come here to see the carvings.'

He was about to go when curiosity got the better of him. 'By the way, can you tell me why someone's put fresh flowers on that old grave over there?' He pointed. 'It's dated 1830.'

The vicar looked surprised. 'No, I can't say I can. Sometimes people leave flowers on the newer graves but I'm afraid that part of the graveyard's been sadly neglected. It's almost impossible to find people willing to look after them nowadays. Over there, you say? Perhaps I'd better have a look.' They went over to the grave together. She bent down, read the inscription, then shook her head. 'I've absolutely no idea why someone should suddenly have taken such an interest.'

'I thought the ground looked as if it might have been disturbed,' Latymer pointed out. 'Nothing major, just as if someone had recently pulled out weeds or scratched the surface of that small patch.'

The vicar looked again. 'I'll have a word with the churchwarden. He might know something about it.' They retraced their steps and she locked the church. 'Where do you live?' He told her. 'Haven't you ever been to Kilpeck then? It's not far from you, just the other side of Monmouth.'

'I've never heard of it.'

'The church there also has carvings all round the roof, even more than ours. You should go and see.' She laughed. 'One is of two gentlemen who seem to be doing something it's better not to try and work out too closely!'

Two

A small but steady stream of people were making their way into one of the small rooms offered for hire at the Conway Hall in Red Lion Square in central London, a venue dedicated to hosting good causes. This particular event was listed as a meeting of the Sustainable Agriculture Forum. The meeting's harassed chairman, Mark Ransom, was frantically shuffling through a pile of papers while at the same time trying to greet people and give last minute instructions to Penelope Cross, who acted as SAF's secretary. She was standing at the door with a clipboard, ticking off the names of those entering the room.

'How many so far?' he called out to her.

She looked down the list and came over to him. 'Twenty-seven. I imagine that must be about it, we know there are a few from the Midlands who can't make it.' She looked at her watch. 'When's this person from Friends of the Earth going to get here? It's half past seven now.'

Mark frowned slightly. 'Didn't I tell you? He rang up this afternoon to say he was very sorry but he couldn't make it. It doesn't really matter, we can manage the protest perfectly well without him.'

In actual fact the adviser from Friends of the Earth had told Mark in no uncertain terms that his proposed action shouldn't go ahead. 'There's been too much activity in the West Midlands recently and landowners are on the lookout for it. Our information is that there are some people based up there only too keen to make an example of those they consider to be wreckers and aren't too fussy about how they set about it. You're a relatively new and inexperienced group, you could even find you've been infiltrated by *agents provocateurs*. You must be on your guard. My advice is to cool it for a while until things have settled down, which they will. After all, there's a wideish window of opportunity, at least another six weeks, before any action need be taken. Also, by then there'll be some of us available to help you. There's no earthly point in risking the wrong sort of publicity. Get in touch again in about four weeks and we'll talk.'

'Surely it would've been better if we could talk it through with them and know we had their full backing,' Penelope persisted. 'I know some of us have had previous experience, but "Friends" are experts. Didn't you ask if they could send someone else?'

'They hadn't got anyone else,' Mark responded, irritably. He looked round the room. Most people were seated, only a handful still standing chatting just inside the door. 'Right, we'll make a start.' He thumped on the table in front of him for silence. 'Have you all got a seat?' There was a scraping of chairs. 'Good evening, everyone. Glad you could make it. Now, Penny will just close the door . . . First off, I'm afraid that Friends of the Earth couldn't send anyone along tonight but since they're confident we know what we're doing, it doesn't really matter all that much. So . . . Penny, will you hand round the photocopies of the actual area with its map reference?' There was a shuffle and muted conversation as the pieces of paper were passed around.

'Everyone got one? Right. You'll see that the farm in question is off the old Cheltenham–Stratford road, not far from the village of Lower Horton. The specific fields on the map reference are about a mile to the west of the village and the lane leading to them is on the right going in the direction of Cheltenham. The area containing the crops is about a quarter of a mile – not sure what it is in metres – from the road. Got it? It's our old friend oilseed rape and the land in question is only a few miles from several of the area's organic farmers. This should give us good local support when the news of our protest breaks.'

'How are we going to get there?' enquired a young man in a neat suit, who looked like an office worker.

'More importantly, how are we going to get there without drawing any attention to ourselves? Between us I reckon we can take most people down by car, though it might be useful if a few of you could go by train to Stratford. We can arrange lifts from there, there's three or four other people involved who live in the area but weren't able to get up to London tonight. Then we'll take it gently. There's no need to meet up until around midnight and the longer we leave it before we do, the less noticeable we'll be. We'll work out who is going in which car and I'll give you my mobile number and one of you can give me yours so that we can all liaise with each other. But be sparing with any calls, you never know who might be listening in. I've bought a new pay as you go one for this trip in the hope it might be slightly more difficult to trace.

'When it gets near the time, the cars can be left in different places, tucked away in back lanes, in the odd lay-by and so on. *X* marks the spot on the map where we finally assemble. There'll be white overalls for everyone and plastic "death's head" masks for those who want to wear one. But they're pretty hot and uncomfortable and I suggest you keep them in a pocket and only use them as a gesture if you're about to get arrested and there are lights and cameras present, which I doubt. We should be so lucky!'

A young woman sitting at the back put up a hand. 'What's the opposition likely to be?'

'I was just coming to that. I'm going to ask James – most of you know James Weaver, I think – to fill us in on who owns the land and so forth. I believe your family used to live near Lower Horton, didn't they, James?'

Weaver, a tall, burly man of about thirty stood up and faced the group. 'Can you all hear me OK? Good. Well, the fields in question belong to a farmer called Bob Wells. Family's been there for umpteen generations. In actual fact he's quite a decent—'

The red-haired man beside him groaned audibly. 'Get on with it. We don't need his family history or a character reference, we've not got all night.'

'I'm explaining the situation, Jeff, because I think it's important and was asked to do so. If the representative from Friends of the Earth was here tonight I'm sure he'd expect us to be as well briefed as possible – there's no point in going at it like a bull at a gate. If you'd been on one of our previous raids you'd know how important this kind of information is. To resume. As I say, Wells is not a bad chap. I understand he's got a short fuse and obviously he'll not be pleased when he finds his experimental crop's been trashed, but he's not vindictive' – Weaver felt his audience becoming restive – 'however . . .' He paused. 'Now please will you listen to this, it really is important.

'Wells's farm used to be the home farm of a large estate and the old manor house nearby belongs to a Lucas Symonds. Symonds and Bob Wells have been close friends since childhood, very close!' This provoked oohs and ahs and a couple of lads gesturing with limp wrists. 'No, I don't mean that. Wells is married with a couple of kids.'

'That doesn't mean anything,' remarked the man in the suit.

'I hadn't realized we were here to discuss people's sexual orientation,' snapped his immediate neighbour.

Mark banged on the table. 'That's enough. Carry on, James, but like the man said, we're not here all night.'

'Not only that,' continued James, raising his voice, 'Bob Wells is married to Symonds' sister. The reason I'm telling you all this is that Symonds is also involved. He now has little land of his own, except for a sizeable garden, because as soon as he inherited the estate he sold most of it off. One chunk is now a golf course, the other went to a housing developer which caused a good bit of local anger at the time. He has business interests in Birmingham and he's seriously rich.'

Jeff yawned loudly. 'I still can't see where the hell all this is leading.' There was a general chorus of assent.

'I understand from my source that it was he who persuaded Wells to join the government's experimental scheme in the first place. He was sorry he'd sold off so much land that he couldn't do it himself as he thinks eventually it'll be a licence to print money. But he's canny with it. You might say he's the acceptable face of GM food. The man they often use on local TV to put the case for it. It might even be that he believes all that stuff about saving the starving in the developing world.

'The fields in question are far closer to Symonds than to Wells and what this is leading to, is that Symonds will treat any attack on Wells' crops as if they were his.

'So while I don't imagine that Wells is given to having any of his fields under surveillance, I wouldn't like to bet on Symonds. He has electronic gates to his own house and a CCTV camera at the back of it. For all we know he might have rigged up some kind of an alarm system so that he can call the police out at the first sign of trouble, or even before if he gets wind that there's something in the offing.' He stopped and turned to Ransom. 'To be honest, Mark, I'm not at all keen on this one.' This produced an outcry. 'Neither of these guys are particularly looking for trouble and, as I've already pointed out, apart from the blip when Symonds sold off the development land, they're well liked; added to which the experimental area itself is a comparatively small one. There are bigger and better targets we could go for later, without so much risk, which would give us really useful publicity. This one might well give us publicity of the wrong sort. However reasonable Wells might be, I couldn't swear the same is true of his farmworkers or neighbours living nearby. Scenes of punch-ups followed by violent arrests on the property of an apparently reasonable farmer whose crops have just been trashed, won't do us any good at all.' He paused. 'I wish the chap from Friends of the Earth had turned up. I'd be really interested to know what he thought after hearing what I've had to say. Didn't he offer you any advice at all?'

Mark shook his head. 'None. Except to wish us well. Are you saying you've got cold feet, James?'

'Not with regard to the campaign as a whole. But I have about this one. Call it instinct or whatever you like – and I've been involved in half a dozen actions of this kind – I just don't like the feel of it.' There was silence as he sat down.

Mark stood up. 'Does anyone else share James's doubts?' Three or four hands went up. 'The rest of you? OK, then we'll get down to the nitty gritty.'

Three quarters of an hour and a number of questions later, Ransom closed the meeting and the members of the group filed out, some coming over to him for a last word, others chatting among themselves. James Weaver was among the last to go and as he came up to the chairman's table hesitated for a moment as if wanting to say something more, then apparently changed his mind and was about to leave the room when Ransom stopped him.

'In view of what you said, James, should we be expecting you to turn up at the weekend or not?'

'I said I'd come and I keep my word. But it's with the greatest reluctance. There's another three days to go, if in the meantime I hear anything else that gives cause for alarm I'll let you know.'

'OK. But I think you're making a mountain out of a molehill. Coming for a drink, Penny?' enquired Ransom as Weaver left.

She shook her head and picked up her coat. 'I don't think so. I'm not in the mood.'

'You haven't let that dismal bugger get to you, have you?'

'He knows a lot more about the area than we do, in fact he knows a lot more about trashing GM crops. Don't you think it might be an idea to get back to Friends of the Earth again and thank them for their backing but telling them what James said. It might be that they'd give you different advice.'

Mark was hardly prepared to admit even to himself that James's advice had so closely mirrored that of Friends of the Earth. He put the thought away. 'I doubt it,' he replied, briskly. 'So far as I'm concerned, the operation's going ahead as planned. Compared to some,' he continued, with the confidence of inexperience, 'this one's relatively simple. Easy-peasy you might say.'

'It was a visitor who drew my attention to it, Fred.' Jane Hutchens, vicar of Lower Horton, was standing with her churchwarden beside the grave of Elizabeth Bidford and her child. 'He asked me why there were fresh flowers on so old a grave and I told him I didn't know and I'd ask you. I meant to mention it last week then other things cropped up and I forgot about it. Anyway, I went back with him to have a look and we both thought that the ground seemed to have been disturbed – just that small patch there immediately in front of the stone. And as you can see the stone itself has been cleaned up.'

The flowers were now well past their best and no longer so noticeable. 'It was the yellow of the daffodils when they were fresh that made him notice the grave.'

The churchwarden knelt down and felt the disturbed patch. 'It's almost as if it's been dug up recently, then flattened again.' He felt down through the soil. 'That's odd. You'd expect to find it overgrown with weeds like all the others but I can't even feel any roots here. Wait there, will you, vicar? There's a trowel in the shed where the mower's kept from the days when they used to let people put plants on the graves.'

He disappeared and Jane Hutchens bent down herself. She felt uneasy. Had something else been buried there? She shivered slightly. At least it didn't look like a hole big enough for a person, but she hoped that they weren't about to unearth the rotting corpse of a family pet, a point she made to the churchwarden when he returned with the trowel.

'Reckon if it was something like that we'd have smelled it by now once the earth was disturbed. Now, I'll just have a go with the trowel and see if there is anything in there which shouldn't be.' He dug around for a few minutes without any success, until suddenly his trowel hit something hard. 'Hang about, now. What's this? I've hit something solid.' He dug away with more energy, throwing up small mounds of soil each side of the grave. Then he reached his hand and arm in. 'It feels like some kind of box.' He grunted. 'Difficult to get out, though, the ground's so heavy down here.' He worked away for another five minutes or so puffing and panting as he did so, then he sat back on his heels. 'Reckon I've got it now, vicar,' he told her, mopping his forehead. 'One more go.' This time, when he reached in, he felt the object move. Very carefully he manoeuvred it out of the ground. 'There you are.' It was a small, highly-varnished, pine box, about a foot square, and very nicely made. It was somewhat stained by earth but the varnish had protected most of it.

Jane looked at it mystified. 'What on earth is it?'

The churchwarden picked it up and shook it slightly. 'It's not very heavy.' He examined it carefully. 'It doesn't look as if it was meant to be opened again – see, it's been firmly screwed down with brass screws. What do you think we should do, vicar?'

'I think we'd better take it along to the police station, tell them where we found it then leave them to decide whether or not to open it.'

By the time Latymer had returned home from Stratford, Tess had already made arrangements with half a dozen estate agents in the Taunton area. She showed him the various leaflets containing the details of property varying from converted cottages to 'executive housing' on new estates. 'Let's see, it's Sunday now, if we go down on Tuesday and stay over the following weekend we could see all these and fix up some more, if we don't find anything suitable and . . .'

'There's no way I can stay over next weekend,' Latymer told her. 'I've a lot to do for the next tour, far more than for the last. They've put some extra venues into the Oxford visit and I've complicated arrangements to make as to who goes to which events for the Shakespeare Birthday celebrations. I can't do it all on email, I actually need to talk to people. If we don't find anything "suitable" then it will have to be left to another time.'

'But suppose we don't find anything we like out of this first batch?'

'It's you who's in this frantic hurry to move, not me. Where's the fire? For God's sake, Tess, can't we leave things as they are for another few weeks?'

'But you promised you'd look at properties with me. And I want to get on with getting an agent round here to give us an idea what this house might fetch.'

Latymer felt the now familiar irritation rising within him. 'I said I'd come down to Somerset with you this week and I'm coming, aren't I? But I'm employed to do a job and there's no way I can spare more than three or four days at most. As to putting this place on the market, surely it would be more sensible to leave all that until we've found something we – or rather you – like.'

She looked at him and shook her head. 'You seem determined to put obstacles in our way.'

'I told you when you first broached the idea that I'm perfectly happy where we are. It's taken all this time to get the house and garden just as we want them yet now you propose selling up. It's a nice place – that's why we chose it, remember? Convenient for Bristol and trains to London. As for Taunton, I wonder if you'll still think moving down there to be on top of your family a good idea after you've spent a couple of years as Diana's unpaid nanny!'

Tess became tearful. 'You're not prepared to make the slightest effort to save our marriage, are you?'

'Do you want it saved? It's you who's been piling on all this pressure, insisting on moving for no good reason. Treating what matters to me as if it's of no account. Perhaps you'll tell me what your input into our marriage has been these last few months? Oh, don't get so upset. Tuesday's OK by me if that's what you want.'

Three

'All right, all right!' shouted Mark Ransom as he ran down the stairs. He flung open the door of his flat to find James and Penny standing outside on the mat. 'There was no need to bang away like that. It's a wonder you haven't had all the neighbours out to see if it's a drugs bust!'

'Your bell still isn't working,' James informed him, 'and we knew you were in as we could see the lights were on, but you didn't seem to hear us.'

'I was busy with some people.' There was a pause.

James looked at him, then through the door. 'Well? Aren't you going to ask us in?'

Looking none too pleased, Mark opened the door wider and his two visitors preceded him up the stairs and into his untidy sitting room, before stopping short. Sitting side by side on the sofa were a couple whose general appearance shrieked 'alternative'. The man, who was white and looked as if he was in his late twenties, sported a Rasta hairstyle of green and orange plaits and a baggy T-shirt so faded that its message was unreadable. The girl sitting next to him wore her hair in two long plaits, had rings through her eyebrows, nose and upper lip and was wearing what looked like an old patchwork quilt. There was a third member of the party, odd too, but in a different way. His face was gaunt and very pale, his eyes deep set, while what remained of his hair, which was receding from his forehead, was dragged back into a thin pony tail. He was dressed with scrupulous neatness entirely in black: black roll-neck sweater, trousers, short black boots. James put his age at about forty-five.

'Sit down, if you can find anywhere. Er . . . these good people have volunteered to take part in our GM crop demo, James. Rowan and Rain – ' he motioned towards the sofa then, to the other man who was sitting in an upright chair – 'and . . . I didn't quite catch your name?'

'Shrieve.'

'And your first name?'

'Shrieve will do.'

Mark was obviously uneasy. 'Well, Rowan, Rain and – er – Shrieve, this is James Weaver and our organization's secretary, Penny Cross.' This was greeted with silence. 'Er . . . coffee anyone?

'Yes,' said James, firmly, 'allow me to help you make it.' He signalled to Penny to stay behind, pushed Mark firmly towards his kitchen, then closed the door behind them. 'Who the hell are they?'

'It seems Jeff told them about our proposed action. He met Rain somewhere or other and he must have said something because she told him she wanted to join the fight against GM crops. So he gave her my phone number and told her to contact me. She called me, so I asked her over and she said could she bring a couple of people she'd met recently at some alternative lifestyle circle. What's wrong with that?'

'Are you quite losing your marbles? You know absolutely nothing about these people. For all you know the Man in Black is from Special Branch.'

Mark filled the kettle. 'You're paranoid.'

'And you're a fool. And why on earth have you changed the date from the Saturday to the Tuesday? After everything'd been decided at the meeting? When Penny came round and told me I didn't believe it, that's why we're here.'

'I've changed it because I've had a better idea. One of the students in the Midlands who's taking part said why didn't we change the action to Tuesday. It's Shakespeare's birthday.'

'Now I've heard everything! When's the next one? Burns' Night?'

'No, you don't understand. On Shakespeare's birthday half the Warwickshire police force will be tied up in Stratford. There's some kind of mega procession during the morning in which a whole pile of dignitaries take part – a representative of the government, possibly the American ambassador, bigwigs from all over the world – and masses of luvvies. There may even be royalty there, Prince Charles's been known to turn up. There's a huge lunchtime thrash in marquees and, I think, some kind of church service, then they all go to the theatre for hours and hours. It's the very last day, therefore, when the local plod'll be going round looking for anti-GM protestors.' The kettle boiled and he poured water into half a dozen mugs.

'I suppose you have a point,' James conceded. 'Have you managed to let everybody know?'

'I've emailed everyone on email and no, I haven't said, "oh by the way, the crop-trashing's been put back a couple of days . . ." I've also seen some people personally and asked them to pass it on. It'll be a bit more difficult for people as it isn't a weekend, that's why I was pleased to get three more volunteers. Help me take this through, will you?'

They re-entered the room to an awkward silence. 'Rain's just been telling us how she spent the summer living in a bender in West Wales,' Penny informed them, rolling her eyes at James.

'So I could get really close to the earth,' she agreed.

'I wish I'd known you then,' said Rowan, his eyes full of admiration. 'It's something I've always wanted to do myself. I'm a vegan too, like you. That's why I think all vegetables should be organic.'

'And you?' enquired James of the gloomy Shrieve. 'Are you a vegan?'

'Shrieve's an expert on old magic,' Rowan put in, before Shrieve had a chance to respond. 'He knows all about the old earth rites and the Mother Goddess and all that sort of thing. He says we have to placate the earth because of what man's doing to it, like they did in the old days. Though, of course, we couldn't do everything they did in the old days. Except in a token way.'

James tried again. 'And what are these rites and such like that can't be done these days, Shrieve?'

Shrieve gave Rain a disparaging look. 'In past times there were rites and ceremonies designed to ensure a good harvest or, in orchard country, a fine and unblemished fruit crop. Even today in parts of the West Country they wassail the cider apples on New Year's Eve, which proves some of the old ways linger on from before the coming of Christianity. Why else do you find green men carved all over our old churches, even cathedrals? Earlier still, of course, more, much more, was demanded by the earth from those who profaned it. Blood was needed to purify it, satisfy it so that it would give plenty in return. It might be that it will take something as drastic as that again to stop the rape of the planet.'

Penny shivered, Mark look embarrassed and James stared at him. 'What on earth do you mean? That we should actually go back to blood sacrifice? What are you proposing? That we dance hand-in-hand in a ring around a wicker man singing "summer is a'cumen in" while the chosen victim fries inside, like in the film?'

'The film of *The Wicker Man* has become a cult because even today people recognize the power of the imagery. But as I've just told you, the ultimate sacrifice demanded from the earth was blood, not ashes. You only have to read *The Golden Bough.* The sacrifice might be willing, or the blood shed in personal combat during a fight to the death. Or it might be that of a scapegoat on behalf of the whole community. Whatever the way, it fed the earth, cleansed the people and gave sustenance to the land.'

Shrieve could hardly have devised a better conversation stopper. After that there was little more to be said except for practicalities. Mark explained that he'd arranged for all those bringing activists in their cars to meet up in the car park of the services by the Pear Tree roundabout just north of Oxford. 'It will be busy, we'll be less noticeable and we can talk in small groups.' The newcomers, however, declined. Mark had given them a photocopy of the map and they would go straight to the rendezvous point about half a mile away. Mark turned to James. 'Oh and as you probably know by now, it'll take place much earlier, about 10.45 while the police are still fully tied up in Stratford.'

Rowan, Rain and Shrieve got up to go and Mark looked at James and Penny as if expecting them to leave at the same time, but they made no effort to move. With a sigh, Mark showed his other three guests downstairs and out of the door.

'I despair,' declared James as he reappeared. 'If "Rowan" and "Rain" – the names sound like a put-on from the start – are who they say they are, then they're the kind of clueless wonders who'll quite likely tell everyone they meet what they're going to be up to.'

'You're prejudiced because of their lifestyle.'

'Maybe. Though you might recall that long ago, before I became a hardworking, freelance graphic artist, I did go to art school where everyone was competing to be alternative. It's not that I object, it's that those two seem so . . . well . . . stagey, too . . . I can't imagine where Jeff met Rain. He works in a City office which she manifestly doesn't, and spends most of his spare time clubbing and that doesn't look like her scene either. As for "Shrieve" . . . the man's a fully paid up nutter.'

'He gave me the creeps,' said Penny, with a shudder. 'I think he actually believed in what he was saying.'

'Make your mind up,' snapped Mark. 'Ten minutes ago you were telling me he might be from Special Branch!'

'That was before all that sick stuff about sacrifices and human blood.'

Mark shook his head in exasperation. 'He was just trying to create an impression. At worst he's a *poseur*. He probably works in a bank. Now I really must get on. I've had to do a deal with a fellow lecturer who's agreed to take my classes for a couple of days when I ring in to say I'm sick and I've a lot of notes to write up. He's a sympathizer and sees this as a way of assisting the cause, so I want to make it as easy for him as possible.'

This time his fellow activists did get up to leave and he went downstairs with them. 'I'll be in touch if there is any change of plan but I'm not anticipating it. Otherwise, see you a week on Tuesday.'

He shut the door firmly behind them and breathed a sigh of relief. He felt the adrenalin running through his veins. He was on a high. He'd been determined, ever since taking part in his first action against GM crop planting, to put on a spectacular of his own and nothing, nothing was going to prevent it.

'What on earth can we do?' asked Penny, looking back at the closed door.

'I think I'll give Friends of the Earth a ring and see exactly what they did say to Mark.'

Before leaving for his second tour of Oxford and Stratford, Latymer rang Berry to arrange where to meet, and after some discussion settled on a pub in the part of Stratford known as the Old Town. 'I think it's recently changed its name,' Berry told him, 'but you can't miss it. I suppose you're in some expensive hotel. Nothing like that for a poor, second-hand bookseller like me, I'm in a B and B five minutes walk from the pub.

Once Latymer knew his people were settled for the rest of the evening of their first night in Stratford, he set off along Waterside, the road beside the river, towards the Old Town. Halfway along it he saw, reflected in the lamplight, a face he vaguely recognized and momentarily halted. The dark young man on the opposite side of the road also stopped, then peered through the gloom. 'Aren't you Mr Latymer?'

'That's right. It's Jonathan Higham, isn't it?' The young man smiled and crossed over to him. 'I believe we met when I first moved into the village,' continued Latymer, 'but I think you've been away almost ever since. I've seen your parents from time to time.' A few times had been more than enough. Higham senior was a local estate agent with whom Latymer had once crossed swords at a dinner party given by mutual acquaintances. The hosts, who Latymer hadn't cared much for either, had been deeply offended, which had upset Tess, who had become very friendly with the wife. This had been another bone of contention. 'Your father told me you were up at university in Warwick.'

In fact, Latymer had run into Higham shortly after hearing that his son had achieved a university place and, in spite of the differences between them, had congratulated him. It was obviously the wrong thing to have done. 'Bloody waste of time,' snarled Higham. 'First he takes a – what do they call it – a gap year where he buggers off to the West Country and does nothing. Then he goes in for this arty farty degree nonsense at Warwick. The boy's an idiot. I was willing to pay for a year's course at one of the best business colleges in the country, after which he'd join me in the business. By the time he was twenty-one, he'd have been driving his own BMW . . . As it is by the time he's finished he'll be twenty-two with a useless qualification and £15,000 worth of debt hung round his neck. Well, he needn't come crying to me.'

'Dad was anything but pleased,' confirmed Jonathan.

'So I rather gathered when I mentioned it to him. What are you reading?'

'English and Drama. It's what I've always wanted. I'm just on my way to the theatre now, but . . . well, I've had a lot on my mind.' He paused. 'Are you here for long, Mr Latymer?'

'Until Wednesday, why?'

'Do you think we might meet up? There's something I'd like to talk over with you.'

'Am I to assume it's something you'd rather not talk over with your parents?'

Jonathan nodded. 'Even if we'd been getting on, I don't think they could help.'

'I'm not at all sure I'll be able to,' Latymer told him.

'I think you might. You used to be a policeman, didn't you?'

'I was. But I'll tell you now that if this has anything to do with drugs or drug laws, I don't want to know. I had enough of that last year when I tried to help someone.'

'No, it's nothing like that, it's . . . Look, can you tell me where you're staying so that I can call you in good time before you leave?'

Latymer's heart sank at the prospect, feeling that he had enough problems of his own. 'Very well, if you really think I can help. Look, I'll give you my mobile number as I'm never sure where I'll be.' Jonathan pulled an old envelope out of his pocket and Latymer wrote it down. 'There. I'll wait to hear from you then. But don't leave it later than Tuesday night.' Jonathan raised his hand in salute and continued on his way towards the theatre. Nice lad, thought Latymer, watching him cross the road. Imagine having a man like Higham for a father. Most parents would be only too pleased in this day and age to have a boy who knew what he wanted to do and was prepared to work hard to achieve it.

He resumed his walk, plunged in gloom. None of the houses he had looked at with Tess remotely appealed to him. The cottage conversions in pretty villages were way above their price range and the 'executive houses' were the kind of brick-built, mock Georgian dwellings about a foot apart that spread like a rash over the whole country. Even Tess hadn't viewed them with enthusiasm, but she was doggedly determined to find something and find it now. She'd refused to return home with him, she told him she would continue the search alone for a few more days and hoped that by the time he returned a week later she would have found something suitable. But so far as she was concerned there was now no going back. The situation had become so fraught that he'd had to ring Becketts Tours, pleading a domestic crisis, and ask if they could send another courier down to Stratford on Tuesday night to see the party safely back to London on Wednesday morning. They had finally agreed but were obviously far from pleased.

He found he'd become more or less resigned to the break-up of their marriage. All he wanted now was for everything to be settled with the minimum of acrimony, after all, he and Tess had enjoyed some good years together. There was also another reason, one he wouldn't even admit to himself. When he returned from Somerset and picked up his emails he found a message from Fiona Garleston. Fiona, who lived near Kirkcudbright in Scotland, had played a major role in the previous year's drama into which he'd been inadvertently drawn. Her husband, a Gulf War veteran who was dying of leukaemia, had set up a website exposing a local hazard which he believed could become a catastrophe, so running himself and others into a great deal of trouble. Latymer had been touched by Fiona's warmth and fierce loyalty to her husband and he'd been shaken by a feeling of attraction towards her he'd never experienced, even in the early days of his relationship with Tess. Her husband had died towards the end of the previous year.

'Any chance of your coming up here again?' she'd written. 'Thought I'd let you know, if you haven't looked lately, that I've managed to keep the fisherking website going, also adding other nasties like pesticides and GM crops to it. James would, I think, be very pleased with me. I still miss him such a lot, we'd planned to do so much together. At least the nightmare of his terrible illness is over. Hopefully, I'll begin to get a life again eventually.'

Latymer was still pondering how best to reply. He was so

deep in thought that he almost walked past the pub before he realized where he was. Berry was sitting at a table towards the back and as he saw Latymer, put down the newspaper he'd been reading. He looked at his watch. 'I'd just about given you up. It's twenty past ten.'

'I'd things to do, then I got stopped by a young lad from our village on my way here.'

'Well, now you are, mine's a pint.'

Latymer went over to the bar, bought the drinks and brought them back to the table. 'I really am sorry I'm so late,' he said as he put them down.

Berry grinned. 'I should think so. I've read the local rag through at least four times while I've been waiting. I can just about recite all the small ads.'

'Anything interesting in it?'

Berry picked up the paper and began to look through it. 'Yes, there is, actually. Quite an intriguing story.'

'What about?'

'Human remains found in a graveyard!'

Four

Latymer settled beside Berry and picked up his pint. 'Do me a favour!'

'No, really. Look for yourself.' He handed over the paper. 'See?'

The story was headlined **'Double Death Discovery in Graveyard'** and continued:

> Police have removed the remains of an infant from a grave in Lower Horton churchyard. The discovery follows an earlier one, several days ago. About two weeks ago the attention of the vicar, the Rev. Jane Hutchens, was drawn to the fact that the earth in front of a 150-year-old tombstone seemed to have been disturbed. 'A visitor to the church pointed out that fresh flowers had been put on the grave, which is in a very overgrown and sadly neglected part of the churchyard, and that the area in front of the tombstone looked as if it had been recently moved,' she told our reporter.
>
> Sometime later she had visited the grave again, along with the churchwarden, who was equally at a loss for an explanation. The churchwarden investigated the disturbance using a trowel, and with difficulty unearthed a small wooden box which, from its condition, did not look as if it had been there very long. It was impossible to ascertain the contents as the top was securely screwed down. The Rev. Hutchens, therefore, took the box to the

police. On investigation by forensic experts, the box was found to contain a cremation.

In view of this, the police visited the site and a search was made in the disturbed area to see if there were any clues as to identity of the cremated remains. But on digging down a little deeper, police discovered what appeared to be a small rotting blanket and it was when this was removed and unfolded that the body of an infant was discovered. An initial examination suggests that it had been in the ground for around two to three years. The grave, that of an Elizabeth Bidford, who died in 1830, has long been neglected and there are no longer any descendents of the Bidford family living either in or near Lower Horton.

The finds are a mystery and the Rev. Hutchens says they make her very sad. 'With regard to the cremation, although there is no longer any room in the graveyard for normal burials, a small space has been set aside for the ashes of those who have expressed a wish to rest here and this could easily have been arranged along with a service, had this been desired. But the finding of the remains of the baby is truly tragic. The most likely explanation must be that it was the child of some desperate young girl. It shows once again that in spite of all the advice now available to teenagers, young girls are still driven to desperation by unwanted pregnancy. If the mother had only sought help at the time this tragedy need never have happened. What she must have gone through hardly bears thinking of.' Investigations continue and anyone who can throw any light on the matter is asked to contact Stratford police station.

'It's a weird one, isn't it?' commented Berry when Latymer had finished reading the report. 'I bet the vicar wishes the person who visited the churchyard and set the whole thing going had stayed home.'

'Actually, it was me,' said Latymer.

Berry was about to come out with a withering comment when he saw his friend's face. 'You're not joking? You mean it really *was* you?'

'Unfortunately it was. I'd time to kill when I was here a couple of weeks ago, so I had a tour around. It was quite fortuitous that I noticed the sign to the church and went to have a look. Apparently they get quite a few visitors as it's quite famous for its unusual carvings. I noticed flowers on an old grave and went to have a look. Curiously enough it was that of a young woman and her unnamed child. It was also by chance I met up with the vicar as I was about to leave the graveyard and so mentioned it to her. I suppose if I hadn't no one would ever have been any the wiser as to what was there. I don't know whether that's a good thing or not, but it'll be interesting to see if there are any developments over the next few days.'

The landlord called last orders and Berry went to replenish their drinks. 'So,' he said as he sat down again, 'how's things?'

Latymer shuddered. 'Don't ask!'

After finishing their drinks, the two men parted and Latymer arranged to look in on the book fair during the next few days.

The tour followed the same pattern as the previous one with a locally based guide organized to take the party round the sites of special interest in the morning, except that this time it was a Sunday and the event started later to allow those who wished to attend church to do so. After breakfast the first part of Latymer's morning was taken up with ensuring that the churchgoers were looked after, explaining which churches or chapels were within easy walking distance and how to get to them, and arranging taxis for those who either wished to go further afield or didn't want to walk. The rest of the party either went out to have a look around the town or stayed in the hotel to write postcards or read the papers, which meant that Latymer had to remain where he was until everyone had returned and was accounted for. Unsurprisingly it all took longer than planned, resulting in a good deal of acrimony among those who had either been waiting in the hotel or had arrived back from church promptly. Eventually, however, to Latymer's relief, he managed to get the whole flock assembled in the foyer just as the coach pulled up outside and was able to hand them over to the capable local guide. Lunch was laid on for the party so he was free until the end of the afternoon.

As soon as he'd seen them off, he went to a nearby newsagents. The sight of the monstrous bulk of the national Sunday papers made his heart sink but his enquiry elicited the information that there was also a local Sunday paper, the *Sunday Mercury*, published in Birmingham. He bought a copy, shook out the unwanted sections (mercifully few) and leafed through it. He was in luck. The report was on page four. Most of the information was the same as that he'd already read in the *Stratford Herald*, but the *Mercury* report also gave the results of the examination carried out on the baby's bones.

> Dr G.J. Wood, who carried out the post mortem, confirmed that the remains were those of a premature newborn baby. It was impossible to tell whether it was stillborn or died shortly after birth, or to determine with certainty its sex. She estimated it had been in the ground from two to three years. Police enquiries continue.

On another page he found a feature linked to the news story setting out the dismal statistics for the rising number of births to very young mothers and asking what more could be done to prevent them. It also referred to other cases similar to that of the Lower Horton baby: a dead infant discovered on a beach at Saltash in Cornwall, another found in a cattle-food sack on a riverbank in Devon, pointing out that such tragedies were not confined to rundown areas of inner cities but were just as likely to occur in the depths of the country.

Elizabeth Bidford and child, mused Latymer. What part did they play in the mystery? It couldn't have been by chance that the desperate mother chose that particular grave in which to bury her child, rather than simply leaving it under a bush or in a field. Did the twenty-first-century mother know something of Elizabeth Bidford's history, or simply find the place appropriate? As for the cremation, were the two burials related? He supposed they must have been, it was simply too much of a coincidence to believe otherwise. So surely, whoever buried the casket must also have known about the baby.

He felt suddenly at a loose end. He'd been fully occupied during the two days in Oxford, there was plenty to do and see and his group had depended on him to guide them round the various places of interest. Tomorrow he would be busy again as the whole group had opted for a day at Warwick Castle, which left only Tuesday, then . . . what? He felt he ought to get in touch with Tess and rang her daughter's number. Mother, Diana informed him, coolly, had returned home after finding a house she felt would suit her. 'Her', he noted, not 'you' or 'both of you'.

So he rang home but there was no reply, his own voice on the answerphone informing him that Tess and John Latymer were unable to take calls at present so would the caller leave their name, telephone number, the time they called and, if necessary, a brief message. 'And *we* will get back to you as soon as possible'. He looked at his watch. It was already half past twelve. Berry had turned down an offer of lunch as there was no one else to man his table while he took a break. He was now doing a fairly successful trade in second-hand, out-of-print, crime fiction and true crime, especially first editions, and Stratford was even more packed with tourists than usual because of the birthday celebrations. 'So I'll see you tomorrow night,' he'd said. 'If I do well, the drinks are on me!'

As John stood considering what to do next, his mobile

rang and, assuming it must be Tess getting back to him, he answered it without looking to see the caller's number. But it wasn't Tess, it was Jonathan Higham. 'I was wondering how you were fixed, Mr Latymer. It's Sunday so obviously I've no lectures. Is there any chance we could meet?'

Why not, thought Latymer, I've nothing better to do. 'Fine, how about lunch? Any suggestions, Stratford's heaving.'

'Most pubs round here are too, everyone seems to go out to Sunday lunch these days. But there's one right in Warwick which might be OK. It's also got quite a big garden and it's fine enough today for people to sit out. Have you got your car?'

'Unusually I have. I left it in Stratford again before going to London to collect my party, which is as well as someone else is seeing them safely to Heathrow. And you?'

'I've got what Dad would consider an old banger,' he replied and gave Latymer the necessary directions.

They met up half an hour later. It was impossible to talk other than generalities over lunch and it was clear that whatever it was Jonathan had on his mind, he wanted to ensure no one overheard any of the conversation. However, by half past two most people had cleared from the garden so, after paying the bill, they took their coffee outside to a table in a corner. It was surprisingly warm for late April.

'So,' enquired Latymer, 'what's the problem?'

Jonathan swallowed. 'I don't honestly know how to start. There's so much I just *can't* tell you. It's all so . . .'

'Look, do your best. I take it that it directly concerns you?'

'Yes. No. In a way. Oh God! Suppose, just suppose, that years ago someone did something really dreadful to someone you know, but you've only just found out about it. What do you do?'

'That's far too vague for me. "Really dreadful" might cover anything from stealing someone's wallet to murder. I'll need more to go on than that. Suppose we say there's a scale, a wallet at three to murder at ten. Where would you put this dreadful thing?'

Jonathan thought a moment. 'About eight, I suppose, or even nine.'

'Do you know the person who did it?'

'I do now.'

'And the person to whom it was done?' Jonathan assented. 'A family member? A friend? A *close* friend?' Jonathan nodded. 'What do they have to say?'

'They can't . . . that is . . . not now . . .'

'Was this thing – I take it you mean a crime – committed recently?'

'No. It was when she was . . .' He stopped short again.

'She? I see. Are we talking about a rape?'

'Not exactly. Oh God, I'm making a terrible mess of this.'

'A serious sexual attack then?' Jonathan made no reply. 'Where did it take place?' demanded Latymer, finding so one-sided a discussion increasingly frustrating.

'I was told about it first when I was down in the West Country before I started at Warwick. Then I learned more, just after Christmas.'

'And you've done nothing about it since? Well, my advice is that you talk to the person concerned and tell her that by far the best thing is for her to go to the police now, even if what happened took place some time ago, particularly if she knows the identity of her attacker. Police forces have specially designated officers these days to deal with such cases and she'd be treated with care and sensitivity. And as you feel so strongly about it, presumably you'll give her all your support.'

'But she can't. You don't understand. She can't.'

'Why not? The passage of time doesn't matter. You must have read of cases where such information has been followed up years after an attack took place.'

Jonathan shook his head. 'I'm sure what you say is right,

but it's impossible. I'm sorry, Mr Latymer. I've wasted your time and messed you about. Thanks for your help, but it's for me to sort out. There is no one else.'

A thought struck Latymer. 'You're not trying to tell me that it's you who was the victim and in reality there's no other person involved?'

'No, honestly, it isn't me. Perhaps one day I'll be able to explain.'

They rose to go. 'Well, I'm sorry I haven't been able to help more. Presumably you feel unable to break this young woman's confidence. But believe me, I've given you the best advice. Go back to her again, try and persuade her and tell her what I've told you. Is her attacker still around?'

'It's not really . . .' Jonathan then paused again but finally admitted, 'yes, he is.'

'Then try and make her see that by going to the police she might well save another young woman from becoming his victim. It rarely stops at one.' A sudden thought struck him. 'I know you *said* you were staying down in the west of England when you were told this story, but in reality does it actually involve someone in our village and that's why you don't want to say any more?'

'No. Definitely not. Thank you again, though.'

They shook hands. 'Think about what I've said, Jonathan,' said Latymer. 'And if you do decide to take it further, you know how to contact me. If you do finally persuade her to go to the police, I'll be more than happy to help in any way I can.'

Driving the short distance back to Stratford he mulled over the conversation. It sounded as if the young woman in question was, or more likely had been, Jonathan's girlfriend and that something had suddenly prompted her to reveal a traumatic event in her past. He said he'd learned of it while he was in the West Country during his gap year, so possibly he'd met her then. Perhaps she was now at college with him. If so, then presumably the university had some sort of counsellor to whom the girl could turn if she didn't want to go to the police. Where she was and whatever their present relationship, he hoped Jonathan would persuade the girl to do something about it. He obviously cared deeply and it would help both of them.

It was late on Sunday evening. Mark Ransom, a can of lager in his hand, was sitting on the sofa with his feet up watching the end of a crime drama on television and summoning up the energy to go to bed, when there was a knock on his door. He looked at his watch. It was 10.45. He wondered who on earth would come calling so late. The knocking continued. He swore, got up, went downstairs and flung the door open. Standing outside was James Weaver.

'Shit! What do you bloody well want this time, James? Can't you effing sleep!'

'You owe me – us – an explanation,' retorted James, pushing his way into the flat and going up the stairs.

'I owe you nothing. Are you drunk? Stoned? What are you on about?'

'You know bloody well what I'm on about. This morning I finally got through to our regular contact at Friends of the Earth.'

'And?'

'And he told me he'd warned you in no uncertain terms not to go ahead with this particular action. That it was in an area where landowners were very much on the lookout at the moment and that it wasn't even a particularly important site. *And*, that given all the circumstances, it could actually be counter-productive. He said you'd been told that there was a much bigger, better organized event being planned for about the same time in Dorset and that you should join forces with them. But if you were absolutely determined to go ahead with a protest in Evesham Vale, then you should at least leave it for a month or so when the local farmers were no longer so edgy and he'd be able to offer you support and up-to-date advice.'

'That may be what he said but I don't have to take his advice. I can run this thing perfectly well without the help of Friends of the Earth.'

'I also told him what I told you about the farmer involved and his brother-in-law next door with a load of electronic equipment.

'Jeff was right. All this stuff's irrelevant.'

'Such information is *never* irrelevant. And I do have a lot of real experience of these kinds of demos. Our contact from Friends of the Earth said that he feels you lack experience and that was another reason for leaving this alone. When I met you on that action in Norfolk and you said you were forming your own group and asked if I'd help, you told me you'd had plenty of experience. Now I discover that was only your second time out. Though from the way you've gone about this, I've had my suspicions.'

'Anything else?'

'Your choice of volunteers. Rain, Rowan and, what did he call himself, Shrieve? Our man suggested I rang a colleague, a woman, who specializes in infiltration. She agreed that the alternative lifestyle couple might be all they say they are, but that it's by no means certain. There are plain clothes cops who can carry that kind of thing off very well. As for Shrieve . . . apparently there are a number of these semi-mystical, occult, back-to-paganism outfits calling themselves by a variety of names. Most are harmless enough but some are deeply unpleasant. There have almost certainly been cases of animal sacrifice, in one instance a cat was found dead in an apple orchard, staked out with apple twigs and mistletoe, and she certainly didn't like the sound of all that stuff about blood. She says he sounds like an obsessive, possibly even a dangerous obsessive.'

'Well there's nothing I can do about him now – I don't even have a contact number.'

'What about Rain or Rowan?'

'I haven't got one for them either. She rang me from a call box.'

'There you are, you see. Mark, if you count me in any way your friend, please call this off. No one will think any the worse of you if you tell them that new information has come your way and it would be better to postpone everything.'

'I shall do no such thing. Do I take it as definite then that if this goes ahead you won't take part?'

'No, I won't take part. But I'm sufficiently concerned for you to act as an official observer. I'll be there and take careful note of what happens. At least that way I might be able to do some good.'

'Oh, suit yourself,' retorted Mark. 'You know your own way out.'

Five

It started to go wrong almost straight away. Heavy rain on the M40 meant slow-moving weekday traffic with the result that Mark Ransom, like almost everyone else, arrived late at the Pear Tree services. Thoroughly frustrated, he could have done without the comments of those there before him pointing out how much easier it would have been for everyone if the action had been undertaken, as originally planned, on the previous Saturday.

For a little while they all stood around in the damp to see if anyone else turned up, then redheaded Jeff made his own mind up. 'I don't know about you lot but I'm going inside for some soup and a coffee. There's surely no point in trying to discuss anything standing out here in the wet.' And so saying he marched off towards the café. Three more figures loomed up out of the gloom and Mark saw it was Rowan, Shrieve and a man he hadn't seen before who seemed to be having some kind of an argument with Rowan. Of Rain there was no sign.

'Where's Rain?' enquired Mark as they reached him.

Rowan yawned. 'Oh, she dipped out. She said she'd something else to do.'

'But she seemed so keen. It was her that got in touch in the first place and asked if she could bring you and Shrieve along.'

Rowan shrugged. 'Nothing to do with me. Anyway I've found you another volunteer. He's given a couple of talks to our circle.'

Mark's heart sank further. Oh God, not another possible nutter like Shrieve.

Altogether, including four volunteers from the Midlands, he and Penny had reckoned there'd be about thirty people involved. He'd wondered if Penny would come given the doubts she shared with James. James had said he'd be there as an observer and although he and Penny weren't an item, they usually shared transport, so presumably she would turn up although there was no sign of them yet. Meanwhile, the others were growing increasingly restive and eventually, as if of one mind, they started moving towards the café. It was too late to try and stop them. However, was he going to be able to discuss last minute arrangements in a motorway services heaving with other people? As he stood wondering what to do next James and Penny arrived having left their car at the other end of the car park. The two men greeted each other coolly.

'I should go after them if I were you,' advised James. 'You don't want them to start chatting to each other loudly while they queue up for their sandwiches.'

'I suppose you can't wait to say "told you so"!' snapped James.

'It's still not too late to call it off.'

Mark just looked at them without saying anything, then made his way towards the café. Several neighbouring tables in one corner had become empty at the same time as a coach party had just left and as he went in through the door he saw they were now being reserved by some of their party whilst the rest queued for food and drink. Well, that's something, thought Mark, at least we're all together and it should be possible to get over what I have to say without drawing too much attention to us. He'd also had the foresight to print off last minute notes of what they needed to know. He saw James and Penny come in and, without giving any sign of recognition, go and sit some distance away. It occurred to him that perhaps he ought to have suggested to the others that they dribbled into the café in twos and threes instead of in a group. He was beginning to feel queasy. For the first time it really hit him just how inexperienced most of them were, except for James, of course, and he wasn't even going to take part.

After getting his own coffee, he went round the tables handing out the notices, saying loudly, for the benefit of anyone listening, that it was the agenda for the next day's sightseeing. He then muttered to them not to start reading the information out loud or to discuss it until they were out in the car park again. Printed on the sheet were the details, once again, of exactly where they were to meet that evening and when, and a note to the effect that as promised there would be sufficient white overalls and 'death's head' rubber masks in the boot of his car for anyone who wanted to wear them and he'd hand them out during the briefing half an hour before the action.

'Shrieve and I have brought our own masks,' Rowan mouthed, quietly. 'It's the face of the green man. He thinks we should all wear his.'

'Suit yourself,' returned Mark, not quietly enough. 'And who's that other fellow sitting with him over there? You really should have told me you were bringing someone else. I'm supposed to have everyone's name.'

'You never said. They don't bother with that kind of thing on the anti-globalization demos,' Rowan told him, his voice rising in indignation.

'*Will you watch what you're saying,*' hissed Mark. Other diners were beginning to turn round and stare, at which point, fortuitously, there was a tremendous crash from the kitchen which drowned out his words.

It took a good twenty minutes before he managed to get everyone back into the car park to find, thankfully, that at least the rain had stopped: indeed the sky was already clearing. The action had been planned for a virtually moonless night, but rain would certainly have made everything more difficult. The improvement in the weather seemed to cheer everyone up and they went off on their separate ways to find their cars with rising spirits. Soon the only people left apart from Mark were Rowan, James and Penny, and Shrieve and the stranger who were standing a little away and, if their body language was anything to go on, in a state of mutual dislike.

Seen in daylight, thought James, Shrieve seemed even more unprepossessing than he had in Mark's flat.

Rowan looked uneasy. 'Aren't you coming, Shrieve? It'll take another hour or so to get to Stratford and the idea is that we all do our own thing until we meet up again tonight. Surely you don't want to hang around here all evening?'

Shrieve made no attempt to move. 'Apparently you can take him or me. He says he won't go any further if I'm in the same car.'

The other man nodded in agreement. 'Thanks for the lift so far, Rowan, but that's it. If you take this maniac any further you're going to find yourself in real trouble. I'd no idea he was involved until you picked me up this afternoon. I don't have a car,' he explained to the others. 'Anyway, don't worry. I'll pack it in now and get a cab to Oxford station and catch the train home.' Rowan looked helplessly at Mark.

'You can come with us if you like,' offered James.

Penny looked far from pleased and pulled him aside. 'What on earth for? If they can't get on, too bad. Left to me, I wouldn't want either of them to go.'

'Left to me none of us would,' said James. 'God knows who he is but it might be a good idea to try and find out and I've a hunch he might come in useful.'

'I don't want to cause a domestic argument,' commented the stranger.

'You haven't,' James told him. 'Do you want a lift or not?'

'All right then. You can come with us,' Penny conceded.

The man gave Shrieve an unpleasant smile. 'Right then, Mark. See you later.'

'For what good you'll be,' he returned and walked off towards his own car.

Although the main Stratford road led directly off the roundabout it had already been agreed that the cars would follow a variety of different routes since it was relatively easy to drive cross-country once into Warwickshire. James decided to go down through Banbury then cut across to the Stratford road just outside the town. As they set off with their unexpected passenger in the back seat, James asked him his name.

'Dee. John Dee,' he replied.

Here we go, thought James, it's another joker. 'As in the sixteenth-century alchemist?'

'And physician. Yes.'

Penny gave James a what-did-I-tell-you look. He ignored it. 'Just what is the problem between you and this Shrieve character?'

'There's no problem as such. It's like I said, I actually believe the guy could be dangerous. As I told young Rowan, if I'd had any idea he was part of this set-up I'd never have come, but when I realized he was I thought it might be useful to keep some kind of tab on him.'

Penny turned round. 'You've obviously met him before.'

'Twice, that's all. The first time was a few months back when I'd been asked to give a talk at what Rowan calls their Green Circle and then I ran into him again the other week. The Green Circle people, by the way, are harmless to the point of being totally ineffective. The last time I was at one of their meetings they spent most of their time arguing about crop circles, most of which are faked, of course, and the rest explicable. But they're heavily into old rites and customs to do with sympathetic magic and fertility and so on; it makes then feel they're in touch with their roots, even if half of it dates from the Victorian notions of pagan prehistory.'

'We had some of that stuff about rites and customs from Shrieve the other night,' Penny informed him. 'I can't say I was keen to know more. It was all about blood sacrifices and scapegoats.'

'That's Shrieve for you, it's his thing. That first time I came across him he was giving the talk after mine and as he looks so manic I hung around to see what he had to say. He's clearly obsessed with blood and sacrifice. He actually started on the subject on the way down in car, telling Rowan and I over and over again that for millennia it was considered the only way to ensure the true cleansing of the earth, placate the gods and ensure a good harvest, and that it was still practised comparatively recently.'

'I presume that by "comparatively recently" he means the Druids and that kind of thing,' commented James.

'No, he doesn't He told us that the last time there was a fully recorded blood sacrifice was on some hill or other close to where we're going tonight and that it took place only half a century or so ago. And that perhaps the time was coming when it should be repeated.'

James was getting seriously alarmed. A lay-by was coming up and he pulled over. 'Look, Dee, what you're saying is beginning to frighten me. I'll tell you now that this whole thing has gone off at half-cock and against my advice; indeed against the specific advice of Friends of the Earth. The last thing we need is for that kind of stuff to be dragged in. The aim of the action is quite simple: to uproot all the experimental plants and trash them. Nothing else. And what is needed above all is positive publicity. Lots of people, most people perhaps, are against GM food and they admire these kind of actions. But if we start getting into black magic and blood sacrifice not only will they be turned off, they'll think we've all raving mad.' He paused. 'What exactly *is* your position in all this, Dee? You seem to know a lot about all this occult stuff and you say yourself you've attended various meetings of this Green Circle, and after all that is where you met Shrieve.'

Dee smiled. 'I'll try and set your mind at rest and reassure you. Honestly, I'm not the least bit sinister. I lecture in ancient history and mythology, that's all. Rowan was one of my students and was doing rather well until he dropped out. When he contacted me and asked if I'd give a couple of talks to his group, I agreed, not least because I was hoping to persuade him to return and finish his course. It was totally fortuitous that Shrieve was there as well the first time I went. Oh, and by the way, my name really *is* Dee. I can't help if it my parents also called me John. And I'm totally against GM foods.'

James heaved a sigh of relief and re-started the engine. 'And what, if anything, does Shrieve do for a living?' he enquired as he drove back on to the road, 'or don't you know?'

'Search me! Apart from hearing him telling people he's some kind of a "consultant", though a consultant in what I've no idea. Oh, and he also claims to be a screer. Presumably he charges for that.'

'What on earth's a screer?'

'Someone who can look into a piece of darkened glass or a pool of black ink and "see" things. They believed in that kind of thing right up to the sixteenth century and even beyond. In fact my poor old namesake just about lost his reputation after being totally taken in by a con man called Kelly who claimed he could do it. Even four hundred years ago Dee should've known better. Kelly had already had his ears cropped for digging up corpses and trying to raise spirits.'

'But you said you'd run into Shrieve again only recently,' persisted Penny.

'That's right.'

She couldn't resist it. 'At a coven, perhaps?'

Dee laughed out loud. 'In the Old Rose off Horseferry Road. Look, since you people have been so good as to give me a lift, let's press on to Stratford and I'll treat us to a decent meal before we start crop trashing.'

* * *

The rain had stopped by the time Detective Constable Wendy Rainbird pulled up outside Lucas Symonds' half-timbered converted farmhouse. The plaits that previously straggled down her back had become a neat coil on the back of her head, all the facial rings had disappeared – they were only clip-on but they'd been most uncomfortable – and she was now dressed in a neat dark sweater and trousers. She rang the bell and the door was opened almost immediately by Symonds' housekeeper who took her straight through to the room where he was waiting for her.

He held out his hand. 'Good of you to come, constable.' Until now they had spoken only over the telephone. He was tall, distinguished-looking, greying at the temples, and one of the most good-looking men she'd ever met. She judged him to be in his late forties. 'Coffee? I don't suppose I can offer you anything stronger?'

'I'm afraid not. It's likely to be a hectic night.'

'I'll ask Joan to make us some then. Do sit down.'

She did so. The room she was sitting in was large, low-ceilinged and tastefully furnished; two of the walls were lined from floor to ceiling with books. A log fire burned in the grate and a beautiful arrangement of spring flowers stood on a carved antique dower chest under the casement window. It was like something out of *Country Life,* she thought, or a lifestyle piece in one of the Sunday supplements. She thought of her own cramped flat. Just think of actually living somewhere like this. She knew he wasn't married or had a partner and wondered why ever not. Perhaps he was gay.

Her reverie was interrupted by Symonds bringing in a tray on which was a cafetiere and two cups and saucers. 'I didn't know if you preferred cream or milk, so there's both. And sugar if you take it.' He smiled at her. No, she thought, he's definitely not gay! In fact he gave off in spades the kind of charm it was impossible to fake. He pressed down on the lid, waited briefly, then poured her a cup of coffee.

'I really am most grateful to you for telling me what was planned.'

'Well, I've been working under cover for some time, making myself useful to the more extreme ecological groups to discover just what is going on. When I got back to the Midlands a couple of days ago and told my boss about this particular action, he saw it as a way of making an example of these people and obviously the best way to do it was to enlist the support of the farmer involved and bring him in on it. Which is why I rang – your brother-in-law, is it? – Bob Wells, because as I understand it the crops are actually being grown on his land, but then he referred me to you.'

'Well it was my idea in the first place that he should take part in the experiment. I'd have volunteered like a shot but most of my land's been sold off, so the next best thing was to persuade Bob. I suggested, in case there was any trouble, that he use a piece of land almost outside my gate so that I could deal with it for him if it arose. His house is about half a mile from here. Also, I've a nice line in electronic gadgets to deter intruders and it was quite easy to rig up what you might call an early warning device. But my original information was that it was all going to happen on Saturday.'

'It was. Then they decided to change it to tonight. The thinking behind that was because they thought we'd be fully tied up with the Shakespeare birthday celebrations, but by late evening most of that will have wound down. I understand it all went well this morning.'

'It certainly did. I took part in the procession myself, then was invited to the lunch, fortunately the rain held off until this afternoon.' He smiled at her again in that almost intimate way and she wondered it if might be possible to stay in touch after the night's event. Keep him informed in case there were any further actions close by. 'I don't want any trouble tonight,' he continued. 'Believe it or not, I don't actually bear these people any ill will. I think they have a point, just as I have myself, that they truly believe that growing GM crops will prove detrimental, dangerous even, to the rest of the ecology. Whereas I am certain it's the only way we'll ever prevent famine in the Developing World. But the way to sort this out is by reasoned argument, not crop trashing. However, as I say, I don't want any trouble.'

'Neither do we. But on the whole these people aren't usually into violence. They tend to roll over and do what they're told when they're caught.'

'What happens afterwards?'

'They'll be arrested, charged and carted off to the police station – or stations, depending on how many there are – and quite likely will come up in the local court tomorrow morning. The magistrates have been warned. Mostly it's a fine and costs. It depends how it goes, some of the ringleaders might be bailed to appear at a later date. Not to worry. We'll wrap this one up quickly, you'll see.' She stood up to go.

'Did you have a coat? No? Then let me see you to the door.'

Yes, quite definitely she would keep in touch.

It was just after half past ten and all those expected were now at the rendezvous point, including four students from Warwick university. At first Jonathan Higham had intended taking them all in his car but then, to his relief, one of the others offered instead. He was feeling very nervous. When the idea was first suggested a couple of weeks ago, it'd had all seemed something of a game, a bit of fun with serious overtones. Now it had actually got to it he wasn't so sure. He wondered what his father would think he if ended up in court. Chances were he wouldn't even know. Oh well, it would soon be over.

Mark was handing out overalls and masks to those, about half of the party, who wanted them. James had brought a clipboard attached to which was a list of most of the names of all those he knew were taking part, and their home telephone numbers, with further blank sheets for further comments.

Penny, now dressed in overalls but without a mask, had joined up with the others. Dee remained on the sidelines with James.

'I'm not too sure what to do,' he told him. 'I suppose I must go with the flow since I've committed myself and got this far, but like you I feel distinctly uneasy.'

'You could stay with me and observe, if you like,' James suggested. 'It's up to you.'

Mark called for silence. 'Everyone ready? Right, let's go.' It was then that a minibus pulled up, its number plates partially concealed. Everyone stared. Oh God, thought Mark, it's the police. But it was worse than the police. The dozen or so people who piled out were dressed from head to foot in black and all were wearing the green man face masks. The one in front pulled off his mask, looking round as he did so. Shrieve immediately did the same then went over to the newcomer.

'We came, you see. We promised we would.'

Shrieve smiled. 'Very good. Very good indeed.'

Mark was beside himself. 'Who the hell are they? What in God's name do you think you're doing asking these people along?'

'I have every right to bring some of my own people down here if I so choose,' retorted Shrieve. 'It's not a private event, is it?' He looked up and saw Dee. 'You still here? I'd have thought you hadn't the guts.' He went over to the newcomers. 'Over there,' he told them, making a sweep with his arm, 'is Meon Hill, where fifty years ago, on the Roman festival of Lupercal and a witches' sabbath, a man was sacrificed to ensure a good fruit crop and replenish the earth. Let that encourage you.'

Dee grabbed Mark by the arm. 'For God's sake stop this. If you haven't wanted to take any advice before, then listen up now! Everything's changed. If you go ahead now, you don't know what shit you'll be getting into. You can see your own people are doubtful. Go over to them, explain, assure them you'll set up something else again soon and apologize. They're not stupid, they'll understand.' He looked across to Shrieve's party who were standing in a circle surrounding him, anonymous now behind the grotesque green masks. 'I know nothing about these people Shrieve has encouraged along. They could be up to anything, at best serious damage, at worst . . . who knows?'

For a moment Mark hesitated. Then he made up his mind. No, he couldn't let it go, not at this late stage. It was too important to him. He walked over to his own group. 'Come on then all of you. We've come here to do something and we're bloody well going to do it.' He turned to the group in their green masks. 'No, I can't stop you taking part if you're determined to go ahead. But if you get into trouble, it's got nothing to do with me.'

James looked at Dee. 'I wish I thought it was as simple as that.'

Six

The persistent sound of his mobile phone woke Latymer from an uneasy and troubled sleep in the early hours of Wednesday morning. He swore, groping for it in the dark. 'Is that you, Mr Latymer?' The voice at the other end of the phone sounded hysterical. 'It's Jonathan Higham. I know I must have woken you up but something awful's happened.'

Latymer shook himself properly awake then sat up, switched on the bedside lamp and looked at his watch. 'What on earth . . . ? For God's sake, don't you realize it's only half past four?'

'But I don't know what to do. I've found something . . . It's . . . he's dead!'

'*Who's* dead?' snapped Latymer.

'A man. I've found a dead man.'

'Then you must tell the police straight away, if you haven't already done so.'

'You're the first person I thought of.'

'But you know I'm not a policeman any more.'

'But it's . . . Oh God, I don't know what to do. You see I took part in a demo against GM crops and it all went terribly wrong and the police were there and people got hurt and I ran away and . . .'

'Did this dead man you say you've found take part in it?'

'Yes. He must have done.'

'Then all the more reason to tell the police at once.' There was a pause. 'Surely you aren't trying to tell me you're involved in some way?'

'No, no, of course not. But are you sure you can't come out here? The dead man . . . It looks like something out of a nightmare. Please? I know it's a lot to ask.'

You can say that again, thought Latymer, savagely. 'Where the hell are you?'

'Near Lower Horton. It's on the road from . . .'

'Yes, yes, I know where it is. Where *exactly* are you?'

'I'm standing in a copse on a small hill about half a mile outside the village. The fields where the demo took place are down a lane, it's got a painted notice at the end saying Horton Manor. I ran across a field behind the manor and up the hill . . . and found . . .'

'But I can't see what on earth you expect *me* to do about it.'

'Help me, that's all. Wait 'til you see what's up here. I daren't send for the police on my own, in case, like you did, they start thinking I'd something to do with it.'

'You're quite sure this man's dead?'

'He must be. Wait 'til you see him.'

'Very well,' growled Latymer. 'Though I can't think why I'm doing this. Where shall we meet?'

'If you go on past the lane to the fields where the demo was, about fifty yards or so further on there's a public footpath sign pointing off the road. If you follow the path it leads up to the hill. I'll come down and wait for you at the bottom. I can't thank you enough.'

The two groups of demonstrators had arrived at the experimental fields, each one of which was surrounded by stout wooden posts with wire stretched in between. It was very dark and absolutely quiet, uncannily quiet; not even the sound of a vehicle travelling along the road they'd just left. Mark produced wire cutters and cut the wire in several places, motioning the people through. Even finding the plants wasn't easy. It had been a cold, wet spring and they were scarcely through the ground and difficult to see. For a few minutes everyone worked in silence, then, without warning, they were drenched in light as a number of police officers appeared out of nowhere. To James and Dee, who had remained standing in the lane, the scene was like something out of an early mediaeval painting of Judgement Day as the bright lights picked out the white figures with their death's heads and the bizarre masks of Shrieve's green men. Several police cars and a large van could be seen standing by, close to a hedge, along with a small TV crew and a photographer. The invaders had manifestly been expected.

The officer in charge strode forward with a loud hailer. 'This is Chief Inspector William Ross of Warwickshire Police speaking and I am ordering you to stop what you are doing immediately. Immediately!'

Another man stepped beside him into the light. 'My name is Lucas Symonds. My brother-in-law, Bob Wells, owns this land and is running the experiment on behalf of DEFRA. I have his authorization to promise that if you do as Inspector Ross here says and go quietly away now, then he personally won't take it further. I can't say fairer than that. So, please, do as the inspector says. Go now.'

'If not,' warned Ross, 'you will immediately be arrested and charged.' He looked around at the demonstrators. 'Who organized this?'

'I did,' Mark told him. 'My name is Mark Ransom and we're members of the Sustainable Agriculture Forum, here to make a point . . .'

As he spoke several members of SAF and what looked like all the people from Shrieve's party returned to pulling up plants. The police at once moved in to prevent them. Scuffles broke out in different parts of the fields between the police and those they were trying to arrest, though on the whole the members of Mark's party either went quietly and were marched off towards the police van or, like Penny and Rowan, simply took off their masks, sat down and refused to move. But a handful of Mark's party and all of Shrieve's green men took no notice and turned instead to attacking the police who they soon realized they outnumbered.

The result was mayhem. Mark grabbed the chief inspector's arm and pointed to the green men. 'I'm not responsible for that lot, they're nothing to do with us. I'd no idea they were going to turn up.'

Ross didn't want to know. 'Take this one, will you?' he called out to the nearest police officer and Mark was hurried away towards the police vehicles.

The fighting was getting uglier by the minute. The TV cameraman narrowly escaped injury from a demonstrator trying to knock his legs from under him. One of the green men picked up a brick and smashed it with all his force into the face of a policeman, before disappearing into the dark beyond.

Ross radioed frantically for back-up, then for the first time noticed James and Dee.

'Who are you? What's your part in all this?'

'I'm here as an observer,' James informed him. 'I am a member of the Sustainable Agriculture Forum, but I did my best to stop this from happening. Right up to the last minute I warned Ransom that he should call it off. Friends of the Earth gave him the same advice. But what he's told you is right. We've got nothing to do with those idiots in green masks. They turned up here in a minibus, you'll find it in a lay-by about half a mile back.'

'Who are they, then?'

'God knows! Dee might have more idea.'

Dee shook his head. 'I can't help much either. I've come across the ringleader a couple of times, that's all. He calls himself Shrieve and I truly believe he's unbalanced. He's into the occult and all that kind of rubbish. I presume this lot are his disciples or adherents, or whatever he likes to call them.'

Ross was about to ask him how it was he knew Shrieve, when Symonds came over to them. 'Is there anything at all I can do, Chief Inspector?' he asked.

'No, sir, you're better out of it. If I'd any idea that it was going to turn out like this, I'd have done my best to bring more officers in spite of the birthday celebrations.' He looked round anxiously, then there was a noise from his phone and he clamped it to his ear. 'Right,' he said into it. 'And not a moment too soon.' He turned to Symonds. 'We should be getting reinforcements any time now.'

As he spoke a 4×4, its headlights on full beam, bumped along the lane towards them. 'This will be my brother-in-law, Bob Wells,' said Symonds. 'I just phoned to tell him what's been happening.'

The vehicle pulled up and Wells jumped out and surveyed the scene, aghast at what he saw, then turned to Symonds. 'God, Lucas, it looks like a battlefield!'

A constable, bleeding from a cut over one eye, ran over gasping for breath. 'I've called an ambulance, sir. Robinson's out there unconscious, one of those green bastards thumped him with a brick. I tried to get a grip on the one that did it, but he broke away and ran off somewhere. We simply haven't got enough people. And Detective Constable Rainbird got knocked down. I think she's cracked a couple of ribs.' He paused briefly. 'Aren't they ever going to send any back-up?'

At that moment, to their relief, there came the sound of police sirens from along the main road and within a couple of minutes two police vans, blue lights flashing, jolted along the lane along the track towards them, followed almost at once by an ambulance. As soon as he realized what was happening, Shrieve pulled off his mask and shouted to the others to run for it and in a matter of seconds they were racing off into the night in all directions. By the time the police reinforcements actually reached the field, the fighting had stopped and the exhausted police officers were either tending the wounded or rounding up the handful of SAF people still left, one or two of whom were also nursing injuries.

'Do you want us to go after them, sir?' asked one of the new arrivals.

'After them where? There's nothing but fields and copses for miles, they could be anywhere. The best thing is for you to take one of the vans and go back on to the road to see if any of them are making for their vehicles. I understand the people in the green masks arrived in a minibus which was left in the old lay-by about half a mile back towards Stratford. Make a start there.' He looked across to where an officer had managed to hold on to a green man and was holding him down on his knees in the churned up earth as he struggled to put handcuffs on. 'I see we've managed to get one of them. Let's hope he'll tell us more.

One of the paramedics from the ambulance came over. 'Where's this policeman who's been knocked out?'

Ross pointed up the field. 'Over there, there's a couple of officers with him.' The paramedic shouted to his colleague and the two went over to the injured man.

Meanwhile, the seated protestors, who had taken no part in the fighting, remained sitting down until forcibly dragged to their feet. As Penny and Rowan were being taken to the police van, they passed an injured policewoman who was being supported by a colleague. As they passed by the light caught her face. Rowan stopped and stared.

'Rain? he queried, uncertainly. Then leaned forward for a closer look. 'You cow! You little *cow*! This is all down to you, isn't it?' He turned to the policeman gripping his arm. 'I wouldn't bloody well be here, if it wasn't for her. She actually contacted the demo people and fixed for us to come. I wondered why the hell she didn't turn up herself. It's – what do they call it, when someone deliberately sets you up to do something? – incitement? I'll tell everyone when I get to court.'

'You do that,' returned the policeman and lugged him away.

The paramedics now had the badly injured policeman on

a stretcher and were carrying him towards the ambulance. 'How bad is it?' asked Ross as he joined them.

'Pretty bad. He could be bleeding from the brain. Hopefully we can keep him stable until we get him to hospital.'

'Can you take this one too?' enquired the policeman supporting Wendy Rainbird. 'I think it's cracked ribs, but she's having difficulty breathing.' The paramedics nodded their assent, the stretcher was loaded into the ambulance and Wendy Rainbird helped inside. As the paramedics were about to close the door Symonds came over.

'I'm sorry to see you like this, constable,' he said to Wendy. 'Bob and I can't thank you enough for all your hard work. Goodness knows what might have happened if you hadn't been able to warn us.' In spite of her pain, she smiled. 'Let me know how you get on. Promise?' he added.

'You seem to have made a conquest there,' joked one of the paramedics as he firmly closed the door. Wendy smiled wanly. But yes, she would let him know; most definitely. The ambulance moved cautiously back up the track, then, as it reached the main road, the driver switched on the blue light and the siren began to blare.

The last of the demonstrators were being loaded into the cars and vans. It was only just over an hour since they had first entered the field. The shaken cameraman, accompanied by the reporter and the photographer, were talking to Symonds and Wells. They then turned their attention to Ross. 'Do you think you could give us a short interview, inspector?' asked the reporter.

'No,' Ross told him, wearily. 'I've had just about enough. You've got your pictures. We'll be issuing an official statement for the early bulletins and late editions as soon as I get back to the office. There'll be a proper press conference in the morning and you can ask me more then.' He turned away and the press, realizing there was no point in hanging about, left without any argument. Ross looked across at the two landowners and shook his head. 'What a night! What a bloody night!'

'I thought you coped very well,' said Wells, 'in part thanks to Lucas. Are you going to need me for anything else tonight?

'I'll want a statement but it'll do tomorrow. I'll send someone out to take it.'

'How about me?' enquired Symonds.

'The same applies to you. We'll see you both in the morning.'

Lucas gave a sigh of relief. 'Fine. Well, if that really is it, I'll be off back to the house. My housekeeper's probably been terrified. Oh, and I'll have a good look round the outbuildings and the garden just in case one of those lunatics is hiding somewhere, though I'd expect the sensor lights to pick them up. But you never know. You're OK, Bob?' Wells nodded, climbed back into his vehicle and drove off.

'I don't think you'll be having any more trouble tonight, Mr Symonds,' Ross told him, 'but if anything worries you or you find some of these people lurking about, call us straight away.' Symonds thanked him and strode off back towards the manor.

'What about us?' demanded James. 'Dee and I have done nothing. We haven't trespassed on the fields or trashed the crop. Do you intend keeping us here all night?'

Ross ran a tired hand across his forehead. 'You'd best come back in the car with me. I'll need statements from both of you.'

As soon as the four university students realized they'd walked into a trap they made a dash for it while the police were busy dealing with the main body of demonstrators. They'd already arranged, if things went wrong, that each should make his own way back to the car. Jonathan had offered to drive over a few days before to see exactly where they were supposed to go and he'd found a spot just off the road, behind a deserted farm building, and it was there they'd left their car. Three of the students, panting for breath, reached it almost at the same time and although Jonathan wasn't with them, they assumed he must be following close behind. But minutes went by and there was still no sign of him. It was while they were discussing what best to do that they heard the sound of police sirens and saw the reinforcements turning into the lane up to the fields. An ambulance followed behind.

'That's it!' said the driver of the car. 'Get in. We can't risk waiting any longer.'

'But what about Jonathan?' queried one of the others.

'The silly sod should've been here by now. He can make his own way back to college. There's no earthly point in us all getting ourselves arrested.'

The night porter raised a surprised eyebrow as Latymer came quietly down the stairs. As there didn't seem to be much he could say in the way of an explanation, he muttered something about being back soon amd went out, leaving the man totally mystified. As he drove over Clopton Bridge on his way to the Cheltenham road, the full scale of his foolishness struck him forcibly. Whatever it was the boy had found, whatever he'd been mixed up in, the obvious thing to do was call the police. It might well be that the supposed corpse was lying in a drunken stupor or had suffered an injury; even more reason to have sent for help straight away.

He found the footpath easily enough and made his way cautiously along it, preferring not to use his torch. Jonathan was waiting for him at the foot of the hill, huddled in his jacket and shivering. Latymer was exasperated. 'Whatever, whoever's up there, Jonathan, you should have called the police. The worst that could happen is that they might do you for trespassing.'

'Wait 'til you see,' returned Jonathan and turned to lead the way.

On the top of the hill was one of those small copses of trees

Latymer remembered being told were planted in past times to guide the drovers across the Midlands on their way south from the Welsh marches. Jonathan stopped as they reached it, then stood back, motioning Latymer forward. 'He . . . it's . . . just in there.'

Latymer got out his torch and shone it down on the ground. At first he could see nothing, then, shatteringly, the beam centred on a grotesque, twisted, green face. As Jonathan had said, it was like something out of a nightmare. Involuntarily he stepped back, the light now focussing further down and it was then he saw the full horror of it. It was the body of a man wearing a green mask. He lay on his back with his arms flung out each side. Some kind of old, sharp farming tool was speared through his chest, which had also been slashed in the shape of a cross, while an equally ancient hayfork had been jammed across his throat, its prongs plunged deep into the ground on each side. He was covered in blood, which had spread into a pool around him.

Dear God, thought Latymer, no wonder the lad had been hysterical. He backed away and returned to Jonathan who was leaning against a tree staring out over the countryside. 'I don't wonder you were in such a state. It's appalling, quite horrible. And why the mask? That makes it look even worse.'

'Some people turned up, nothing to do with the organizers, and they were all wearing those green masks. They had some kind of leader who was egging them on to bash up the police. He was a tall, thin chap. I think that must be him.'

'Well, whoever it is we have to get the police here straight away. You didn't touch anything, did you?'

'When I first saw it . . . him . . . I bent down and put my hand on the ground. When I got up I wiped it on my jeans. I just thought it was wet from the grass then I realized it was blood. His blood. But I didn't actually touch him. After that I threw up. Then I called you.'

Latymer took out his mobile, dialled 999 and asked to be put through to the police. There was a slight pause, then he was asked why he was calling. He explained that he'd found a body and, in answer to the next question, told them where it was.

'Are we to understand you are one of those who was taking part in an anti-GM crops action tonight, then?' enquired the voice at the other end.

'Certainly not,' snapped Latymer. 'Look, I'll explain everything just as soon as you can get someone out here.'

'And you are sure this person really is dead?'

'Oh yes,' replied Latymer. 'He's as dead as anyone you're ever likely to see. In fact, you've a full scale murder enquiry on your hands.' He put the phone back in his pocket. As he did so, something began to nag at the back of his mind. A place name he'd noticed when he'd visited the church a couple of weeks ago. Lower Quinton. Dear God, he thought, this has all happened before.

Seven

At about four o'clock in the morning the policemen in the patrol car radioed in to say that all was quiet, there had been no reports of stragglers from the demonstration and they had seen no sign of anything amiss. They had been to the lay-by where the cars and minibus had been left, but the bus had gone. 'Presumably they realized we'd come looking for it and arranged a pick-up somewhere else and we've no registration number for it.' Ross, after a brief consideration, felt there was little point in continuing the patrol and called them back in.

He felt exhausted. The police officer with head injuries was now in intensive care in the district general hospital, his condition described as critical. Half a dozen other officers, including Wendy Rainbird, had also been to the hospital to be treated for various minor injuries, along with several of the protestors, meanwhile the press were already on his back wanting to know more. On top of that there were around twenty of the arrested demonstrators still waiting to be processed. James Weaver and John Dee were slumped in the waiting room intermittently dozing off, their request, that since they were not under arrest, surely they could be allowed to go if they undertook to return in the morning, having been turned down.

News that a body had been found not far from where the demonstration had taken place was just the last straw. 'You're sure this isn't some kind of a hoax?' Ross had demanded of the sergeant who had brought the unwelcome news. 'That it's not some idiot from the demo trying to get his own back and this is his idea of a joke?'

The sergeant who had taken the call didn't think so. 'The chap who rang in sounded genuine enough. It seems he'd been called up by some youngster who'd been on the demo and stumbled across it. He says he didn't really believe it either but the lad was so hysterical he went and took a look and there's no doubt about it. And it must be one of the demonstrators because the face is covered by some kind of green mask.'

For a moment Ross considered sending someone else then, reluctantly, changed his mind. 'OK. Then we'd better take a look. Who the hell am I going to take? Everyone who isn't dealing with the arrests here is down the hospital.' He paused. 'If the corpse is someone from the demo then the sooner it's identified the better. We'd better take that fellow who calls himself an observer and has a list of names and addresses.'

'What about the press?' asked the sergeant. 'There's been about a dozen calls already wanting a statement for tomorrow morning.'

'Tell them it's in hand and get them to ring back in half an hour. Our press people should have got something together by then. And tell them that I'll be holding a press conference at eleven o'clock. If the news is no better on Robinson it might well be that the Deputy Chief Constable will want to attend. I don't even want to think about how we'll cope with a possible murder on top of everything else.'

'The evening papers won't like waiting until eleven for the main info, sir.'

'I don't give a toss whether the evening papers like it or not,' roared Ross and left the office.

To Latymer and Jonathan, shivering on the hillside, it seemed an age before they saw the lights of a car making its way up the lane towards the manor where all was dark and silent. As it reached the drive to the house itself, sensor lights came on and lit the parking area outside, but there was no sign of life. Presumably, thought Ross, the occupants slept at the back of the house and were fast asleep., but he was still surprised Symonds hadn't reacted to the noise of their arrival. He climbed wearily out of the car and was joined by James who'd dozed off in the back beside an equally sleepy constable. The driver was a sergeant who'd lived in that part of Warwickshire all his life and now pointed to a small hill, capped with trees. 'Up there, sir. It's not as far as it looks if we use the gate at the back.'

As Latymer saw the torches coming towards him he found the most prominent position he could, switched on his own and waved it. Within a few minutes he was joined by the three police officers and a man in civilian clothes.

'Chief Inspector Ross,' barked Ross in way of a greeting. 'This is Sergeant Wilkins. Well then, where is this body you say you've found?' he demanded, without further preamble.

'Over there,' said Latymer. 'I'll show you. I think Jonathan here would prefer not to see it again.'

'And you are . . . ?'

'John Latymer.'

'And what's your role in this?'

'Very little. Jonathan here, was one of those taking part in the demonstration. It seems he and his friends split up and ran off when it began to get rough and he ended up here, found the body, and called me.'

Ross looked at Jonathan. 'And your name?'

'Jonathan Higham. I'm a student at Warwick.'

'And why did you call Mr Latymer?'

'Because I know him. He lives in the same village as my parents and I knew he was in Stratford.'

Ross turned to James. 'Do you know this lad?'

'I knew of him,' replied James, 'and that he supported SAF. We spoke on the phone when I was trying to make up a list of who exactly was going to take part. He said he'd bring some others along but I don't have their names.'

Ross nodded. 'Let's have a look then. And this had better be good.'

'Oh it'll be "good", all right,' retorted Latymer, nettled by his tone.

He led the way, Ross following close behind until they reached the small clearing in the middle of which it was just possible to make out a dark shape on the ground. The policemen aimed the beams of their torches on to it.

'Christ Almighty!' gasped the constable. They all stared down appalled at the monstrous figure. 'What's wrong with his face?'

James swallowed, his stomach queasy. 'It's a mask. The other lot, the people in the minibus we didn't know were coming, were all wearing them. You saw for yourself, Chief Inspector. It's supposed to represent the Green Man.' The constable went into the bushes and was quietly sick.

Ross nodded. 'So it follows that this must be one of them?'

'It has to be. We didn't have any masks like that.' Reluctantly he peered closer. 'I think it could be the leader of the group, the man we told you about who called himself Shrieve. He was capering about like a madman and it was him who told them to cut and run when the reinforcements arrived. He's the right build and height.'

'Shrieve who?' asked Ross.

'Just Shrieve, that's all. He never gave me another name. As I've already told you, I'd only met him once before until tonight. He said the earth had to be cleansed by blood. He'd a thing about blood sacrifice.'

Ross gave a bleak smile. 'Well now he's an expert.' Then, to Wilkins: 'Get that thing off, will you? The first thing we'd better do is check it really *is* this guy, Shrieve.'

Wilkins knelt down and carefully removed the mask.

But it wasn't Shrieve. It was Lucas Symonds.

There was a prolonged silence, finally broken by Ross. 'But

I don't understand. I left him at about one o'clock. I saw him go straight back to the house.'

'It certainly doesn't look as if he's been dead very long,' commented Latymer. 'Not from the state of the blood. I imagine he must still be quite warm.'

'Do I take it you have medical training, Latymer?

He was about to explain when Sergeant Wilkins, who had been looking closely at the corpse, straightened up. 'It's very odd . . .' he began.

Ross rolled his eyes. 'Oh, really?'

'I don't mean it like that, sir, obviously it's odd. It's just that there was a murder like this near here once before, towards the end of the war. A man was found over there, on the top of Meon Hill, killed in almost exactly the same way: billhook through the heart and a pitchfork in his throat.

'It became known, I believe, as the Witchcraft Murder,' added Latymer.

Ross gave him a weary look. 'Not an expert in the occult as well?'

'No,' snapped Latymer, 'but, as I was about to explain when the sergeant spoke, I retired from the force about three years ago and I still retain a few odds and ends of information. The case to which the sergeant refers was notorious at the time. I'd have thought you might have heard of it, not least because it remains unsolved.'

Ross, who had only recently joined the Warwickshire force from up north, had to admit he never had. 'Well, we can go into all that later. Let's get moving. We'll need the whole lot: doctor, ambulance, SOCO. No wonder there was no reaction at the manor. Make a start, will you, sergeant? I'd better get on to the top brass. Constable, take Mr Weaver and these two gentlemen back to Warwick so that they can make statements. Weaver needs to make one too.'

James groaned. 'Am I never going to get any sleep?'

'Once you've given us a statement and let us have all your

details, you and your friend Mr Dee are free to go. You aren't under arrest.'

'Look, Inspector Ross,' said Latymer, 'I've got my own responsibilities. I must get back to the hotel to see to my party. We're at the Black Swan, you can check it out if you like. They leave for London at half past ten and as it happens this time I'm not going with them.' He took out his official badge and his driving licence and a card on which he scribbled his mobile number. 'See? That's who I am. And that's how you can reach me. I promise I'll be at the police station by eleven or thereabouts, just as soon as I've seen them safely away.'

Ross thought for a moment. 'Very well, then. I'll expect you in the morning.'

As the three men accompanied the young constable down the hill to the car, the sky was lightening rapidly with the coming dawn. 'I was sick too,' Jonathan confided to the young policeman.

'I suppose I'll have to get used to it,' he replied. 'People do.'

'It won't always be as bad as that,' Latymer assured him. 'It was ghastly by any standards.'

The constable gave a wan smile. 'Why did you leave the force, sir?'

'Because I didn't like the way things were going, all the bureaucracy, the mountains of paper . . .'

'Do you miss it?'

Latymer had to admit that he did.

Jonathan and James got into the police car and Latymer watched it set off up the lane. It was now almost light and he was easily able to make his way across the field to his car. As he reached it, the sun rose into a clear, pale blue sky. Before him lay the rich rolling green countryside of Warwickshire, every tree and bush standing out as if newly-painted. Over the copse which contained the horror, a lark rose effortlessly into the sky, singing its heart out.

As he drove back to Stratford he switched on the radio to learn that the night's activities had made the early bulletins. A policeman had been seriously injured during an attack by demonstrators on a GM crop trial in Warwickshire and was now critically ill in hospital. Several other officers and a number of demonstrators had also been treated, mainly for minor injuries and there had been over twenty arrests. It was hoped that more details would be made available later in the programme. No wonder Ross had been so short tempered. Latymer switched it off and yawned. What a night.

The news had obviously got around for he found it being eagerly discussed over breakfast. The Americans in the party simply could not understand what all the fuss was about. GM crops were OK, they were grown all over the States and the only condemnation had come from ecology cranks. So why the protests? And all that violence! What, Latymer was asked by several people, will happen if that poor police officer dies?

'Whether he does or not, the police will be going flat out to find out who attacked him,' he told them, 'not least because it's one of their own. But unfortunately, as is often the case with this kind of thing, although there must have been plenty of people involved, it can be difficult to pin down a specific suspect amid so much confusion.'

'But if he does die and you get the culprit, then what?' one woman persisted.

'If he's found guilty, he'll go to prison for life.'

She stared at him in amazement. 'Is that all?'

'They don't have the death penalty here,' explained her friend.

She shook her head. 'There you are then!'

He heaved a sigh of relief as the coach carrying his party finally disappeared out of the hotel car park. He looked at his watch. Obviously he had to go to Warwick, as promised, but after that the day was his. In the event that Tess was at home, she would have assumed he'd have gone to London with his charges and wouldn't expect him back until that evening.

Meon Hill . . . the Witchcraft Murder. He mulled over the references in his mind. He'd noticed a sign that said 'Record Office'. After he'd made his statement to the police, he'd call in and see if they had anything on it. Before setting off for Warwick he rang Berry.

'Heard on the radio there'd been a bit of excitement your way last night, John,' his friend commented, cheerfully. 'Crop trashers and so on. Looks pretty bad for the officer, though. Not that you'd have seen anything of it.'

'Well . . . not *exactly*,' responded Latymer.

'Uh uh, what do you mean "not exactly"?'

'I didn't see anything of the crop trashing. But I did find a corpse. On a hill nearby where it happened.'

'*You what*?'

'Found a corpse. In a little wood on a hill near Lower Horton. At about five o'clock this morning. I'm just on my way to Warwick to make a statement.'

'Can't you go *anywhere* without falling over a body? You just happened to be passing by, I suppose?'

'No. I'd had a phone call from a young man who lives in my village. He'd been on the demo, ran away when it got nasty, and stumbled over it. He called me up in the small hours and begged me to come and see for myself.'

'It didn't occur to you that he might have been having you on? Or that he was just plain wrong and the guy wasn't dead?'

'Don't be daft. *Both* thoughts occurred to me. But anyway I went, God knows why. In the event it was as well I did.'

'And found . . .'

'A dead man wearing a grotesque green mask. With some kind of old agricultural bayonet-type thing through his heart and the prongs of a pitchfork each side of his neck.'

'My God!' There was a pause, then he heard Berry draw in his breath. 'Hang about? Wasn't there something like that near Stratford once before, years ago? Unsolved? Got it! The Meon Hill murder.'

'Bang on the nail!' agreed Latymer.

He rang off after promising to come over to Bristol to see him as soon as he could. He looked at the time. Better get going. But knowing how such things could drag on, he bought a copy of the *Post* to read while he waited. It was as well he did for when he arrived in Warwick he was asked to take a seat and wait as there was a press conference going on. He noticed that the door to the room was ajar, a reporter leaning against it, and sat down as close as he could so that he could hear something of what was going on.

The questioning was following a predictable course, interest focussing mainly around the injured policeman. So far there had been no change in his condition. Ross, who had finally managed to grab a couple of hours sleep, was fielding questions rather well. No, he'd had no warning that matters were likely to get so out of hand, it seemed another group, looking for trouble, had latched on to the initial protest.

Latymer yawned and unfolded the paper. There was a fuzzy picture on the front page under the headline 'Policeman Critical Following Demo', followed by a brief account of what had happened, a few words from Ross, and short statements from Mr Lucas Symonds (47) who lived nearby, whose brother-in-law, Mr Bob Wells (51), owned the land on which the crops were being grown.

'We all did our best to prevent things getting out of hand,' Symonds was quoted as saying. 'I told the demonstrators that if they packed up and left quietly my brother-in-law was prepared to leave it at that and take no further action. We hoped they'd listen to reason. I believe that most of those taking part were sincere about what they wrongly see as a threat to the environment, but unfortunately it looks as if their action was hi-jacked by people of a very different sort, out to cause as much damage as possible.'

Latymer turned to the inside pages. At the bottom of page

three under 'Inquest On Infant Death' there was a brief note to the effect that the Warwickshire coroner had set a date for the inquest into the remains of the newborn baby found recently in an old grave in the cemetery at Lower Horton. It would take place on 30th April. Latymer gave a wry smile, wondering what Ross would make of it if he revealed himself as both the visitor to Lower Horton churchyard whose curiousity had led to the discovery of the remains of the dead baby, as well as the man on the spot at the scene of a particularly gruesome murder.

A change in the noise in the conference room drew his attention back to what was going on. Ross had obviously been winding things down. There was the sound of chairs scraping on the floor amid general conversation, when out of the blue there was a question from the reporter who had been leaning against the door. 'Would Chief Inspector Ross confirm that a body has been found close to the site of last night's demonstration?'

There was immediate uproar.

'What makes you think that?' queried Ross, stalling for time.

'Word gets around. I've a contact living in Lower Horton who told me that when he went out very early this morning to take his dog for a walk across the fields near Horton Manor, there were police cars, a doctor's car and an ambulance in the manor driveway and the hill behind was crawling with people, some in white suits. You don't need to be Sherlock Holmes to realize there's something funny going on.'

There was more noise. It was the very last thing Ross had wanted. He'd hoped against hope that he could have kept it out of the news for another few hours. 'Very well, then,' he shouted. 'All I can tell you at this stage is that the body of a man was discovered in woodland close to Horton Manor in the early hours of this morning, that we are treating it as a suspicious death, and that it is hoped that a post mortem can be carried out later today. And no,' he declared firmly when asked if it was that of one of the demonstrators, 'the body hasn't yet been formally identified. Now, that's all you're getting for now. I've nothing more to say.'

He swept out, accompanied by two police officers. As he came through the door, Latymer stood up. Ross motioned him to follow. 'I suppose we'd better get it over with.' He turned to a constable. 'You'd better come along and take the statement.' He took Latymer into his office, sent for coffee. 'After we've taken your statement I intend going home for a couple of hours. I'll have the media on to me again soon enough. My boss is appalled. It seems he used to play golf with Symonds.'

Latymer then gave Ross his personal details and his reason for being in Stratford.

Ross heard him out. 'You said you already knew this lad, Jonathan Higham?'

'Yes, but not well. His family live near me, his father's a local estate agent, but Jonathan has hardly been home recently. He told me he's reading English and Drama at Warwick.'

'And you just ran in to him?'

'That's right. We exchanged a few words and I asked him if he'd like to meet up for a meal, knowing how broke students always are. I gave him my mobile number so that he could check his timetable and let me know when he was free. Obviously I never expected him to use it again, let alone call me in the middle of the night.'

'And did you meet up with him?'

'Yes, we had Sunday lunch in a pub in Warwick.'

'Did he tell you he was going to take part in the protest?'

Latymer smiled. 'It was hardly likely, seeing he knows I used to be a police officer.'

They then turned to the details of Latymer's discovery of the body up until the time the police arrived on the scene. After he'd finished Latymer asked after Jonathan.

'He didn't want his family told and insisted on going back

to the university. He's twenty years of age and we can't make him tell his people, although I stressed very strongly that he should. He'll be wanted at the inquest of course and so will you, I'm afraid.' He turned to the constable. 'Get that statement sorted then bring it back here for Mr Latymer to sign. And ask them where the hell's that coffee?'

It arrived as the constable left and Ross handed a cup to Latymer. 'I'll almost certainly have to talk to Higham again pretty soon – there's a gap of about three hours between his running away from the demo and phoning you to say he'd found the body. I need to know why.'

'You must have had a pretty bloody night, one way or another,' commented Latymer.

'I can't believe this is happening,' agreed Ross. 'A demo that went wrong, an officer who might well die, half a dozen others with various injuries and now a man murdered in a most bizarre manner, and not just any man, but a well known local figure. God, I must be paying for something I did in another life.This other murder, the one at . . . Meon Hill, is it? Can you tell me any more about it?'

'Not much off hand. All I can recall is that the corpse was found murdered in almost exactly the same way and that there seemed to be no possible motive for it. Though, of course, the war was on and compared with what else was going on at the time it hardly had priority.'

'So what's all this stuff about witchcraft?'

'Someone somewhere suggested early on that it might be connected to black magic, the occult. The date, which I can't remember, was supposed to be some kind of a witches' sabbath and there was lots of stuff about a throwback to pagan times, blood sacrifice to placate the ground and ensure good crops. That kind of thing. Of course, others immediately took and ran with the notion and I imagine the story grew in the telling.' He hesitated briefly. 'Actually, for my own interest, I thought I might have a look in the local records before I went home. See what actually did happen, perhaps do some research into it. There must be a good bit on the witchcraft angle as well. Not that I believe in it, but once or twice over the years I came across some deeply unpleasant people who did. No doubt you have too.'

Ross agreed. 'Look, if you do find out anything among your researches you think might be useful, will you let me know? I've enough on my plate as it is.' Latymer promised he would.

After he'd signed his statement the two men shook hands and he returned to his car. Yes, he'd see if they'd anything in the Record Office on the Meon Hill murder. As to the occult angle, both Jonathan and the man, Weaver, who Ross had brought with him to view the body, had assumed it was that of someone who'd been on the demo and who was heavily into all that kind of thing. Since he wasn't the corpse, might he not be the killer? Yes, it was certainly worth looking into. He looked forward to talking it all over with Berry.

Eight

The librarian at the Record Office reacted with weary resignation when Latymer asked if by any chance they had any information on the Meon Hill murder. 'I gather you have,' he commented on seeing the man's expression.

'I reckon at least once or twice a year someone turns up here asking about it,' the librarian replied. 'It's amazing how it still goes on and on.' The Record Office did not hold a vast amount of information but they did have the relevant copies of the *Stratford Herald* of the day on which the murder was first reported, plus subsequent further reports into the investigation. Latymer was shown through to a reading room and a little while later the librarian appeared with bound copies of the newspaper. After telling Latymer that should he want to copy anything then he must use a pencil (which could be provided), he left him to it.

Given wartime newsprint rationing the stories were hardly difficult to find and the first was on the front page and dated 16th February, 1945, two days after the discovery of the body. It was headed:

OLD MAN'S TERRIBLE INJURIES INFLICTED WITH BILLHOOK AND PITCHFORK

> Warwickshire police are investigating what may be a murder of a peculiarly brutal character. On Wednesday night, following a search, the body of 74-year-old labourer Charles Walton of Lower Quinton was found

> with terrible injuries on Meon Hill where he had been engaged in hedge-laying. A trouncing hook had been embedded in his body.
>
> Walton, a widower for many years, lived alone with his much younger niece. He'd spent all his life in the village, and in spite of his age still did odd jobs for local farmers. Neighbours described him as 'a quiet inoffensive old man', saying he was unlikely to have had any enemies in the village.
>
> It seems impossible to impute any motive for the murder. Miss Walton, his niece, is engaged to a Stratford man and after the discovery left home for Stratford. Police are continuing with their enquiries. Later it was stated that the police regarded the crime as the work of a lunatic or someone maddened by drink.

Lunatic, yes, thought Latymer, someone 'maddened by drink' reeling out of the pub, crossing a number of fields and climbing Meon Hill before running amok, not very likely.

'**NO DEVELOPMENTS IN MURDER CASE**' was the message a week later. But all was not lost. Warwickshire constabulary had called in no lesser person than Fabian of the Yard, Britain's most famous detective and his colleague, Sergeant Webb. More details were given of the injuries. Both instruments had been used ferociously. Three slashes had been made across the body with the hook while the pitchfork had been driven through the neck, pinning the body to the ground. A bloodstained walking stick nearby suggested that Walton had been hit on the head with it.

At the inquest, Miss Walton told the coroner how she'd instituted a search when her uncle didn't come in for supper and had set out to find him, accompanied by their neighbour of twenty-three years. But first they'd gone to see the farmer, a Mr Potter, for whom Walton had been working. He told them that Walton had been hedge-laying on Meon Hill and the three then set off. Potter was the first to find the body and seeing the state it was in, went back to the others as he did not think Miss Walton should see it. There was a lot of blood and a big gash on Walton's neck. They then saw a man working in a field lower down and asked him to send for the police.

Professor J. Webster, who carried out the post mortem, reported that the cause of death was shock and haemorrhage due to injuries caused to the neck and chest. Several ribs had been broken and the front of his clothing had been undone. All the blood vessels of the neck had been severed. Walton was, however, remarkably healthy for his age. The inquest was then adjourned.

After this there was nothing until 23rd March, and it was immediately obvious that Fabian of the Yard, brilliant as he might have been at solving major crime in big cities, had not got very far with the Warwickshire villagers of well over half a century earlier. Latymer smiled, recalling from his own experience the reactions of some rural villages to local crime, even today. To the inhabitants of Lower Quinton, Fabian of the Yard must have seemed like an alien from Planet Zog.

QUINTON MURDER ADDED TO LIST OF UNSOLVED CRIMES? queried the next headline. The coroner had wrapped up the inquest with a verdict of murder by person or persons unknown. Very little more had come to light, it seemed that the villagers were not saying anything; anything at all. Walton's watch was said to have been missing but it was unlikely he'd been attacked with robbery in mind as he rarely had more than a pound's worth of change on him.

The farmer, Potter, had been recalled to the resumed inquest, because he'd known that Walton was working up on Meon Hill. No, at no time had he quarrelled with the man and no, when he found the body, he'd touched nothing. Asked why he'd changed his story as to what he'd been doing earlier in the day, he told the coroner that he put this down to the fact that he had been suffering from the shock of the discovery. To which the coroner replied, 'One has to give you credit for being so distressed.' And that, it seemed, was that.

Except, of course, that it wasn't. The witchcraft story must have originated somewhere and there must be more information available. Having copied down what he needed and thanking the librarian, Latymer, after providing himself with paper and an envelope, called in at the office of the *Herald* and penned a brief note to the Letters Editor saying that he was interested in any information anyone might have on the 1945 Meon Hill murder, giving his email address. Since the last thing he wanted at the moment was for Tess to discover he was meddling in such matters again, he emphasized to the editor that although he had given his home address and telephone number as requested, he didn't want either published.

He felt increasingly depressed as he drove home. To avoid the Severn Bridge and its tolls, he'd cut across to Gloucester before turning west on to the road to Chepstow. As he drove through the now familiar villages and countryside, he wondered yet again why on earth Tess had set out with such urgency on such a drastic course. As ever when he was away from it, he mused on whether or not it might have been possible to retrieve the situation. But since nothing would have induced him to move to Somerset, then it really was all over. It might have been better in every way if they'd left things as they were in the early days of their relationship and never bothered to marry.

He turned right off the main road then left into the narrow road, still called a lane, to his house, one of several looking out across open countryside. The first thing to hit him was the sight of an estate agent's sign nailed to the gate, the second that Tess had put the agency into the hands of Higham Estates. He swung the car into the drive and burst in to find Tess and Higham, who was holding a clipboard, deep in conversation. They looked at him in surprise and there was an awkward pause.

'I didn't expect you until later,' declared Tess.

'Evidently.' Latymer didn't attempt any formalities.

Higham looked from one to the other and Latymer guessed that Tess had apprised him of the situation. 'Ah, well, I'll be running along, then,' he said, fingering his tie. 'I've told . . . er . . . Tess you should easily get £285 grand for it at today's prices.' He turned to Tess. 'I'll make sure all prospective buyers ring first, as you asked.' He saw the copy of the paper under Latymer's arm. 'Heard about that demo, I suppose? Policeman half-dead. As I've said before, until they bring back hanging it'll never get any better. As for the rest of them, they all want locking up.'

Latymer was infuriated but made no comment as Tess showed Higham to the door and let him out. 'What the hell do you think you're doing putting the house on the market before we've even discussed it?' he demanded as soon as she came back into the room.

'You don't need to shout. What is there to discuss? You've made it crystal clear you won't move to Somerset with me. Obviously I can't buy the house I thought might have suited both of us, but I've found a smaller one which will do. Property's selling fast there and I was advised to make an offer on it straight away. Which I have.'

'And what am I supposed to do?'

She shrugged. 'That's up to you. Now you're here, do you intend staying the night?'

'I intend staying here every night until the house is sold,' he told her. 'I'll move into the back bedroom, I've been sleeping in there half the time as it is.'

'Very well. Then in the meantime, let's try and be civilized about it. Dave Higham thinks we'll sell straight away and it could all be settled within about two months. I'll be spending a good deal of time with Diana, anyway. Her doctor says the baby might come early and that she should give up work now.'

The thought of starting house or flat-hunting again on his own account filled him with despair. He walked through to his study, comforted by its familiarity. It was unlikely he'd be able to afford anything offering him such space again. He then went out to the kitchen to make a cup of tea to find Tess had already done so. She put out two mugs and poured the tea in to them. 'I know what you think of Dave Higham,' she said, in a more placatory tone, 'but he's been most helpful.'

It was on the tip of his tongue to tell her that Higham might soon be needing help himself, but sadly realized he couldn't trust her with the story. Ross was right. Jonathan would need to account for the hours between the end of the protest, and the call he had made. Surely he couldn't have hidden up there for three hours? In fact, if he had, then he'd have been there when the murder actually took place. Yes, if he'd been in charge of the investigation, he'd certainly want to know what the lad had been up to. And if he wasn't able to come up with an adequate explanation, then Higham senior would have to be involved, if only to provide him with a decent solicitor. It would be interesting to see how Higham would react if he felt his own flesh and blood had been wrongly accused. Yet for the life of him Latymer couldn't imagine Jonathan carrying out such a bestial attack. John and Tess exchanged a few more words, Tess told him that she had enough food in for two and they agreed that they would eat together. How civilized, thought Latymer, how absolutely bloody civilised.

He returned to the study, switched on his computer and checked his email. He learned that he would be wanted for a tour of the Shropshire and Welsh Marches in three weeks' time, and after that two more based in Oxford. Would he please confirm. In the meantime there was nothing. On an impulse he emailed Fiona Garleston:

> I seem to have become involved, without meaning to, in some more strange goings-on. Not drugs or depleted uranium this time though, and hopefully not MI5! But you say you have info on GM crops. Do you have any details of protest groups? In strict confidence, of course. Or, more specifically, the more way-out ones, those into

> crop circles, fertility rites, Druids and so on? And have you ever come across someone calling himself Shrieve? The matter also touches on the occult. I hope to get more on this within the next few days and will mail you again then. I don't know how long I'll be at my home address, though the email will remain the same. Tess has decided that she must move to Somerset to be close to her daughter and I don't want to go. Might have been different earlier on, but last year seems to have driven us permanently apart. So, there you go, a second broken marriage. At least you and James were happy together. Yours, John L.'

The next morning he walked down to the village shop and newsagent and stopped, rooted to the spot, at the array of dramatic headlines spread across the newspaper racks. It had been a slack day for news and the media had fallen on the Symonds murder like a flock of vultures, almost all of them picking up the association with the Meon Hill murder.

IS THIS A RITUAL KILLING? queried the *Express*. WITCHCRAFT CURSE STRIKES AGAIN howled the *Mirror.* SADISTIC SLAYER STALKS WARWICKSHIRE the *Star* informed its readers. The *Telegraph* had a resumé of the story on the front page under the restrained heading BIZARRE MURDER, then pointed its readers in the direction of page 5 where they would learn more of the obsession with the occult that was sweeping the country. An obituary of Lucas Symonds could be found on page 9.

The *Guardian* contented itself with MURDER VICTIM FOUND FOLLOWING ANTI-GM CROP PROTEST in smallish type towards the bottom of the front page. No sensationalism there then. Indeed, there was no mention of a possible connection with the occult until the end of the report when readers were promised that the next day's *G2* supplement would carry a whole host of goodies: features on pagan fertility beliefs, the influence of the cult movie,

The Wicker Man; comments from their stable of columnists; and an interview with a practising witch, coven member and lifestyle author, Hecate Teesdale.

He bought half a dozen and took them home with him and, on meeting Tess in the hall, handed her over a copy of the *Telegraph.*

She scanned the front page. 'What a dreadful thing!' She looked at the wodge of papers under his arm. 'How can you be so ghoulish. I suppose next thing you'll be telling me you're off trying to solve it.' There was no answer to that. 'It's where that anti-GM demo was, isn't it? Where that policeman was so badly hurt. At least it's just said on the news that he's improving slightly. I'm in the little bedroom sorting out some of my stuff there,' she told him, changing the subject. 'I'll put yours on one side.'

Throughout the day he and Tess were coldly civil to each other, each trying to keep out of the other's way. Two prospective buyers came to look over the property without committing themselves, meanwhile Tess's offer on the Somerset house had been accepted. Oh God, thought Latymer, I'll have to get myself together. Possibly the best thing would be to find somewhere to rent to give himself a breathing space. He rang Berry and arranged to meet him for lunch the next day.

After breakfast the following morning he switched on his computer and couldn't believe his eyes. There must have been at least twenty emails, each one headed 'Meon Hill murder'. There were letters, stories, half a dozen lengthy attachments which turned out to be copies of magazine articles and chapters from books. It took him well over an hour to print it all off; he didn't want to risk saving them only on the computer in case for some reason he couldn't get at them again. Anyway, they were easier to read as hard copies.

One correspondent had drawn his attention to a website which, he was promised, would tell him all he needed to know. Better take a look then. He went on to it and waited. At first nothing happened, then gradually the screen turned black and eyes began to come at him out of the darkness, all kinds of eyes. They'd grow bigger and bigger then dissolve and more eyes would come, accompanied by creepy music. Next came the menu. None of the items listed looked particularly appetising and he wondered what heading Meon Hill would come under. Eventually he chose 'Ritual Murder'. There followed a long list and about halfway down he came across 'Witchcraft at Meon Hill'. He downloaded the item, then quickly ran through what else was on offer, some of which he thought quite sick. He was astonished to find at the very end that the owners of the domain also ran a dating agency. 'Are you single? Looking for a suitable partner?' it queried. 'Click here and fill in your details.' He wondered who on earth, or rather *what* on earth, might turn up if you did. A vampire? A practising Druid? He didn't want to know. He'd take the whole lot over to Berry and see what he made of it.

For the police the situation was rapidly turning into a media nightmare in which the only gleam of light was that the policeman was now expected to live. Most of the arrested protestors had been dealt with fairly quickly and while, had things been different, more of them might have faced charges, at the end of the day the number charged and bailed to appear before local magistrates amounted to less than a dozen. Several of the protestors had witnessed the attack on the policeman but none of them had any idea of the identity of the attacker, masked as he was as a green man. As for the murder of Symonds, since he'd manifestly been alive after all those arrested were safely in police custody, they could all be eliminated from that particular investigation. The single arrested green man, who gave his name simply as Jez, was still being held for further questioning in an effort to find out the names of those he had travelled down with.

A suitably chastened Mark Ransom, informed of Symonds'

murder, had already been questioned at length in the hope that he could throw more light on the identity of Shrieve and his organization, but he was genuinely unable to help. 'Why don't you ask your police constable?' he asked eventually, in frustration. 'She brought that nutter to my flat in the first place. She must have met him somewhere.' But Detective Constable Rainbird had been sent home to nurse her cracked ribs and was now weeping copiously over the report of Symonds' death. However, Mark, Penny and James had done their best to come up with a description of Shrieve.

James had also provided them with a list of those members of the Sustainable Agriculture Forum who had taken part, all of which were known either to himself or Ransom, if only by name, and he could personally vouch that none of them had arrived in the minibus or worn a green mask. Dee gave the police the name of the person who had invited him to give the talk when Shrieve had been the other speaker, but even if he'd kept a note of the person's telephone number, which he doubted, it would be back at his home. The meetings had been held in a room in a defunct school building in Fulham. He couldn't remember the name of the road but he could take police to it if necessary.

The patrol car had checked out the vehicles at the lay-by and all the cars did belong to those who claimed they did. They were all taxed and in order. As for the missing minibus, a message had gone out to look for it but the search was hampered by the fact that its registration number wasn't known.

Jez was then questioned again. 'You deaf or stupid or something?' he enquired belligerently. 'I've told you all I know.'

'Well you can tell us again,' Ross informed him and asked the constable present to switch on the tape recorder.

It was pretty much a waste of time. No, he didn't belong to no group. No, he hadn't taken part in nothing like it before. Who did they think he was? Swampy? Asked how, in that case, he'd got to know about the demo, he replied that he'd heard it from someone in a pub.

As ever, groaned Ross to himself, it was the stock answer to everything.

Yeah, the person in the pub had been on the minibus. His name? Kevin? Dick? He couldn't remember. If he'd never taken any interest in anti-GM crop protests before, then why was he there? Thought it'd be a bit of a laugh. And he'd been pretty wrecked when he'd agreed to come. No, he hadn't seen who whacked the copper, the first he knew was when he'd seen him lying on the ground. 'After that two of your plods thumped me on the back of the 'ead and pushed my face into the ground.'

Ross ended the interview. 'Take him back,' he said to the constable. 'We'll have another attempt later, then we'll have to let him go.'

Ross's thought processes had mirrored Latymer's. If Shrieve, whoever he was, wasn't the victim as Weaver and Higham had thought, then he was certainly in the running to be the killer. If he truly believed all that stuff about blood sacrifice, then Symonds, the owner of the crop trial land, would be a prime target. But there must be other motives? A strong-minded entrepreneur like Symonds might well have made enemies during his career and someone had mentioned to him that there'd been trouble in the past when he sold his land for development. Though surely, if someone had had it in for him then, they wouldn't have waited this long to do something about it? Perhaps Wells would be able to come up with some suggestions. A more recent enemy then? But why a carbon copy of a half-century-old murder? Unless it was to throw the police off the scent.

Certainly, what was proving the worst aspect of it all was the glaring spotlight shone on the investigation by the gruesome nature of the murder and all the baggage that went with it. It had taken only a matter of hours for the first papers to link it to that of the Meon Hill murder and even less time thereafter for all the stuff about witchcraft to be dragged out. In the hope that it might throw some light on the subject Ross had got Wilkins to dig out the basic facts of the case which were still on file.

He wondered if it was worth sending a man out to Lower Quinton to see if anything useful might be found there, but he doubted it. At the time speculation had been rife, facts hard to come by, and anyway those living in the village when the murder took place, and had been adults at the time, must now be either very old or dead. Younger locals, those who had been children, were unlikely to have known much about what was going on and could only report on what they'd learned later. Not only that, it was common knowledge that no one had been prepared to say anything back in 1945 and from what he had read in the media so far, it was soon made plain to reporters that no one was prepared to say anything much now.

In normal circumstances the idea of using John Latymer in a consultative capacity would never have crossed Ross's mind. But given the tremendous pressure he and his colleagues were now under and the welter of stuff on the Meon Hill murder which was now muddying the waters, it might be useful to have a trained mind examine the old material and see if it did yield anything that might be of use. He would give Latymer a call.

'Cripes!' exclaimed Berry when Latymer put the folder of printouts down in front of him. 'What on earth did you do to get this lot?'

'Put a letter in the local Stratford rag giving my email address and asking for any information on the Meon Hill murder and it poured in. It probably still is. I seem to have tapped into a rich seam. I suppose interest in Meon Hill is at a premium: it was horrific in its own right, was apparently motiveless, had a strong element of ritual, and was never solved. And look here . . .' Latymer pulled out the copies he had made of the original newspaper reports.

Berry ran his eye down them. 'Good God! Fabian of the Yard. My customers would love this. What a picture it conjures up! The great man from London in his trench coat, a trilby hat on his head – did he smoke a pipe? – and his sidekick, driving down to Warwickshire to solve a little local murder. I wonder where they stayed? Presumably at a posh Cotswolds hotel like something out of Agatha Christie.'

'I'm glad you find it entertaining,' observed Latymer. 'You'll find the rest less so.'

Half an hour and a good deal of reading later, Berry agreed. 'I hate this kind of stuff. No wonder the press are over the moon. It's going to run and run if they don't get the killer very soon, and it doesn't look as if it's going to be an easy one, does it?' He picked up one of the printouts. 'This one's right off the tree. Who sent it to you?'

'I downloaded it from a weird website. I don't think I'll be going on to it again, it was full of really sick stuff.' Then, in spite of himself, he had to smile. 'But do you know, it even ran a *dating agency*!'

Berry made photocopies of all the material and the two men arranged to meet again soon. 'Obviously I must be out of my mind,' said Latymer, 'but I thought I'd go to the inquest on that baby they found in Lower Horton churchyard since it was partly down to me that the discovery was made; though I intend keeping a low profile. I did wonder what Chief Inspector Ross would say if he knew I'd been instrumental in bringing that to their notice as well.'

'I don't suppose there could be a link in any way?' suggested Berry. 'Apart from yourself, and the fact that there's been so many strange goings-on in Lower Horton within a very few weeks.'

'I wondered about that too, but I can't honestly see it.'

They were at the bookshop door when Berry stopped and smote himself on the head. 'What am I thinking of? Is it absolutely definite that you and Tess are splitting up?'

Latymer nodded. 'I came home to find she'd put the house on the market.'

'That's what I meant to tell you. A friend of ours has some property in the city that he lets out to careful tenants and there's an unfurnished flat coming up soon on the other side of Bristol. Between Whiteladies Road and the zoo, quite a nice area and, I understand, quite a nice flat. It might be a useful stopgap measure for you while you look for something else. Hang on a moment and I'll give him a call.' He disappeared back into his office leaving Latymer to browse round the shelves at the hundreds of volumes, new and second hand, fiction and true crime. Murder, he thought, never lost its popularity.

Nine

Latymer drove back from Bristol deep in thought. He had to admit the flat, on the ground floor of a detached Victorian house, was very pleasant. It was empty and the landlord was having some minor alterations and repairs done but if Latymer wanted it he could take it over in about six weeks' time. For what it was the rent was not unreasonable. Faced with finally having to make such a decision he almost said he'd go away and think it over, but when it came down to it he asked himself why. Think *what* over? One way or another he was forced to move. Why not get it over with even if the house sale hadn't yet gone through. He agreed to take it and the landlord said he'd post the necessary paperwork to him then fix a time to meet again.

Tess had told Laymer she'd be out for lunch but when he returned her car was parked outside and he went in to find her showing a couple round the house. She gave him a warning look. 'It really is lovely, isn't it, Don,' beamed the young woman, 'and not overlooked or anything.' She turned to Latymer. 'You must be really sad to leave it.' He agreed that he was, gave her what he hoped was an encouraging smile, and retired to his study.

A little while later Tess came to find him. 'They've made an offer,' she told him. 'It's almost all our asking price. You'd better come.'

'*Your* asking price,' he reminded her. 'If I remember rightly, I wasn't even consulted on that either.'

They found the young woman standing by the French

window leading into the garden. 'Oh, and you've done so much to the garden too. Is there a nice one where you're going?' Latymer made some non-committal response. After asking a few more details and exchanging the names of solicitors, the couple left.

'Have they got one to sell?' he asked as they drove away.

'No,' said Tess, shortly. 'They're both divorced. There's no chain.'

He smiled bleakly. 'Sounds like us when we bought it. Let's hope they have better luck.'

'It isn't my fault,' she said, her face set. 'You could have come to Somerset with me.'

'After all that's happened? I don't think so.'

She went over to the table and came back with a piece of paper which she handed to him. 'Oh, by the way, there was a phone call for you this morning just after you left. From a Chief Inspector Ross of Warwickshire police. He wants to talk to you urgently. Presumably he wants you to solve his murder for him. I'll ring our solicitor and put him in the picture.'

Towards the end of the afternoon of the previous frustrating day, Ross had finally gone over to Lower Horton to interview Bob Wells and ask him if he'd formally identify the body. He'd also rung Horton Manor and arranged to see Symonds' housekeeper and her husband who had their own quarters in the house. Wells lived in a substantial, three-storey Warwickshire farmhouse, prompting the young detective constable who was driving Ross to mutter darkly about moaning farmers and subsidies.

The farmer opened the door to them himself and ushered them into a pleasant and comfortably furnished room. 'I'll get Liddy, who helps us, to make some tea. As you can imagine my wife's in a pretty shattered state.' He reappeared a couple of minutes later and invited them to sit down.

'Do you think your wife is up to having a word with us in a little while?' enquired Ross.

Wells looked doubtful. 'I'll have to see what she says. It's been an almighty shock.' He looked from one to the other. 'So where do you want me to start?'

'From wherever you think is relevant,' Ross told him. 'Perhaps it might be as well to start with your decision to take part in the experiment. It might help.'

Wells explained how he'd been persuaded by Symonds to undertake one of the government's crop trials. 'To be honest, I don't think I'd have bothered but he was very keen. He can – could – be very persuasive and he really did believe it was the way forward for the future. After your Detective Constable warned us there might be trouble, he said not to worry. He'd fix up lights and some kind of a device to give us some warning; he was into that kind of thing. He also suggested dealing with the protest himself, leaving me out of it as much as possible.'

'Why was that?'

'He said he felt guilty because it was all his idea and he didn't want me to suffer as a result of it. As much as anything for Marian's sake, he's always been the big, capable brother. Their own father died when they were children. She's going to miss Lucas dreadfully.'

'I know this is an obvious question, but do you know if your brother-in-law had any enemies? Such a successful, wealthy man can rouse all kinds of passions, not least envy. No aggrieved employee or bitter business colleague?'

'Not so far as I'm aware. If there was then he never said anything to me and we discussed most things.'

'How about when he sold off the land for development? I understand some people were very upset?'

'But that was five years ago. It's all died down since. I can give you the name of the man who organized the campaign against it, if you like, but I'm not even sure he still lives in the area.' Wells frowned. 'But surely this is the work of a psychopath? No sane person could possibly do such a thing.'

'One would think so,' agreed Ross. 'Naturally we're investigating the possibility that the murder was directly connected to the protest.'

'But it must have been. You saw those maniacs in green masks for yourself. I wouldn't think you'd have to look much further for the killer, they were off their heads.'

'Possibly not,' Ross agreed, 'if we can find any of them. The original protest had been properly organized – if that's the right term to use – by an outfit calling itself the Sustainable Agriculture Forum. They brought an observer with them who gave us an accurate list of all those taking part, none of whom were wearing green masks. More to the point they were all being held at police headquarters at the time the doctor estimates the murder took place, which rules out all those we arrested. As to the green men, unfortunately all but one successfully got away. We trying to find the minibus they used and since they all came down from London, the Met are helping.'

The door opened and a young woman came in with the tea. 'Help yourselves,' Wells told them. 'I'll go and see if Marian's up to seeing you.'

'Doesn't seem much to go on here, sir,' commented the constable as the door shut behind him.

Ross had to admit that there wasn't. He looked round the room again, which he thought looked cluttered, but homelike. Framed reproductions of classics such as *The Hay Wain* hung on the walls and there were a number of framed photographs on shelves either side of the fireplace: a younger Wells and his bride at their wedding; the bridal couple again with Symonds, who must have been best man; Marian Wells holding a baby; again with another baby and a toddler; also a young man in cap and gown, presumably the Wells' son; and a large photograph of a pretty, dark-haired girl in school uniform, who must be the daughter of the house.

The door opened and Wells ushered in his wife. Ross estimated Marian Wells to be in her mid-forties. She would normally, he thought, have been a good-looking woman but now her face was swollen and blotched with tears. As she saw the policeman her eyes brimmed again. 'I'm sorry,' she whispered. Her husband sat beside her and poured her a cup of tea.

'We realize how hard this must be for you,' said Ross, gently, 'but if we're to find who did this terrible thing to your brother, we'll need all the help we can get. I've just asked your husband if your brother had any enemies, anyone who might have borne him a grudge.'

Marian Wells shook her head. 'No. There's never been anything like that. Lucas has always been so popular locally. Always willing to help out with anything and put his hand in his pocket for good causes. You can ask anyone.'

Ross nodded. 'Do I take it he never married?'

'No,' she replied. 'It's really rather sad. He was engaged to a lovely girl ages ago, the date had been set for the wedding and everything, then without any warning, she suddenly broke it off. We never learned why and he's never talked about it. He's had several relationships since, but nothing permanent.' She became tearful again. 'It's such a shame. I could never understand it. And he'd have made such a good father, he's never been able to do enough for our two.'

Ross looked across at the photograph of the young graduate. 'I take it that's your son.'

This brought a brief smile. 'Yes, that's Michael. He graduated from Bristol last year. He got a first in physics. He's in America now on a Fulbright scholarship. We're very proud of him.'

'And the young girl in the silver frame's your daughter?'

There was a sudden and definite change in the atmosphere. 'Yes,' responded Wells, shortly.

There's something funny here, thought Ross, then continued: 'Is she at college now or still at school?'

'She's away,' said Wells, whereupon Marian Wells burst

into a further flood of tears. He turned to Ross. 'Is this necessary? You can see the state my wife is in.'

'I'm sorry,' said Ross. 'We won't keep you any longer, Mrs Wells. I'm sorry it's proved so upsetting but we need to get as full a picture of your brother as possible.' She nodded and, with her handkerchief still pressed to her face, left the room.

Ross stood up. 'We'll leave it for now then, Mr Wells, until we've arranged a time convenient for you to formally identify the body.'

'I could come over in a couple of hours,' Wells told him, 'when I've finished what I'm doing on the farm. I might as well get it over with.'

'Thank you, that would be helpful. In the meantime if you can think of anything else that might be useful, let us know. Once you've identified the body, we should be able to get a date for the inquest quite soon. Little more than a formality, of course, it'll be opened and adjourned.'

Wells went out to the door with them, but as Ross was about to get into his car he called him back. 'It's got nothing at all to do with this business, Chief Inspector, but there's something perhaps you should know so that you don't upset Marian again. It's about our daughter, Lucy. Three years ago, when she was coming up to taking her GCSEs, she left home without warning. She was only fifteen at the time. It was a great shock. There'd been no quarrel, no ill-feeling. She took some clothes and, we think, about £50 in cash, and left us a note saying she was sorry and loved us very much. And we've never heard another word.'

'Did you report that she was missing to the police?'

'Of course. And they asked us what you'd expect. Had there been any trouble at home? We assured them there hadn't. Under too much pressure at school, perhaps? Not at all, she's very bright and she'd no difficulties with her schoolwork. Did we think there was a boy involved? Not so far as we knew, at least no particular one. She was lively and popular with boys and girls.'

'And you say you've heard nothing since?'

Wells shook his head. 'Because she'd taken clothes and money with her and left us a note, the police in Stratford didn't think she'd been abducted or anything like that. They told us how many hundreds, thousands, of youngsters go missing every year. Some are found, some not. I believe she's still on the Missing Persons Register.'

It was a sad story Ross had heard all too often from bewildered parents. 'I'm very sorry,' he said. 'I can see how her brother's death must have hit your wife particularly hard in the circumstances. But, you know, there are many, many cases where youngsters do turn up again. Or at the very least contact their homes through organizations like the Salvation Army.' He climbed into the car. 'See you later, Mr Wells. I promise you, we'll do all we can to bring this killer to book.'

The next port of call was Horton Manor, where they found the housekeeper, Mrs Hodgkins, as bewildered as she was upset. She asked them to come in and called out to her husband who joined them. 'George does all Mr Symonds' odd jobs about the house,' she explained. 'He's a good carpenter too and there always seems to be something for him to do.' Ross asked her how long they had been at the manor. 'Oh, it must be ten years, perhaps a bit more.'

'I was made redundant from the furniture firm I'd worked for all my life,' Hodgkins told him, 'and Joan was doing school dinners. Then she saw an advertisement in *The Lady* for a cook housekeeper. She applied, told Mr Symonds about me, and he took both of us on. He's been very good to us. Goodness knows what we're going to do now.'

'Can you tell me what happened last night?'

George looked at his wife. 'You tell him, Joan.' Then to Wells: 'She tells things better than me.

According to Joan, Symonds had warned them that night

that an attempt might be made to destroy the GM crops, however everything was in hand. He understood from the police that the demonstration was expected to be peaceful, but in the circumstances it might be a good idea if they stayed inside and kept all the doors locked, which they'd done. 'We heard all the noise and carry-on and after a bit George did go out to see what was happening but by that time you were putting people into police vans. He said there was someone lying on the ground. It must've been that poor policeman who was so badly hurt. Then it all went quiet.'

After having a good look round, Symonds had come in and reassured them everything was under control and that if anyone was lurking about the place it would trigger off the sensor lights and he'd ring the police straight away. 'He told us to go and get some sleep.'

'And what did he do?'

'He said he'd stay up for a bit. He usually goes to bed late. He said he'd have a large scotch – or two – put some music on and read a book until he felt ready for bed. Then he went into the lounge. As we were going up the stairs I heard his mobile phone ring, but I didn't hear what he said. Whatever it was he wasn't on for long.' The first they'd known that something was wrong was when the police cars drew up outside.

Ross asked the usual questions. Had there been any strangers hanging around recently? Had they seen anything remotely suspicious? Were they aware of any bad blood between Symonds and any of his neighbours? Or anyone else for that matter? To all the questions, the answer was no.

Latymer rang Ross back straight away but was told the chief inspector was out. However, a couple of hours later he called back and explained what he had in mind. 'I'd like, if it's possible, for you to do some work for us in a consultative capacity. You said something about doing some research into the original Meon Hill murder. Do you think you could do that as a start? It's a long shot but there just might be a clue in there somewhere which would help us with this one. At the very least someone knew exactly how the other victim had been killed and reproduced it as closely as possible. Then there's all the witchcraft stuff as well.'

'Actually I already made a start,' Latymer told him. 'I got hold of the copies of the original reports in the local newspaper when it happened, along with a great deal more I didn't expect.' And he told Ross about the response to his letter in the *Herald.* 'I'm drowning in stuff on witchcraft.'

'Well, if you can take this on, you'll relieve my mind of a weight.' The sound of a yawn came down the line. 'I'm so tired I can't think straight.'

Latymer marshalled his material in front of him, the growing pile of printouts of letters (they were still coming), the magazine articles and book chapters, the downloaded document from the website. Then he set about some serious reading. Towards the end of the afternoon Tess looked in and informed him that she'd got hold of their solicitor and that the house sale was being set in motion. 'In view of our situation, Bill Latham wants us to go in and see him so that he can draw up the necessary paperwork to give us each a half share of the purchase price of the house, after the settlement of all the usual fees. Oh, and we'll need to sort out the furniture and other things.' She seemed very matter of fact about it all.

'I'm not going to start arguing,' he told her. 'I'll need some basic stuff for the flat . . .'

'Flat? What flat?'

'The one I agreed to rent this morning.'

'You never said anything.'

'Why should I? For God's sake, I have to live somewhere!'

For the first time since she'd made her decision she looked disconcerted, as if the full implications were finally sinking in. 'Yes, of course.'

'OK, so you're buying a house. I thought I'd mark time for a bit while I decide what to do, whether to rent or buy again. So, as I said, I'd like to take some basic stuff, I'll not quarrel over what. And everything from my study, of course. And my books and the pictures I had when we married.'

She stared at him without saying anything. Ever since his return from Scotland the previous year she'd refused to talk properly about anything. For months she'd nursed a grievance which had finally resulted in her decision to move to Somerset, with or without him, and once her mind had been made up, she'd gone ahead apparently without a second thought. Yet, he thought, it was Tess who had so enthusiastically worked on the house and garden, involved herself so closely in village affairs, had made friends (if so they could be called) with others who'd taken early retirement or who, like the Highams, had bought a house in the village 'to enjoy country life'. Country life being a subscription to the nearby golf club and embarking on a round of competitive dinner parties.

'All right then, fix it up with Latham.' He looked at the calendar in front of him. 'Any day except the 30th. I've something else on then.' She looked for a moment as if she was finally going to say something, then changed her mind and went out.

He returned to his task. First, the basic story. This as least was the same in all the many accounts. Charles Walton had gone up on Meon Hill to do some hedge-laying, taking with him the necessary tools, a kind of billhook and a pitchfork. His niece, who had lived with him since she was three years old, had become concerned when it grew dark and he hadn't come in for his tea. She and the neighbour had gone to ask the farmer for whom he was working where he might be, and the farmer had then joined them on a search of Meon Hill where almost immediately they'd found the body.

Next came the investigation. The local police, getting nowhere, had called in Fabian of the Yard and he and his sergeant, assisted by Superintendent Spooner of Warwickshire police, had taken hundreds of statements, all leading nowhere.

It was quite clear that no one was prepared to say anything. The only suspect brought in for questioning had been an unfortunate Italian prisoner of war from a local POW camp who was working nearby at the time, and there'd been a good deal of excitement at the possibility that not only had a foreigner done it, but an *enemy* foreigner at that. However, it transpired that the Italian could not possibly have carried out the murder. Finally Fabian and Webb returned to the Yard, the case unsolved, a case which so obsessed Spooner that for the rest of his life on the 14th February, the anniversary of the murder, he revisited Meon Hill.

The brief details of Charles Walton's life were also spelled out for all to see. How he'd been walking out with a farmer's daughter with marriage in mind, but in 1913 had suddenly dumped her and married 'out of the blue' his own cousin. He was then forty-three, she twelve years younger. There were no children from the marriage and she'd died in 1927. At some stage Walton had taken in her sister's three-year-old child, the niece who had been living with him at the time of his death. Possible motives? His wife had left him about £200 in her will, a quite considerable sum at the time. Walton had put it in a Building Society and, so people averred, had never touched it. Yet, after his death, only £2.11s.9d. was found in it, though no withdrawals had been made after his death. What had he needed the money for?

But it seemed that ever since most people had made up their minds as to why it happened, only the reasons differed: satanism, black magic, witchcraft, ancient sacrificial rites; you could take your pick. After all, the date was significant. 14th February was not only St Valentine's Day but the date of the Roman festival of Lupercal, also of one of the great witches' sabbaths, and a day devoted to some obscure Anglo-Saxon ceremony. The spilling of blood, as many commentators pointed out, had played a key role. For centuries in ancient times sacrifices had been made to ensure a good harvest and placate the earth, the Earth Mother or a variety of other Gods. Throw in Druidism, or legends of human sacrifice at the Rollright Stones, not far from Lower Quinton, and there you had it. After all, 1944 had been a very poor year for the fruit crop, and 1945 hadn't shaped up to be much better; Walton had been a blood sacrifice.

Or not, if you went for the witchcraft theory. His attacker had been killing a witch or warlock. Apparently in Warwickshire, as late as 1875, a disturbed young man had killed a woman, Anne Turner, with a pitchfork, claiming that she was a witch and that this was the right way of dealing with them. He'd also slashed a cross on her chest similar to that found on Walton, claiming it was the only way of stopping them rising from the grave. Judge and jury were unimpressed, however, and he was hanged. But there was enough stuff on witchcraft, ancient and modern, to write a book on Meon Hill.

Finally, ghosts and the supernatural and one story in particular had grown in the telling over the years. The earliest version was that a young ploughboy, working fields in Alveston, near Stratford in the 1880s had, over the course of the week, met up with a large black dog every night on his way home. Altogether he crossed its path eight times then, on the ninth, instead of a black dog a headless woman had rushed past him and the very next day his sister died. Not only that, the lad's name was *Charlie Walton!* Was it the same one? asked the various storytellers. But oddly enough no one seemed to have been bothered enough to find out and anyway Alveston was a fair distance from Lower Quinton and it was also said Walton had only ever worked in and around his home village.

Not to worry. Soon the tale of the black dog (and headless woman) had been transposed to Meon Hill and needless to say there had been a spate of sightings of black dogs ever since, not to mention rushing, headless women. Even Fabian of the Yard was supposed to have encountered 'the Black Dog'. Spectral black dogs were not infrequent in folk lore, Latymer learned as he read on. As well as the nationwide legend of the Wild Hunt, the Yorkshire Moors had a spectral hound, the Barguest, while Dartmoor boasted the original for the Hound of the Baskervilles. He recalled seeing a play in Stratford some years back, *The Witch of Edmonton*, in which the devil had appeared to the poor old woman accused of witchcraft in the form of a black dog.

He went through it all again. Surely, the killer *had* to have been a local person and a good many people must have had a fair idea of who it was, and the reason for the murder, even if they didn't know for certain. He thought again about the missing money that had leaked away from Walton's account but which it appeared he hadn't noticeably spent. Blackmail? If so, over what? Whatever the real reason, however, all that witchcraft and supernatural business must have been a godsend to the murderer. He was sad to see that in the end even Fabian appeared to have gone along with it, issuing a statement published later in several of the magazine pieces:

> I advise anybody who is tempted at any time to venture into black magic, witchcraft, satanism – call it what you will – to remember Charles Walton and to think of his death, which was so clearly the ghastly climax of a pagan rite. There is no stronger argument for keeping as far away as possible from the villains with their swords, incense, and mumbo-jumbo. It is prudence on which your future peace of mind and even your life could depend.

Good God, thought Latymer, how over the top. But then, so far as Fabian was concerned, his investigation had been a total failure. It was, he supposed, one way of letting himself off the hook.

Ten

At least, thought Ross the following morning, there was some good news. The injured police officer was now out of intensive care and expected to make a full recovery though no progress had been made in finding his assailant. On the other hand, Detective Constable Wendy Rainbird was found to have punctured a lung and was likely to be off for some time, but she had rung in the previous day to say that she was back home and up to being interviewed, indeed, eager to help in any way she could since she had, after all, met the ringleader of the green men. For some reason, for which no one was able to come up with an adequate explanation, the message had only just reached Ross and, after giving all and sundry his views on the subject, he called her up.

Yes, she told him, she was sure she could provide a description of Shrieve and help put together a computer likeness of him but no, she had no information as to his whereabouts. She had met him through Rowan, who'd told her about the demo and introduced her to the Sustainable Agriculture Forum people. But surely they knew that? She herself had seen Rowan being arrested and presumably he had information about Shrieve that was worth following up?

'I'll look into it,' said Ross. 'In the meantime I'll send Wilkins round now with a graphics man in the hope you can come up with something good.'

'I should be able to,' she told him, 'he was a really weird-looking guy.'

After ringing off, Ross checked with the records but Rowan

Ash (surely an assumed name?) was not one of those bailed to attend court and had therefore been allowed to go without being charged. He had left an address and telephone number but Ross was not surprised when informed later by the constable detailed to follow them up that the address didn't exist and the phone number was unobtainable. He knew he was being unfair but he couldn't help feeling annoyed that Rainbird had got herself carted off to hospital before giving him a potentially useful piece of the information which, if he'd had it earlier, might have resulted in their being able to question Rowan further.

Wendy Rainbird had been surprised at just how upset she had been to learn of Symonds' death. On the briefest of acquaintances, he had come across as a genuinely decent person with that rare gift, genuine charm, a point she made to Wilkins. 'He came over to the ambulance and actually told me I must let him know how I was. It's hard to imagine how anyone could do that to him.'

Wilkins grunted. She was, he thought, still comparatively wet behind the ears however good she might be at infiltrating eco-warriors. Briskly, he changed the subject to that of Shrieve.

'I met him a couple of times,' she told him. 'The first time with Rowan when I went with him to his "Green Circle" and then again, just before the demo when the three of us went to Mark Ransom's flat to find out what the plans were. But he's so bloody odd it surely shouldn't be difficult to find him.' She then offered a detailed description, after which the artist produced his laptop and they got down to producing an image. 'He had what I think they used to call in books a cadaverous face,' she told them. 'Quite gaunt, with highish cheekbones. Rather pale. His eyes were dark and deep-set. His hair was weird. He was kind of balding at the front but he'd grown what there was and wore it pulled back into a thin, greyish-brown ponytail. Age? I'd say, probably late forties. Far too old for a hairstyle like that and anyway it's out of date.' The artist worked away and, quite soon, came up with an image that she agreed was very like Shrieve. 'He was quite tall too, around six one or two,' she added, 'and thin.'

The two men looked at the image. 'Well, at least that gives us something to go on,' commented Wilkins. 'Pity we didn't have it sooner, Rainbird.'

'I didn't even know how important it was until yesterday,' she retorted, 'and as soon as I realized what had happened I rang the boss. It's not my fault he didn't get the message until this morning.'

'All right, all right, keep your hair on,' snapped Wilkins, who'd borne the brunt of Ross's wrath. 'We'll go back and show him what we've got. It's up to him what he does with it.'

'So you see,' Latymer observed to Berry, 'whether the original Meon Hill murder has anything to teach us or not, I must admit I couldn't resist Ross's offer. I couldn't help but think that by agreeing to it we might be able to have some unofficial input into the case.'

'I take your point,' his friend agreed. 'But to be honest I'm not sure there's all that much mystery surrounding the Lower Horton death. Just from reading the papers, I'd put my money on that oddball with the ritual sacrifice fantasies being the prime suspect. Just think about it. What a publicity triumph! The killing of a pro-GM crops landowner in a spectacular way which makes headlines in all the papers. Did Ross tell you if they were making any progress towards tracking him down?'

'Apparently none. I rang him this morning before coming over. They found the minibus parked in a quiet road on the outskirts of Oxford. It seems it was hired from a rundown rental firm in Balham by a Mr Jones.'

'But surely they must have asked for some real proof of identity before hiring the vehicle out . . .' Berry began, then checked himself. 'What am I saying? Quite likely not.'

'You're right. It wasn't that kind of a set-up. It was a ramshackle old heap and whoever rented it paid cash upfront. As for Shrieve and the rest, they seem to have vanished into thin air. Ross got nowhere at all with the only one of his lot they arrested, who really does seem to have been nothing more than a young yob who came along for the ride looking for trouble.'

'You've no contacts with any of the others involved then? How about the person they brought out to take a look at the body? Or the young lad who phoned you?'

'Jonathan wouldn't be much help, but as to the man they brought with them, then that's a thought,' admitted Latymer. 'I think he said his name was Weaver. He belonged to the other lot and he'd done his best to stop the demo from happening at all. But when his advice was turned down, he went along to check up who was taking part and observe what went on. Now, he might not be able to help much but he told me he'd been taken to the nick with another non-participant, a college lecturer who'd come across Shrieve before as his subject is ancient history, myths, beliefs and so on. He might be useful.'

'I could look into it a bit if you like,' Berry suggested. 'Running a bookshop like mine brings you into contact with those who have other specialities and there's a real market today for anything to do with the New Age, the occult, and so on. If you think it worthwhile, I'll go up to London and make some enquiries. It could be that someone in one of these shops might have heard of this nutter and his set-up.'

It was what Latymer had hoped he'd say. 'So long as we don't step on anyone's feet at police headquarters then that sounds like a good idea. I wonder now . . . suppose I say to Ross that I understand he picked up an academic with knowledge of myths and cults and that kind of thing and it might be useful to me if he could run an expert eye over the Meon Hill material and advise me, and would he be prepared to give me a contact number for him. It's worth a try.'

Berry grinned. 'Great! I'll have a go then.' He looked at Latymer. 'Sorry, but I'll really enjoy getting my teeth into this one, like we did last time. Do I take it you believe the two murders are linked in some way? Other than by the method of killing, that is.'

'I don't know. I have this hunch, but there's really nothing to go on apart from the obvious angle of ritual sacrifice to placate the earth. Anyway, I'll have a word with Ross and see what he says. I'll play it very carefully, I don't want him going off the whole idea of using me and, indirectly, you. Oh, by the way, I'm going to look in on that inquest, the one on the baby.' He groaned. 'Which reminds me, I'll be called to give evidence for Symonds once they've sorted out a date. I just hope they can get it over before I start work again and before I move house.'

'I was told you liked the flat.'

'It's very pleasant. At least it offers a solution to my housing problems while I'm thinking what to do next.'

In the event, Ross was quite happy to give Dee's contact telephone number to Latymer so long as it was made clear to him that he wasn't being pressured in any way. 'He was very frank with us, told us everything he knew about Shrieve, though it wasn't much. His name's John Dee and apparently he's well respected in his field and as a result often receives invitations to give talks to a variety of groups and organizations, which is how he came to be invited along by these weirdos and met up with Shrieve.'

At first Dee was somewhat startled when Latymer got through to him at his college, though he listened with some amusement to his account of the response he'd had to his query about the Meon Hill murder. 'Tell me about it,' he said, with a laugh. 'Any enquiry of that sort always provokes a torrent of information. So what's your particular interest in this? And how come you're involved with the Warwickshire police?'

'I discovered Symonds' body, or rather a young student of my acquaintance found the body and contacted me in the middle of the night to come out and deal with it, since he knew I was in Stratford and that I'm an ex-copper. I was interested in the similarity with the Meon Hill murder and told Chief Inspector Ross that it might be useful to look into it again to see if it might offer any clues to the present day; a long shot, I admit. So as he's got enough to do, he told me to go ahead. Obviously whoever killed Symonds went to great lengths to duplicate what happened to the Meon Hill victim, Charles Walton, in every detail.'

Dee picked up on the thought. 'So what you're saying is that a certain amount of planning must have gone in to it?'

'That's right. And to a lesser extent I think that might also have been the case with the original one as well. The first statement from the local police was to the effect that it must have been done by a punter who'd rolled out of a pub blind drunk, which seems as unlikely as the black dogs and headless women which accrued to it later. But it would be useful if you could run your eye over the material and see if it's possible to separate fact from myth.'

'And so you'd like me to meet up with this friend of yours who runs a bookshop in Bristol?'

'If you could. We worked together in the force some years back and, more recently, on something else which turned rather nasty. He's free to go up to London and also has contacts with specialist bookshops, while I think I'm more useful down here at the moment. Though I'd prefer Chief Inspector Ross didn't know I was sending a proxy or that my interest has now strayed outside the bounds of the occult and a murder which took place half a century ago.'

'Well, I'm more than willing to meet your colleague though tell him I can't promise I'll be able to help much. I've already told Ross all I know about Shrieve.' He laughed again. 'I didn't know the police were so understaffed they'd taken to using private detectives!'

'They haven't,' declared Latymer. 'Apart from the myths and legends, anything else is strictly between ourselves.'

It was raining as Latymer reached the coroner's court in Stratford but it obviously hadn't put off those members of the public determined to attend and there were a surprising number of them, most of which were women, as well as a couple of reporters. Almost any inquest into a violent death or scandalous death draws in both the simply curious and the ghouls, but he wasn't surprised that the strange circumstances surrounding the discovery of the dead baby had prompted more than usual interest among women. Were any of those comfortable-looking matrons sitting quietly chatting to each other, he wondered, fearful that the child might possibly be the sad outcome of a liaison involving a daughter or granddaughter?

Since the last thing he wanted was to draw attention to himself, he stationed himself at the side of the back row of public seats. At the last minute, just before the proceedings started, a group of young people came in and sat down and among them was Jonathan Higham. Presumably he was with a group of fellow students, but what on earth had induced them to attend this particular inquest?

He had no time for further surmise as the coroner then entered the room. The proceedings began with a brief note of the finding of the dead baby after which the first witness was called to give evidence: the police sergeant who had discovered it. The reason he'd investigated the grave, he informed the coroner, was because the vicar had brought a wooden box into the police station which, when examined, turned out to contain cremated human remains.

'Apart from where it was found, was there anything unusual about the casket and its contents?' enquired the coroner.

The sergeant shook his head. 'No, sir. With regard to the cremation, there is no doubt that it was carried out as is usual in any of the country's crematoria. As to the casket or box, while cremated remains are often put in standard containers, some families prefer a casket perhaps because they want the ashes buried in a churchyard or cemetery. The pine box was a standard one. Most undertakers will supply them and obviously we checked with all the local firms, but only one of them had made up such a box in the previous twelve months and that was for the interment of someone who wanted the ashes to be buried in Scotland, while forensics say the box found at Lower Horton had only been in the grave at most a matter of weeks.'

The coroner nodded. 'Thank you, officer. Now to the case in point.'

The policeman explained how he'd removed with a trowel some of the earth beneath where the casket had been in the hope that it might yield some information as to who might have put it there, and had then noticed what appeared to be a piece of dirty cloth. 'So I dug down deeper and found what turned out to be either a cot blanket or a shawl, but very discoloured and rotted. It wasn't until I started trying to get it out that I realized it contained the skeletal remains of a very young infant.'

'I take it that there was absolutely no clue as to the identity of the child?'

'None at all, sir. There were no remnants of clothing on the body, no trinket, nothing but the actual remains.'

'I presume you have been making enquiries with regard to finding the mother?'

'Yes, sir. And we publicized it in the local paper too, but no one has come forward. They rarely do, even when it's a newborn and the body is found immediately and the mother in real need of medical help. DNA samples have, however, been taken for possible future use.'

'I see. Thank you.'

The last witness was the pathologist who confirmed the remains were those of a newborn infant, born at around the seventh month of pregnancy, and that it was impossible to say whether it had been stillborn or died immediately after birth of natural causes. 'Given the circumstances, its prematurity and the lack of medical care, that would not be surprising,' she told the coroner. It was only guesswork, but experience suggested that the mother was most likely to have been very young herself, had not known how to deal with the situation she found herself in and panicked.

'Is it possible that the child was related to the person whose cremated remains were also found in the grave?'

'That might well be a possibility but the cremated remains were reduced almost to fine ash. It would be almost impossible to get a DNA sample from them,' she replied.

The last witness was the vicar, the Rev Jane Hutchens. Her attention had been drawn, she told the court, to the slightly disturbed state of the grave by a passing visitor who had noticed that fresh flowers had been left in a very neglected part of the graveyard. She, in turn, had asked her churchwarden if he knew anything about it. He did not, so they had gone and looked at the grave together. Their subsequent investigations had unearthed the pine box, which they had taken straight away to the local police station.

'Is it usual for flowers to be put on that particular grave?' enquired the coroner.

Jane Hutchens replied that it was not. It dated from 1830 and no one related to the family of the woman whose grave it was lived in the locality any longer.

'I imagine you have no idea why either the cremation or the child's remains should have been put there?'

'Absolutely none. I made some discreet enquiries and also put a note in the parish magazine encouraging anyone who could throw light on the matter that they could talk it over with me in the strictest confidence, but so far nothing's come of it. However, when it is possible to release the remains of the infant for burial, I would like to hold a small funeral service and see to it that the child is properly and decently interred in the churchyard, even if it is "known only unto God".'

The coroner thanked her. 'It must have been most upsetting for you.'

'It was. I agree with the pathologist that the most likely explanation is that it was the child of some poor, desperate girl, too frightened to seek help.' She paused. 'Following the discovery I went back through parish records to see if I could trace the original occupant of the grave, Elizabeth Bidford. It seems she died in childbirth at the age of eighteen and that her child was stillborn. As she is described as a spinster of this parish, I imagine this too is a sad story, though someone must have seen to it that she was decently buried and remembered.'

The coroner conferred with his clerk and ruffled through the papers, then addressed the court. 'I see no point in adjourning this inquest since there is so little chance of discovering the identity of the infant. I must therefore return an open verdict.'

So that was that, thought Latymer. But a strange tale all the same. Surely there had to be a connection between the cremated remains and the child, and therefore someone must know what it was. He left the room behind a group of women who were chattering like magpies. A variety of young local girls were being put through the rumour mill. 'That Janice from Luddington's a right little madam. Chasing the lads from twelve years old even though her dad threatened to lock her in her bedroom and put bars on the windows!'

'And what about that family on the council estate – two of their girls had kids before they'd even left school,' offered another.

'That's hardly surprising,' her friend broke in, 'half the family were down the precinct in Coventry touting for trade of a night.' She put her head out of the door. 'It's stopped raining. What about a coffee?'

The small crowd set off, leaving behind an older woman

in its wake who turned to Latymer. 'I think they're all wrong. Girls like they describe either aren't bothered these days about having a child out of wedlock or know too much to get caught out. I think the doctor and vicar were right. It's far more likely to be some poor little soul who didn't dare tell anyone. I do some work for a young people's charity, which is why I came along. It's so hard to reach them when they need help.' She smiled. 'And what was your interest?'

He decided to tell her the truth. 'I was the visitor who noticed the flowers on the old grave, though obviously I'd no idea it would lead to anything like this. I suppose you could say I'm here out of simple curiousity.'

The group of young people, of which Jonathan was one, were among the last to leave the court room. From the look of surprise on his face, he'd obviously not noticed Latymer as he had been in a dark corner at the back. There was an awkward pause.

'Before the other week I hardly saw you from one year's end to the next,' Jonathan managed, eventually. 'Now we keep meeting up in the strangest of circumstances. What's brought you here today?'

'I happened to be the visitor that noticed the grave had been disturbed. It was out of interest, nothing more.'

'You coming for a coffee, Jon?' asked one of his friends. 'Yes . . . yes . . .' Then to Latymer: 'Perhaps you'd like to join us?'

Why not, thought Latymer, since this whole business is getting odder by the minute. They decided to make their way down to the theatre café where they spread out around several tables. 'Are you all drama students?' Latymer asked Jonathan, who confirmed that was the case. 'So why the interest in the inquest.'

'Greta, here, saw the story in the paper and thought it would make a good improvised piece of drama. You know, who the mother was, why she was so desperate, how she'd got into such a predicament, and all that kind of thing, which is why she thought we should see if anything more came out today.'

'Actually it was you who suggested we came over for the inquest,' returned Greta.

Jonathan frowned. 'Was it? I seem to recall we all thought it was a good idea. Anyway, as it's turned out, we haven't learned much.'

'Except for that cremation. That's really weird. I'm sure we can make something of that as well.'

As his fellow students began talking animatedly among themselves, Jonathan turned to Latymer. 'Don't leave your friends on my account,' Latymer told him.

'It's OK. We're all free now until this afternoon when we all have to be in college for lectures. Actually I'm glad to have bumped in to you. I wouldn't have bothered you again, honest, but I'm sure Chief Inspector Ross thinks I know a lot more about that . . . other business than I do. He's asked me to go in and see him again the day after tomorrow. He keeps asking me what I did in the time between my running away from the demo and finding Symonds' body. He says it must have been three hours or more before I rang you.'

'It's a reasonable enough request,' Latymer told him. 'What *were* you doing?'

'I don't know. I mean, it's all such a muddle. All that violence really scared me and I got into a panic. All I know is that I ran off somewhere or other, across some fields, I don't know where except that I ended up quite close to the river and I stayed there for what seemed like ages waiting for everything to die down. Then I thought I'd better make my way back to the car, but I'd lost all sense of direction. If you remember it was very dark and there was no moon. It'd been raining earlier and the ground was already pretty waterlogged and my feet kept getting clogged up in the mud, and what looked as if it had once been a path had been cut in half by a huge, new ditch. Then I saw what looked like a small hill in front of me and thought that if I went up it

I'd be able to get some idea of where I was, possibly see Lower Horton Manor and, if the police were still there. If they weren't then at least I'd be able to make my way back to the road. It took me longer to get to the top than I thought as there was barbed wire in places. I was really tired. I'd been up very late the night before, so I sat down for a bit on a log to get my breath back. I reckon I must have nodded off for a few minutes as I woke up very stiff and cold and then I went to the edge of the copse to have a good look round.

'I could see the house down below, so then I knew exactly where I was. Everything was quiet, there was no sign of any cars. I thought, Blow it, if the police are still lurking down there waiting to catch any stragglers, then too bad. I knew my friends must have buggered off back to Warwick by that time and I'd have to get back as best as I could. The quickest way was through the copse and straight down the hill, so I started running to keep warm and that was when I fell over . . . it. Then I rang you. I've no idea how long all this took.'

Latymer conceded that what he'd recounted was thin but possibly the truth; at the very least it would be difficult to prove it wasn't. 'Then you must tell the chief inspector exactly what you've told me,' he said.

'I already have. But he doesn't seem to want to believe it.'

'Then you'll have to tell him again, in even more detail if necessary.'

'Coming, Jon?' one of his friends called across.

He signalled to them that he was. 'I have to go, Mr Latymer.' He gave him a bleak smile. 'I suppose I'll see you again at the other inquest, the one on Mr Symonds. Perhaps one day we'll actually meet in normal circumstances.'

Latymer watched him go. Now, I wonder, he asked himself, what I should make of all that?

Eleven

'Not sure where you are so am emailing this as suggested,' wrote Fiona Garleston. 'Thing is, an old friend who lives in Bristol has invited me down for a few days and I thought it would do me good to have a break. I've hardly been away from home since James died. Any chance of us meeting up? Give me a call if you can.'

Tess was out so Latymer rang her straight away. 'You're still at home then?' she enquired. 'I didn't quite know what I should do.'

'I'll be here for another month or so, I reckon,' he told her. 'When will you be in Bristol?'

Within a few days, she told him, as soon as she could make the necessary arrangements for someone to look after the dogs and keep an eye on her house. 'Obviously I'd like to see you but not if it's likely to be difficult.'

'Not at all, it's easy enough for me to get over to Bristol. I expect Keith Berry would like to meet up with you again as well.' He thought for a moment. 'Look, you know I asked you about people who were anti GM crops? Well, since then there's been a rather weird development, in fact I seem to have become involved in a rather odd series of events.'

'Again?' He could hear the amusement in her voice.

'Well yes, I suppose you could say that. Except that I don't think it's as dangerous as last time round, though it is distinctly strange. There's recently been a murder near Stratford-upon-Avon, following a GM crops protest. What's strange about it is that the victim was killed in a most bizarre way, identical in fact to another murder over half a century ago, which has become known over the years as the Witchcraft Murder. I've been doing some research into it and now I'm beginning to feel I can't see the wood for the trees. Would it be OK if I sent you some of the material to have a look at before you come up to Bristol?'

'I've no expertise in witchcraft or anything like that,' she told him, 'indeed quite the reverse. I try and steer clear of anything that suggests fisherking is just another cranky website.'

'You don't need to have. What I'd like you to do is to cast your eye over the old story – the murder was never solved – and see if anything particularly strikes you about it, apart from the obvious; whether you might see a possible motive. No one could come up with anything much at the time, other than that it was done in a moment of drunken frenzy, which is why all the stuff has grown up about witchcraft, earth sacrifice and so on. Your intuitive eye, coupled with common sense, is probably just what I need.'

'But what's it got to do with the murder you say happened recently?'

'I'm not at all sure, but I suppose it could just be that there was something common to both, apart from the fact that both men were killed in exactly the same bizarre way. Although I must warn you, this isn't how the police see it. They think they know why it was done and who probably did it. Anyway, I'll do some photocopying and send the stuff off straight away, express delivery.'

'All right, I admit to being intrigued,' she conceded, 'though I'm not at all sure I'll be of any use. At least it will give me something to do on the train journey.' Before she rang off she gave him the phone number of her friend in Bristol, leaving him to contact her. Neither of them mentioned the personal situation he now found himself in.

Berry went up to London the next day armed with a list of

shops specializing in the occult, witchcraft, astrology, New Age or associated subjects. There seemed to be an alarming number of them and as it was obviously impossible for him to go round them all, he spent the journey reducing it to those he thought sounded most likely and which were also easily accessible. Two of those on his list turned out to be in the same small side street close to the British Museum. The first looked dauntingly upmarket, the volumes on the shelves old, mostly bound in leather and astronomically expensive. No, their trade was almost entirely rare books and *incunabula* and no, they had never heard of anyone called Shrieve who was interested in ritual sacrifice and had a group of followers who may or may not call themselves the Green Men.

'It sounds like something you've read in the *News of the World* or the *Daily Mail*,' the shop's manager told him, haughtily. 'Most of our books deal with 16th-century astrology, horoscope casting, the use of astrology in the medicine of the day and what were known in that period as the New Sciences. The notices we display are solely for academic lectures, nothing remotely resembling what you seem to be looking for.'

After such a reception he didn't even go into the second shop which, if anything, looked even grander than the first. The third, near St Giles' Circus, wanted to sell him magic crystals and books on Druids and offered him lists of events taking place at next summer's solstice. The fourth, at the top end of St Martin's Lane, was closed, indeed it looked as if it had been closed for months. He went and had a coffee and referred to his list again. He noted that there was another shop, not far away off New Row in what looked like a back alley in something or other – he couldn't read the tiny print properly – Court. After which, if he drew a blank there, he would have to go further afield to Hampstead or Kensington. For what seemed like an eternity he trudged up and down New Row and the streets both sides looking for 'Miasma', without success, until a helpful postman kindly pointed the entrance out to him. It wasn't surprising that he'd missed it, it looked like a door into someone's back yard.

'Don't mention it,' the postman replied when Berry thanked him. 'People who've worked round here for years don't know where it is.'

Webb's Court proved to be a tiny cul-de-sac, with three small shops or offices on one side opening directly out on to the pavement, and a small double-fronted house on the other bearing a blue plaque. He supposed the whole could be described as quaint. 'Miasma' was the middle one of the three and at first he thought it, too, was closed as it looked so dark inside, but when he tried the door it opened. He went in. The interior was lit by a couple of dim lamps standing on a shelf at the back beside a curtain and there was a heavy smell of incense; at least he hoped it was incense. Immediately inside the door, on the left-hand wall, was a notice board advertising various events, while the shop itself was piled high with paperbacks on everything from the religion of Wicca to the more respectable Feng Shui, along with crystals, candles, pottery and figurines. There was scarcely room to move. Berry screwed up his eyes and was beginning to read his way through the notices when a young woman, robed in purple velvet and wearing a great deal of black eye make-up, appeared from behind the curtain and enquired if she could help him.

'I'm not sure,' he told her. 'You see a friend of mine went to a couple of meetings on the subject of ancient rituals to do with the earth, the Green Man and so on, and how this fits in with the way we're polluting the planet today. He said the person who gave one of the talks was very interesting and ran some kind of group or society. I know this sounds rather vague,' he added, busking away for dear life as she fixed him with a bored stare, 'but I've been trying to locate the speaker as I thought he might be interested in coming down to Bristol some time.'

'What's his name then?' enquired the young woman.

'I think my friend said it was Shrove or something . . . No, Shrieve, that's it, Shrieve. I was looking at your board as I thought there might be a note of another meeting where he was speaking.'

She gave him a disparaging look. 'You don't seem very sure who it is you want. Anyway, couldn't your friend tell you how to get hold of him? If he's that interested, presumably he'd know when this person was likely to be speaking again and where.'

'My friend's travelling in the States,' Berry informed her, 'otherwise I wouldn't need to trouble you.'

She sighed heavily, came round from behind the counter and scoured the board with him. 'Oh, very well, there's a pile of stuff round the back I haven't had time to put out yet. I'll go and get it.'

She returned a minute or two later with a pile of leaflets and pamphlets which they started working their way through. Suddenly she stopped and waved a small notice at him. It was rather badly printed on pale green paper and informed the reader that over a period of three days there would be a course on the subject 'Back to the Past – the Only Way to Save the Planet?', consisting of a series of talks and workshops on the myths and rituals surrounding the placating of the earth and the worship of nature. Subjects to be covered would include fertility rites, the primitive use of sacrifice, customs and folklore, and the place of the Green Man in religious art. He looked at the dates. Today was the third day of the course and the final lecture, at 7 p.m. that evening, was to be given by a very special guest speaker, Duncan Herviser, who the writer was sure would be known to some of those taking part in the events. However, it was to be an open lecture and the venue a hall in Camden Town.

Berry had hoped to return home by mid-evening but it did look as if the meeting might at least offer a possibility of his being able to find out more if he went along.

'Are you going to stand there for the rest of the morning?'

enquired the young woman tartly, bringing him back to earth. 'This isn't a public library. It's a *shop*.'

He mumbled an apology, asked if he could take the flyer with him then, noticing a small paperback on the subject of the green man, he bought it and hurriedly left the premises. He looked at his watch. It was already well after one and he'd arranged to meet John Dee for a late lunch in a pub near the university so he'd better make his way there. Perhaps Dee would have some idea whether or not it was worth his while to turn up for the lecture. The two men had exchanged descriptions of themselves over the phone but the pub was fairly crowded and Berry was beginning to think they should have worked out a more efficient method of recognition when a voice behind him said, 'You have to be Keith Berry! I can't imagine anyone else would be brandishing a book on the Green Man.'

He turned round to find Dee smiling broadly. 'And you're John Dee.' The two men shook hands. 'I didn't intend to buy it,' admitted Berry. 'It was just that I spent so long in the shop asking for information and so on that I felt shamed into buying something.'

Eventually they found a corner where they were able to talk and Berry told him of his search and produced the leaflet. 'Could be,' commented Dee. 'I don't know anything about this particular course but these offbeat events go on all the time. It's worth a try. You could spend weeks trying to find Shrieve and his group and still not succeed. I've been making enquiries myself ever since the protest, but without success. I went out to Fulham with a couple of detectives immediately afterwards but the place where we gave our respective talks was boarded up "for redevelopment" and no one round about seemed to know anything of what went on there. As for Shrieve and co., in view of what happened I imagine they'll be lying pretty low, whether the murder was down to one of them or not.'

'I'm not sure what to do,' Berry confessed. 'This is all quite unofficial.'

'Why get involved then?'

Berry shook his head. 'I don't really know except for the fact that John Latymer and I've both got the taste back for this kind of thing; it's very addictive, you know.'

Dee nodded. 'Look, I've nothing important on tonight. Why don't we meet up there? Whoever this Duncan Herviser is – and the name doesn't ring any bells with me – it would be interesting to see how he reacts if we ask him if he's come across Shrieve. And even if he doesn't know or want to tell us, there might be someone there who can or that I might recognize from the Fulham meetings. Not that I'd be able to prove any of them were at the actual protest since they were all wearing those green masks. One did remove his briefly at the start, but it was dark and I certainly wouldn't swear I could identify him again.'

'I'll see how easy it will be to get home,' said Berry, taking out a railway timetable. He ran his finger down the column. 'There's a train at 10.30 which would get me into Bristol by just after half eleven. How long do you reckon it would take me from the hall to get to Paddington?'

Dee shrugged. 'Depends on our lousy tube service. Let's see, Northern Line on to Circle or Metropolitan – three quarters of an hour?'

'OK then. I'll give my wife a call and ask her if she'll meet me at the station.'

'She must be very long-suffering.'

'She is. But I imagine this will cost me dinner out!'

Berry duly arrived at the hall in Camden at about a quarter to seven, making sure his book on the Green Man was clearly visible, to find that the hall was already more than half full. He made his way to a seat a few rows from the back, sat down beside a middle-aged woman, and after giving her was what he hoped was a confident smile, asked if she'd heard the lecturer before.

'No, he's new to me,' she told him, 'but they say he's very interesting. Haven't seen you at any of the other events or workshops over the last few days,' she added.

'It's difficult for me to get to things,' he told her. 'I don't live in London, you see.'

'Your particular interest is the Green Man?' she continued, glancing at his book.

'Er yes . . . he appears on carvings in a number of churches around me. I saw the book in a bookshop near Covent Garden and saw a notice about the meeting tonight, so I decided to come along to learn more.'

'You were asking about the lecturer,' broke in a younger woman, sitting behind. 'He's really devoted to his subject. I heard him some months ago and he knows his stuff.'

Berry looked at his watch, it was nearly seven. Where was Dee? He hoped he hadn't decided to give it a miss. The hall was rapidly filling up and he was beginning to get complaints about his 'keeping a seat for a friend'. Eventually, as the meeting was just about to start, Dee finally arrived. 'Sorry, got held up at college,' he apologized in a whisper, sitting down beside Berry, just as a bearded man with shoulder-length grey hair walked on to the platform and up to the microphone and called for quiet.

'It's good to see so many of you here tonight,' he began, looking round the hall. 'However, it seems our guest lecturer has been held up, so while we're waiting, I thought, as organizer of "Back to the Past", I'd offer a brief summary of how it's gone. I think those of you who attended all, or even part, of the three-day event will agree that it's been a great success.' Unfortunately, in spite of promising a brief summary he was one of those people who are incapable of being concise and as time passed and he droned on it was evident that the audience was becoming restive. He was halfway through a resumé of day two when the door opened at the back and two young men came in and made their way straight to the front and on to the platform, stopping the speaker in his tracks.

'Trouble?' suggested Dee.

'I don't think so,' said Berry. 'No, it looks as if the old bore knows them.'

An animated conversation was now taking place, involving much hand waving on the part of the organizer. Finally he shook his head, shrugged, and stepped forward. 'Ladies and gentlemen,' he began, 'I'm sorry to have to tell you that tonight's speaker, Duncan Herviser, can't make it after all.' There was an immediate hum of complaint. 'I really am sorry but I've only just been informed.'

'What's the problem?' someone called out from behind Latymer. 'Whatever it is, surely he should have let you know before now? I've come halfway across London.'

The conference organizer looked helplessly at the two men who merely shook their heads. 'It seems something has cropped up. Obviously we'll refund the ticket money for tonight's event or, if you prefer, we can credit you with the ticket so that it can be used for another event.'

'That's not good enough,' declared Latymer's female neighbour. 'Even if something has "cropped up" , then whatever it is Herviser knew he was committed to coming here tonight. Most of us booked our tickets in advance, the lecture was supposed to round off the course. Has he been taken ill?'

'Look, I'm really sorry,' the organizer responded, in exasperation. 'I know no more than I've been told and that is that it was simply not possible for Duncan to be here with us tonight.' There was a noise of chairs scraping across the floor and the audience began to leave, a slow business as most of them queued at the door to get their money back.

'Perhaps a few questions might be in order,' suggested Berry and they made their way towards the organizer, who was still in deep conversation with the two men who had brought the news. On seeing the newcomers, the conversation ended abruptly. The organizer looked extremely uneasy.

Herviser's friends were singularly unprepossessing. Berry

put their ages at around thirty, both were burly, had close-cropped hair and the smaller of the two had a ring through one eyebrow. They were both dressed in black. The only word Berry had caught was 'television'.

'Sorry to bother you,' he apologized, 'but I've come a long way tonight to hear this particular talk.' He looked at the man with the face ring. 'Can you tell me if Mr Herviser is giving his talk anywhere else in the near future?'

The man shrugged. 'Dunno,' he responded, disinterestedly.

'I hope he can come and give his talk again here soon,' the organizer responded. 'It's very disappointing.'

'I'm a college lecturer myself,' Dee informed him. 'My subject's ancient history and myth and I was particularly interested in hearing Herviser, though to be honest I've never previously come across him which is unusual.'

As he spoke the man with the ring looked at him. 'Haven't I come across you before?' He narrowed his eyes. 'So you reckon you're a lecturer?'

'I don't "reckon" I'm a lecturer,' Dee retorted, 'I am. I also give talks to interested groups. Perhaps you saw me at one of them.' His interrogator muttered something in his colleague's ear.

'Presumably you have a contact number for Mr Herviser,' persisted Berry. 'If you can let me have it then I can contact him direct and ask if he'd be prepared to come down to Bristol.'

The two men glowered at the organizer, who was growing more uncomfortable by the minute. 'Er, I think it would be better if you left your name and telephone with me,' he stuttered, 'and I'll let you know. Now, like I said, if you go up to Tom on the door you can have either a refund or a credit.'

This was obviously as far as they were going to get and Berry was about to hand out a business card when he suddenly felt uneasy. 'I think I'll leave it for now,' he told the organiser.

'My friend here will keep an eye open for any publicity in London.' Then he decided on a last, full frontal, attempt. 'By the way, you wouldn't happen to know where I might come across a man called Shrieve, would you?'

You could have cut the air with a knife. 'No,' replied the organizer, with all the authority he could muster. 'I know no one of that name. Now, if you don't mind, I'd like to close up the hall and get off home.'

'There's definitely something funny there,' commented Dee as they went out into the street. 'I wonder if the one who said he'd seen me before was one of the green men at the demo?'

'It's a possibility,' Berry agreed. 'Where do we go now?'

Dee looked round. 'I think if we go down here by the side of the hall, we'll find it's a short cut to the tube.' As they turned to do so, two figures loomed up in front of them out of a side alley. Even in the gloom it was possible to see the glint of the ring in the eyebrow of the smaller of the two.

'Get in there,' said the bigger of the two and hustled Dee and Latymer into the alleyway.

'What the hell do you think you're playing at?' demanded Berry.

'That's what we want to ask you,' snapped the man with the ring. 'Police, are you?'

'*Police*!' Dee protested. 'Why on earth should you think we're police? Is it usual for plain clothes cops to turn up at your meetings then? They've never been to mine, or at least not that I've been aware of.'

'Why did you ask all those questions, then?' barked his companion. 'Why did you want to know Duncan's telephone number?'

'For the reason I gave the organizer, what else?' retorted Berry. 'What's the problem with that? Your man in trouble or something? If this is the way his friends carry on, then I'm not surprised.' As he spoke, he began to push his way between the two men at which point the man with the ring hit him hard in the face, adding to his friend, 'Let's see them off.'

Berry spat the blood out of his mouth and kicked ring man hard in the crotch then, as his assailant howled and clutched himself, he knocked his legs from under him so that he fell heavily to the ground. His companion, taken by surprise at the speed of events, took a step back, whereupon Berry pushed him hard against the wall, knocking the breath out of him. 'Come on,' he said to Dee, as they ran down the road as fast as they could, but it was soon apparent that there was no pursuit.

'Now what the hell was all that about?' queried Dee. 'Talk about drawing attention to themselves! If they'd just left things alone, it's unlikely we'd have bothered to do much more about it.'

'They're obviously panicky about something,' replied Berry, feeling his face. 'Shit, that bastard seems to have loosened a tooth. Presumably it was my mentioning Shrieve that did it. Perhaps this guy Herviser's a close friend of his or something.'

'You didn't half do well,' declared Dee as they reached the tube station. 'God knows what I'd have done if I'd been on my own. I've never been any good in a fight.'

'I seem to have retained some of the old skills,' Berry agreed, 'though I doubt what I did comes within normal police procedure.'

He awoke the next morning, much to his wife's concern, with a stiff and swollen face but before trying to get an appointment with his dentist, he rang Latymer to tell him of the events of the previous night.

'Well, you certainly rattled someone's cage,' Latymer responded, 'and I think I might know why. Haven't you seen today's *Western Mail*?'

'Not yet,' responded Berry, automatically shaking his head, then wincing. 'Sorry, but my mouth's quite painful. Mind you, it's nothing to what my assailant's balls must feel like like this morning . . . Wait, I'll just get it.'

'Turn to page three,' said Latymer when Berry returned to the phone.

Berry did so. Staring out at him was an artist's impression of a gaunt-faced man with receding hair and a ponytail. The heading above the picture was: 'Warwickshire Police Seek Man In Murder Inquiry.' Under it, it said, 'Above is an artist's impression of a man Warwickshire police would like to question with regard to a murder which took place on 23rd April at Lower Horton, near Stratford-upon-Avon, shortly after a demonstration against the growing of GM crops. It is thought he is from the London area and the police would like him to come forward so that he might be eliminated from their enquiries.' A telephone number was given for anyone who might wish to contact the Warwickshire police. No name was given.

'It could be your man, Herviser, was one of the green men who took part in the Lower Horton demo and that someone had tipped him off they were going to the press about Shrieve and he thought it better to cry off in case he was asked awkward questions. The behaviour of his pals seems pretty crass, though that was all of a piece with the green men on the demo, so it does look as if you were on to something. Anyway I'll let Ross know about it, then I'll come over to see you. It's always a risk going for a picture though, isn't it?'

Berry agreed. 'They're bound to get dozens of useless calls, as is always the way.'

'Oh, and by the way,' added Latymer, 'Fiona Garleston's coming down to Bristol in a day or so to visit an old friend. I've sent her some of the stuff on Meon Hill as I thought she might come up with a few ideas and suggested to her we all meet up.' In fact, he'd sent Fiona more than just a selection of the material about the Meon Hill murder, he'd also enclosed a note of the events at Lower Horton and a brief account of the inquest on the dead baby, and the strange circumstances in which it was found. He had the house to himself for Tess was in Somerset for a few days, measuring up her new property for carpets and curtains and seeing what she would need elsewhere, so he didn't feel under quite so much pressure. It was a fine day and he took himself off for a long walk, stopping off in a pub for lunch.

The information on his answerphone, when he finally got back home, told him that he had two messages. The first was from Fiona Garleston to say she would be in Bristol the following day. The second was from an excited John Dee asking Latymer to ring him back 'for I think I've cracked it'.

'I've just been on to Keith Berry and he said to tell you myself,' Dee told him, when Latymer got through. 'I must have been particularly stupid yesterday. Did Keith tell you the name of the lecturer who didn't turn up?'

'I made a note of it. He said his name was Herviser, Duncan Herviser.'

'Didn't you think it an odd name?'

'Not particularly. We have a Scrimshaw and a Pargeter just in this village.'

'Think about it. H-E-R-V-I-S-E-R.'

'So?'

'Don't you see? It's an anagram of Shrieve! Surely it's too much to be a coincidence. So he has at least two names, Shrieve and Herviser. Presumably he didn't turn up last night and his friends got so heavy because some evening papers ran an artist's impression of him asking for him to come forward and it was also on one of the local TV bulletins. It's in the dailies today.'

Latymer had to agree it was a definite possibility. 'Look,' he said after thanking Dee, 'I was going to ring Chief Inspector Ross in the morning anyway, but I'll tell him now. I'm sure he'll be very grateful, though how I explain how we found out, I'm not too sure.' He put down the phone and rang Warwick straight away, but Ross was out and not expected back for some time. Did he want to leave a message? Yes, would the chief inspector ring him back as he had some information for him. Good old Keith, he thought, and yes, he would have to tell Ross the part played by his friend and John Dee.

He returned again to his many notes. It would be good to talk it all through with Fiona. He had to admit that the way he was feeling, it would be good to talk *anything* through with Fiona . . . After a while he made himself a snack supper and slumped in front of the television. It was unlikely Ross would get back to him now, he'd ring him again first thing in the morning. How easy it all looked, he thought, as he watched the most recent police saga, marvellous how television detectives racked up an almost one hundred per cent clear-up rate however complex the crime. He also wondered why there was such a vogue at present for serial killers when in reality they were so rare. He was just about to go to bed when the phone rang and, to his surprise, it was Ross.

'Sorry to call so late,' he said, 'but I got your message and thought you might like to know we think we've found Shrieve.'

So Dee *was* right, thought Latymer. No wonder Shrieve hadn't turned up in Camden Town. There must have been an immediate response to the publication of the artist's impression. 'Good for you,' he responded. 'Where is he then?'

'In the mortuary at the Radcliffe Hospital.'

'*What*!'

'Our picture went in today's *Oxford Mail* and we were contacted by the hospital late this afternoon. There was no identification on him and they'd been trying to find out who he was. Detective Constable Wendy Rainbird went up there with a colleague this evening and identified him.'

'But how . . . ?' began Latymer.

'He was brought into the Radcliffe around six o'clock on the morning of April 24th – alive. It seems he flagged down a couple of railwaymen who were on their way to work, just outside Oxford railway station. At first they took him for a drunk or one of the beggars that congregate up there, but then one of them thought there was something really wrong and so they stopped. He was gasping for breath, clutching his chest and could hardly speak. So they put him in their van and took him straight to casualty at the Radclifffe Hospital. About ten minutes after they got him there he had a massive heart attack and died. I understand it wouldn't have made any difference if they'd called an ambulance rather than take him in themselves as the post mortem showed he had chronic heart disease. The doctor who did it said he must have been well aware of his condition and was surprised he'd no medication on him. Of course if there had been, at least it would have had his name on it.'

'So if these men found him at around six o'clock, he could easily have murdered Symonds before he was taken ill,' responded Latymer. 'Didn't you say you found their minibus just outside Oxford? It wouldn't have taken long for it to be driven up there at that time of night. Presumably after they'd dumped it they all split up and Shrieve was intending to get back to London by an earlier train but was taken ill.'

Ross agreed. 'Of course I asked if there'd been blood on his clothes and whether they still had them. It turned out they did. They were pretty foul, muddy and covered in vomit, which apparently can happen in the run up to a major heart attack, but there wasn't any blood. Perhaps he'd worn something over the top of them. However, once the hospital checked no identification was possible from them and there was nothing in the pockets, they were supposed to have gone into the incinerator. Luckily for us they got forgotten so they're now with forensics. At least it gives us something to go on. Perhaps someone will come up now with his full name and address.'

Latymer smiled to himself. 'I've no idea where he lived, Chief Inspector, but I think I can help you with his name. That's why I called you. Instead of Shrieve, see what happens when you ask for information with regard to a Duncan Herviser.'

Twelve

Latymer put down the phone on Ross in a thoughtful mood. The chief inspector had been somewhat startled by his edited version of the events, but could hardly complain since it had resulted in his being able to put a name to the prime suspect. He was placated to some extent when Latymer reminded him that he naturally had a continuing interest in the Lower Horton murder since he'd had the misfortune to see the corpse and that it was fortuitous that his friend and John Dee, discovering that a meeting was being held in London on myths and rituals, had decided to go along to see what they could find out. 'They certainly didn't expect to be set on by Herviser's mates,' said Latymer, 'but at least they came up with the goods, or rather Dee did when he realized Shrieve was an anagram of Herviser. I certainly wouldn't have done.'

Ross had to admit that neither would he and was sufficiently mollified, when Latymer enquired as to whether or not he now wanted him to present some kind of précis of events at Meon Hill in 1945, to suggest he brought it over in the morning if that was convenient as there were a number of points he would like to go over with him regarding the discovery of Symonds' body. 'I've thought for some time that two people must have been involved in actually getting Symonds up there, if not in the actual murder, and I'm still far from happy with Jonathan Higham's account of what he did between leaving the demonstration and contacting you.' But apart from his distrust of Jonathan Higham it was clear that he was now fully convinced that Herviser had murdered Symonds.

When Latymer switched on the radio to listen to the news the following day, events had moved on dramatically. Now he was safely dead and there were no worries about contempt charges, Duncan Herviser was openly being named as the prime suspect in the Lower Horton murder and Latymer had to admit there was a good deal going for the notion. Once his identity had been circulated to the press, a number of people had come forward with an address for him, that of a flat in a block on an estate in Stockwell in south London. By the evening police had entered the flat and what they found certainly suggested that the case was as good as solved. Herviser had adorned the walls of his rooms with large pictures of subject matter such as the Aztec human sacrifice rituals in which priests held high dripping human hearts, and there were shelves of books on the occult, Satanism, sadistic unsolved murders (including, naturally, Jack the Ripper), methods of torture and scrapbooks of cuttings of the more notorious recent cases such as that of Fred and Rosemary West. Herviser had also downloaded material from the Internet which caused the police officers who had looked at some of it to say it had made them feel physically sick. But the only reference they'd found to the Meon Hill murder so far was a brief account at the bottom of an Internet document on twentieth-century witchcraft.

At the end of the afternoon Fiona Garleston rang to say she had arrived safely in Bristol and Latymer arranged to meet at her friend's house the next day and take her over to meet up with Berry. 'I'm beginning to wonder if I haven't put you to a great deal of trouble for nothing,' he told her. 'The man suspected of the recent murder has been found dead from natural causes and as it seems he had a very dodgy history, the police officer in charge obviously thinks it's as good as solved, give or take a few loose ends. But . . .'

She picked up at once on his hesitation. '*But*, you don't sound too sure . . .'

'It's this feeling I have. To me it's just all to easy. Anyway, to other matters, have you had any thoughts after reading through the material I sent?'

'Actually, I have. I think there could be an explanation for what happened at Meon Hill which has nothing whatsoever to do with the occult, but to do with family relationships. Though it might all be fantasy, of course.'

'Keep on going,' he told her, 'I've got a feeling we might have been thinking along the same lines.' After her call he rang Berry and arranged a time for them all to meet. 'After reading up the Meon Hill stuff it seems she's come up with some ideas of her own.'

'It'll be nice to see her again but is it worth pursuing it further now?' Berry objected. 'Whatever happened at Meon Hill seems pretty irrelevant since it does look as if they've got their man.' There was a silence from the other end of the phone. 'Don't you think so then?'

'I just don't know,' returned Latymer. 'They might well be right.'

Somewhat to his surprise Tess arrived back unannounced an hour or so later, looking far from happy. 'I've been gazumped,' she told him, shortly, as soon as she had let herself in. 'And that after I'd even had the survey done and they'd let me go in and measure up. Apparently this other buyer offered £2000 more, which is, of course, impossible for me since I'll only have half the money from this house.'

'So what do you intend to do?' enquired Latymer.

'Well, I'm still determined to go to Somerset if that's what you mean and I'll have to start looking all over again from scratch. I must ring Dave Higham and see if he'll be able to hang on to our own buyers for a bit longer.'

'Can't you rent in Somerset to give yourself a breathing space until you find what you want?'

'I don't *want* to rent with all the hassle of moving twice. What about your plans?'

'I still intend moving out as soon as it's practicable. It's just about manageable between two tours. However, you're obviously welcome to stay here for as long as it takes.'

For a moment it looked to him almost as if she hoped he might make another plea for them to stay together but then she shook her head. 'I'll give Dave Higham a call,' she said, briskly. 'He won't mind my ringing him at home.' As she left the room his heart sank at the prospect of an evening *á deux.* What on earth were they going to talk about? She returned a few minutes later, looking puzzled. 'It's very odd. There's no reply.'

'What's odd about that?' he enquired. 'Presumably they've gone out.'

'But when they do, they always leave the answerphone on in case it's a possible client. But the phone just rang and rang.'

'Well, you're bound to be able to get him in the morning,' he told her, then changed the subject. 'I didn't expect you back tonight, but there are enough sausages for two in the fridge so it seems sensible to have supper together.' She agreed and suggested he left her to do it. The subsequent meal was eaten almost in silence, apart from a few desultory comments on both sides on subjects unlikely to provoke any controversy. Afterwards, while Tess watched television, he washed up before retreating to the haven of his study. It was just after eleven o'clock when he heard the doorbell ring. He frowned, surprised that anyone was likely to call on them at such an hour, then it rang again, even more insistently as Tess came in to him.

'Will you answer that, John. I don't like to. I can't think who it can be at this time of night.'

He opened the door to find a white-faced David Higham on the step. Latymer looked at his watch. 'It's a bit late for a business call, isn't it?'

Higham shook his head. 'For God's sake, Latymer, can I come in? I need your advice.'

'Why, Dave,' exclaimed Tess, who had come up behind Latymer, 'of course you can come in even if it is late. In fact, I've been trying to get hold of you, you see . . .' She stopped when she saw the expression on his face. 'Whatever's the matter?'

Higham grabbed Latymer's arm. 'You've got to help me. It's Jonathan . . .'

'Jonathan?' queried Latymer. 'What's happened to Jonathan? And how do you think I can help you?'

'He's been arrested. It seems the police think he's an accessory to a murder.' Then he turned on him: 'And you've known about this all along, haven't you?'

'Well, are you going to do anything about it?' demanded Tess over the coffee the next morning.

'There's not a great deal I can do at this stage,' Latymer told her.

She shook her head. 'I simply can't believe it. All this time you knew he'd been involved in that awful GM demo where the policeman was so badly injured, but worse than that, that it was Jonathan who found the body of the man who was murdered afterwards and that you'd actually been there with him! Yet you said nothing at all to his parents. Why not? And why on earth did he call you anyway?'

'In answer to your first question because he begged me not to, and since he's an adult and in his right mind, I respected his wishes. As to the second, as I explained to Higham at least ten times last night, we'd already met up by chance while I was in Stratford and I'd bought him lunch and I'd given him my mobile number so we could make arrangements for that. You heard what I said to Higham – Jonathan rang me because he was in a panic, he knew me, and he didn't know what to do. I told him right from the start that he should go straight to the police but people rarely behave rationally in such situations. Oh, and incidentally, I really did try to persuade him to contact his parents.'

'But surely you can help in some way? He's desperately worried.'

He gave her a bitter smile. 'Help Higham, you say? This from the man who some months back bragged that he'd be only too happy to act as a hangman even if he ended up hanging innocent people, since it was better to execute a few by mistake rather than let someone that might be guilty go free. I'd be interested in his views on the subject now.'

'A lot of people share them, you know. I don't think you realize how many.'

He wondered if he had ever really known her, if they'd ever truly shared anything that mattered. He sighed. 'Until something like this happens to them. You see, you never think it will.'

'So you'll go over there now, won't you? Talk to the police, find out what's happening?'

'I can't. I've an appointment in Bristol.'

'Well put it off.'

'I've no intention of putting it off. I've told Higham what he should do. Get the best possible solicitor and leave it to him to deal with. There's a limit to how long they can hold Jonathan without charging him. I was thinking of going over to see Ross tomorrow anyway and nothing dramatic is likely to happen before then. At present there's nothing more to say about it.' He went and fetched his coat. 'I was just going out to get a paper. Shall I get you one, too?' She nodded, without saying anything, and he left the house.

Once again there was an array of headlines across the racks outside the newsagent. The new 'witchcraft' murder had been relegated during the preceding days to short downpage pieces, if it was mentioned at all, but now the discoveries at Herviser's flat were splashed across all the tabloids and there was even some coverage in the broadsheets. 'House of Horror!' yelled the *Sun*. 'Strange Life and Death of the

Warwickshire Witchcraft Murderer' – See pages 4 and 5' promised the *Daily Mail*. They were solving the mystery in one stroke now there was no longer any chance of being accused of prejudicing a fair trial. It was obvious that the popular press, in line with the *Mail*, had already made up its mind: a particularly nasty murder had been perpetrated by a particularly nasty person who had now saved the taxpayer a great deal of money by dying himself. Bingo!

Latymer bought a selection and took them home. It seemed that a good deal of new material had been dug up on Herviser once the press got busy. In the past he'd belonged to various far-right groups, but of recent years had concentrated his energies on the occult, after spending some time attending a Satanist 'church' near Colchester. He'd also had a number of convictions earlier in his life for violence, including one, back in the 1970s, for causing an affray. But, as is often the way with such people, he had built up something of a following, not least because he now operated under the guise of an 'expert' in arcane beliefs and practices and had seen the protests against GM crops as a useful bandwagon on which to climb. The *Express* had also tracked down his doctor who had no idea of his patient's views but confirmed that he'd been suffering from a coronary heart problem for some time. 'If he wasn't taking his medication, then he would certainly be at risk of either a heart attack or a stroke, either of which could be fatal,' he told the *Express* reporter.

'I still can't see what's so important to you in Bristol that you can't cancel your appointment,' snapped Tess as he prepared to leave. 'What do I tell the Highams if they contact us while you're out?'

'That I'm not here and that you're not sure when I'll be back, but that I'll try and find out what's happening tomorrow. I imagine Higham must have got hold of a competent solicitor by now. Tell him he can call me later, if he wants to. I imagine the problem is that Jonathan is unable to satisfy the police as to why so much time passed between his leaving the demo and finding the body,' he told her, 'and I must admit it sounded pretty vague to me. But unless they have information I don't know about, that in itself isn't sufficient for them to charge him and since he was on his own during those hours, or claims to have been, and admits to being in something of a state, it's going to be difficult for them to prove he's lying.' What he didn't add was that the more he considered it, the less convinced he was by Jonathan's explanation. He felt there had to be more to it.

Fiona Garleston greeted him warmly when he arrived in Bristol, and introduced him to her friend, Gillian. 'I'm really pleased to meet you,' her friend assured him. 'Fiona's told me how you did all you could to help James, and that poor young woman the police didn't believe.'

'But not enough to really do any good for either of them,' he admitted to her. 'Anyway that's all in the past. Let's hope for a better future.'

Gillian smiled. 'Well, off you go. Good sleuthing!'

Latymer glanced at Fiona as he started the car. She was looking noticeably better than when he'd seen her last, immediately after the death of her husband. On the way to the bookshop they chatted comfortably and she told him how pleased she was that she had managed successfully to keep her husband's ecology website going. 'However, it's becoming something of a full time job,' she told him, 'which is all very well but I really do need to earn some money.' She was planning to sell the farm, she went on, and buy somewhere smaller and more manageable. 'It's too big for one person. As you know, we'd plans for an organic herb farm on the land but that all went by the board when James was taken ill.'

On arrival she greeted Berry like an old friend and they all sat down to hear what she had to say. 'I read through all the material several times,' she began, 'and I don't need to tell you that it's obvious how the idea of some kind of a "witchcraft" murder took off – I particularly liked the black dogs and headless women – as the way the man was killed was so strange and no one was able to come up with a motive. Or perhaps there's something I've missed. Unlike the two of you I don't have any expertise in police procedure so I don't know if any mistakes or wrong assumptions were made.'

'That's one of the reasons I asked you if you'd look at it,' Latymer commented. 'When it's an official inquiry it's all too easy to form an opinion early on which then turns into mindset.'

She smiled. 'I see. Well, what seems to me to be important, after reading through it all, is why no one was prepared to say anything. It wasn't like today when, for instance, witnesses to a major crime are too frightened to come forward. This was a sleepy little village in the depths of the countryside over half a century ago and the murder was sensational. The impression I got was that the truth was that most people had a very good idea who did it, why it was done and possibly even approved of it. I noticed that there weren't many suspects: there was the unfortunate Italian prisoner-of-war who was completely exonerated; some murmurs about the farmer on whose land the murder took place and who therefore knew where Walton was working and, incidentally, changed his story somewhat by the time it got to the inquest; and some mystery person who may or may not have drawn most of Charlie Walton's money out of his deposit account.'

'Unfortunately we don't know if they suspected anyone else,' commented Berry. 'It's quite possible that they did, but if so there doesn't appear to be any record of it.'

'Now I'm coming to the part where you might well think I'm being fanciful,' Fiona continued, 'but looking at it from a woman's angle, after all the stuff that's made the headlines in recent years, what struck me forcibly was the strange relationship between Walton and his niece and the nature of it. How very odd that a widower in his late forties, a person of a reclusive nature and without children of his own, should want to bring up a little girl without the help of a woman.' She hesitated briefly.

'Go on,' said Latymer, 'we're listening.'

Fiona nodded briefly, then continued. 'Now I admit this is very much a fictional scenario. But say the relationship between Walton and his niece was one of sexual abuse, not necessarily violent even, but accepted by the child as being expected of her in exchange for being taken in and cared for. Time passes, she grows up and falls almost into the situation of a wife. We know she looked after Walton, prepared his meals and indeed had his tea waiting for him the day he failed to return home, and that when he didn't turn up she was genuinely concerned for him. But at some time during this period she meets a young man, falls in love and becomes engaged to be married. Personally, I find it odd that so far as we know the fiancé was never questioned as to any part he might have possibly played in subsequent events, but there you go.

'By February 1945 the time was fast approaching when she was due to be married and suppose, let's just suppose, that she finally feels forced to tell him of her relationship with her uncle, something forced on her because quite possibly there had been gossip for years. We simply don't know.'

'When it comes to incest and child abuse, people often ask if there's more of it nowadays or whether it either wasn't known or wasn't talked about in past times,' said Berry. 'Personally, I believe it was proportionately just as prevalent but it didn't get anything like today's media coverage when examples came to light and no one talked about it, at least not openly. I've often thought there must have been abusers who were dealt with by a local populace which took the matter into its own hands.'

Latymer agreed. 'It would explain a lot in this case. Suppose it was the enraged fiancé, or if not him someone in the village who, on having his own suspicions confirmed, felt that such a sin required drastic punishment, but rather than rushing round to the cottage straight away and accusing Walton to his face, bided his time. It was known that Walton was out hedge-laying and ditching during that period and it would have been relatively easy to discover when he was likely to be in a place just about as remote from the village as possible. Not to mention that the murder weapons were conveniently to hand. I wonder if he just set on Walton or told him what he intended to do and why.'

'As you know I did wonder if the money that had gone from Walton's account had been some kind of blackmail payments leaked out a little at a time, John,' Berry reminded him. 'It could be that if that was the case it was the blackmailer who told the killer what was going on, not the niece, once the money had run out.'

'That's a possibility,' Latymer conceded.

'It might also explain why it did look like some kind of a ritual killing,' added Fiona. 'Perhaps it was. Not so much witchcraft or a blood offering to the earth and the old gods, but a throwback perhaps to the days when the need was felt, as it were, to peg down evil. Like they used to do with suicides and some murderers, who were buried at the crossroads, sometimes with a stake through the heart to prevent an evil spirit walking abroad. We know that went on certainly up until the late seventeenth century. It would make some kind of sense. But if we're anything like right, it certainly explains why no one said anything to the local police, let alone Fabian of the Yard. So far as they were concerned he deserved it.'

They sat back and looked at each other. 'Do you know,' said Latymer, 'I think we really might be on to something, though I doubt people living there today, or the descendents of those involved, would be happy to have it made public.' He grinned at Fiona then turned to Berry. 'I said she'd bring a fresh eye to it. I can't pretend it throws any more light on the present case but then, officially, that's got nothing to do with us, apart from the fact that I was the second person to come across the body, and anyway Ross is convinced he's solved it.' Then he suddenly remembered what else he'd intended to tell Berry. 'In all the excitement I forgot to tell you that they've arrested Jonathan Higham, the lad who called me up in the first place. They have got some bee in their bonnet that he might have been an accessory to the murder.'

'Why?' enquired Fiona.

'Largely, I think, because his account of where he was and what he was doing during the few hours before the murder happened doesn't stand up too well. Though from what I know of him, I simply don't see him being attracted to a man like Herviser and blindly doing what he said. So now I'm at the receiving end of that too. The lad's father, who I've never been able to stand and who has always been a hanger and flogger, is singing a different tune now someone in the family's become directly involved in a crime investigation. He never thought it could happen to him.' He stopped short. 'I wonder . . . the reason the lad called me that night was because we'd met up shortly before it happened and when we did he'd embarked on some story about a girl he knew (who I assume must have been his girlfriend), who had suffered some kind of dreadful experience which I took to be rape, though he said it was more complicated than that.'

'Date rape?' suggested Fiona.

'Perhaps. I also thought that the girl must be a fellow student at Warwick but from what he said, it seemed more likely she was someone he got to know when he was staying in the West Country during his gap year and that the incident happened there.' He paused. 'But no, whatever it was, it can't have any relevance to the Lower Horton murder.'

'What are you going to tell Ross?' asked Berry.

'I think I might give him the bones of what we've said here, along with the breakdown I'd already done of the Meon Hill material. I don't imagine he'll have much use for it now since they seem convinced the murderer was Herviser, crazed with the idea of ritual sacrifice and using the opportunity to get the maximum possible publicity. Jonathan apart, it's all very neat.'

As he drove Fiona back to her friend's house he asked her how long she was likely to be staying in Bristol and she told him that it would only be for three or four days. 'I can't leave my friend with the dogs for too long, it's not fair, and I don't like the thought of putting them in a kennels.'

'So I'll be able to see you again?' he persisted, as he drew up outside her friend's door. 'Tomorrow?'

'Probably, though I'll have to see what plans my friend might have.' She turned and looked him squarely in the face. 'Look, John, I'm not sure how to say this but I'm simply not ready yet for any kind of emotional involvement. James's death and the events leading up to it are still too raw.'

'I'm sorry,' said Latymer. 'Is it that obvious?'

She smiled. 'Let's say I'm aware of your feelings. But nor am I saying that something might not come of it, given time. I really do like you, if I didn't I wouldn't be here. I know it sounds corny, but in the meantime I hope we can be good friends. After all, you've your own situation to sort out and it seems sensible to get that over and you'll need time to draw breath. We met when both of us were feeling very vulnerable and we both need some space.' She opened the car door. 'In the meantime you've got me really intrigued. You never know, what we've concluded about the Meon Hill murder might yet come in useful, if only for the plot of a radio play!'

Thirteen

When Latymer arrived home he found Tess had a visitor. Dawn Higham was sitting on the sofa in the lounge clutching a mug of coffee, her eyes red and swollen, while Tess was sitting opposite glancing through what appeared to be a photograph album. They both turned and looked up as he came into the room. On the few occasions on which Latymer had met Dawn previously he'd found her irritating, the kind of woman who has no views of her own and is incapable of saying anything that doesn't either echo everything her husband says or merely repeats what she happens to have read that day in the morning paper or a women's magazine. If asked to describe her, the picture he'd retained in his mind was how she had appeared the last time he saw her, a somewhat overweight woman in her late forties, heavily made up, and unsuitably dressed in a décolleté lattice-work black sweater with fake fur round the top, tight black trousers and red shoes with stiletto heels. Now, dressed in old trousers and a shabby sweater, her face bare of make-up and her usually immaculate blonde hair scraped back from her face, he felt sorry for her.

'Any news of Jonathan?' he enquired.

She shook her head. 'He's still at the police station in Warwick.' Her eyes filled with tears. 'Dave's got him the best solicitor he could find, someone highly recommended by a friend of ours. I can't think why he's still there or what the police are doing. Jonathan wouldn't hurt anyone, let alone murder them.'

'I don't imagine they think he did,' responded Latymer. 'They seem pretty sure they've got their man, or rather the body of their man since he's now dead. It's just that Jonathan doesn't seem to be able to come up with a satisfactory account of how he spent his time before he found Lucas Symonds' body, and in a murder investigation they have to check everything out. If it's of any comfort, I don't believe for one moment that he would get himself involved with someone like Herviser, or Shrieve as he called himself, and I accept what he told me, that he was at Lower Horton with several of his friends quite simply to protest against GM crops because he thinks growing them is wrong. But . . .'

'But what?' demanded Tess.

'But it is a bit hard to believe he could really have been lost for three or four hours so near to a main road and a village, even if he was feeling panic-stricken and disorientated in the dark. That's the sticking point. I have wondered if he might not be covering up for someone else, possibly for something that has nothing to do with the murder. Anyway,' he continued, 'they'll have to either release him soon or charge him and I feel pretty sure they'll let him go.'

'Dave says you met up with Jonathan in Stratford, before all this happened, and took him out to lunch,' said Dawn, 'and that's why he called you when he found the body. Did he tell you when you were having lunch that he was going on this stupid protest?'

'He never said anything to me about it,' Latymer assured her, 'but then, as I pointed out to the police, he was hardly likely to, knowing that I'd been a police officer myself.'

Dawn became tearful again. 'But you didn't even tell us when you knew very well that he'd got mixed up in a murder. That he'd actually found the body. How could you have left us in the dark and not said anything?'

'Because he made me promise not to. He's an intelligent, independent young man who appears to know his own mind and he didn't want you to know. I thought he was wrong and advised him to contact you straight away, but he refused and I couldn't make him do it.'

Dawn shook her head in bewilderment. 'I simply don't understand any of it.' She turned to them both. 'We've always done everything we could for both our children, given them the very best. We lived on the Birmingham side of Warwick, you know, before we moved here and Jon went to the private grammar school there as a day pupil. His sister's in private education too, as a weekly boarder in a school near Bristol.' She pursed her lips. 'We don't believe in state education, you never know what sort of people they're going to mix with.'

Latymer suppressed a smile and restrained himself from asking if she meant the sort of people whose actions brought them to the attention of the police. 'And then, I understand, he took a gap year?'

'Yes. Dave was very against it. He was against his going to university at all, let alone taking a year off before he did so. And the course he's chosen! English and *Drama*! What good's that going to be to him? Dave wanted him to go to a good business school, then join him in the agency.'

'I rather gathered that from Jonathan,' said Latymer.

'Well, it seems a lot more practical than drama,' commented Tess.

Latymer looked thoughtfully at Dawn. 'I don't want to betray a confidence, particularly as I realize that the relationship between your husband and your son hasn't been a very good one, but I do wonder what happened during that gap year. When we met it was obvious Jonathan had something on his mind, something that worried him very much. But I couldn't get him to tell me properly what it was.'

Dawn looked startled. 'Why? What did he say?'

'It was to do with a girl, a girl with whom he'd obviously had a close relationship of some kind. From what I gathered she'd suffered a pretty awful experience, which I took to be of a sexual nature. I asked him the obvious thing, if he was talking of rape, but he said not. Or child abuse.

I explained that if this girl had suffered physical or sexual abuse as a child it wasn't too late even now to expose the perpetrator. In fact it was almost her duty to do so to try and avoid it happening to someone else, and that the police these days have specially designated officers who would treat her sympathetically. But he kept saying that was impossible, that it was far more complicated than that. At first I thought he was talking about a girl at college with him but from what he said later, it would seem it was someone he met during his time in the West Country.'

Dawn was obviously mystified. 'He's never mentioned anything like that to us.' Then she stopped for a moment, as if coming to a decision. 'Look, if I tell you something, can we keep this conversation confidential? Even from Dave? Or rather, especially from Dave. He's never been able to discuss, well, the things that really matter. About the gap year, we never did know why Jonathan suddenly decided to take a year off before going to Warwick, he'd worked so hard from his GCSE year onwards to enable him to do the university course that he wanted. Then, towards the end of his last year at school, something made him change his mind and he told us he was going to defer taking up his university place for a year. We tried to talk him out of it but he was so determined that in the end we had to give in. Dave said it was my fault as I'd always indulged him.'

'What did he do with himself during that time?'

'To be honest, John, we don't know. Or why he chose to go down to Devon. Knowing how his father felt about it all, he was very good, very independent. He never asked us for any financial support and seems to have got by one way or another. I think he picked up some work in the tourist trade, did a bit of bar work and so on. He finally came back home at the end of the August before he started at Warwick, but told us very little. He'd changed quite a lot, but then that was bound to happen after a year away from home, but once he'd started on his course, from what we saw of him, he seemed very happy. He didn't come home much, though, and got some kind of holiday job in Stratford during the long vacation last summer, so we were both pleased when he decided to join the family back here last Christmas. All things considered, everything went quite well, and he was really pleased to see Alice (his sister), again, but then just after Boxing Day he came down at breakfast time and said he had to go to Plymouth.

'He gave us no explanation, he just went. We heard nothing from him and thought he must have gone straight back from there to college, but a couple of weeks later the university rang us to ask where he was. Two days later he turned up at home looking absolutely dreadful, still saying nothing, and simply collected his things and returned to the university.' She became tearful again. 'I'm not a complete fool. What John says rings true. I think something really bad happened to him in Plymouth, something he couldn't even talk to me about. But I can't see that it could possibly have anything to do with that business at Lower Horton.'

'Well, all I can suggest,' commented Latymer, 'is that when you next have a chance to talk to him on his own, you ask him straight out what's been troubling him. After recent events and his time in police custody, you might well find he's far more willing to open up than he was before.'

Dawn wiped her eyes and gave him a watery smile. 'Thank you. You've been really helpful and I know you and Dave don't really get on.' She stood up. 'I'd better get back home. Dave's at the office but there might have been a call from the solicitor or the police.' She frowned and looked round the room.

'If you're looking for your photograph album it's here.' Tess picked it up and handed it to her. 'I can see how proud you are of your family.'

'I know it's a bit silly, John, but I brought it over to show you both just how normal a boy Jonathan is; that you could tell by looking at him that he wouldn't be party to a terrible murder.'

Latymer didn't say that all too many murderers looked quite normal and ordinary. Contrary to some fiction they didn't have low foreheads, tiny cunning eyes, or walk around with a permanent snarl. But to please her, he opened the album and skimmed through it. It was much as he expected. Various school photographs of Jonathan and his sister, family holiday snaps, several birthday parties, Jonathan in various school productions, one of which looked like an open air production of a Shakespeare play.

'That was in his last year in the sixth form,' Dawn told him. 'They did *Twelfth Night* in the garden of a big old house outside Warwick. I'm not very good on Shakespeare, but I think he played someone called Orsino. Look, there's a couple more. He was very good.' There were two pictures of Jonathan in doublet and hose, in one of which he was holding the hands of the girl who must have played Viola; very pretty, very young.

'Who's this?' asked Latymer.

Dawn shook her head. 'I can't remember her name. I think we have the programme somewhere if you really want to know. I don't think they were particularly close friends. He certainly never brought her home.'

'Well, don't worry about it,' Latymer told her. 'What matters now is getting your son sorted out.' He gave her back the album and Tess showed her out of the front door.

The atmosphere cooled as soon as she returned. 'So how did your vital appointment go?'

'Fine. I can't see why it concerns you so much. I'd arranged a meeting with someone who's only in Bristol for a few days and didn't want to cancel it. End of story.'

'And it was more important than that poor young boy? You've seen the state his mother's in.'

'And I've told you that there's nothing I can do. It's now in the hands of the police and his solicitor.'

She refused to be placated. 'Oh and by the way, that Chief Inspector Ross rang. He said the inquest would be opened tomorrow and he hadn't got round to letting you know before as you didn't have to go, since it would only be a formality this time, but he was telling you in case you wanted to.'

Back in Warwick, Ross was holding a meeting with those officers most closely involved in the Lower Horton murder investigation. He was also considering what to do about Jonathan Higham. He felt certain that he wasn't being told the whole truth, but there didn't seem to be any link between the boy and Herviser, apart from the fact that they were both on the demo at the same time and both left before it ended. 'And we can't prove he *didn't* just wander around for several hours before finding Symonds,' he told them. 'I suppose we could ask for more time, but I'm beginning to think it simply isn't worth it. So I've had a word upstairs and propose releasing him on police bail.' There was a general murmur of assent. He then moved on to more important matters. 'Various names and addresses have been found in Herviser's flat as a result of which the Met has picked up several members of Herviser's "circle" as he liked to call it. Detective Sergeant Smith's been liaising. Can you give us your report, sergeant?'

Smith looked at his notes. 'The Met say they all seem to be a pretty unprepossessing lot and had little to say for themselves, but two of them – I have their names here – actually admitted to being on the demo, though naturally both deny using violence and neither was able, or prepared, to say who put our colleague into intensive care. I suppose they genuinely might not know since everyone was wearing masks. Anyway those two are now under arrest and the officer who did the preliminary interview says they've told him how their part of the action was set up, how Herviser made contact with the SAF people and arranged a lift to Lower Horton, thus giving the impression that he would be on his own.

'They then got as many supporters together as they could

and hired the minibus, rightly expecting that their arrival would take the other lot by surprise. They'd already thought about what they should do if things went really wrong and decided that if they did, they'd dump the bus somewhere near Oxford so that they could split and get back home by other means. Anyway, we'll soon be able to ask them what we want to know, they're being brought down here this evening. It wasn't possible to do it sooner due to manpower shortages.'

'Well, you can make a start on them first thing in the morning,' declared Ross. 'I have to go to the inquest, though that shouldn't take long. I'll let the coroner know that we soon expect to have a great deal more information. I'd like to clear this up now as soon as possible.'

Latymer rang up and caught Ross immediately after his meeting and told him that he would indeed like to come along to the inquest. Ross then informed him that he was expecting the arrival of two of the two men under arrest some time that evening. 'There were others,' he told him, 'but these were the most talkative.'

'I wonder if my friend Berry would be able to identify the yobs who attacked him and John Dee among those picked up?' commented Latymer.

'Hadn't thought of that,' said Ross. 'I'll see what I can do. Anyway, I'll see you tomorrow morning. Oh, by the way,' he added, 'I'm going to release young Higham on police bail.'

So that at least was sorted for the time being. As for the following day, it would be useful to meet up with Ross again anyway, thought Latymer. In view of the turn of events, the research he'd done into the Meon Hill murder now seemed more or less irrelevant and his work on it of little use since it was obvious that Ross was more or less convinced that Herviser had killed Symonds. Anyway, for what it was worth, he'd take a copy of the notes he'd made, to which he'd added Fiona Garleston's theory. The more he thought about it the more he thought she might be right. However, so far as he could see his own part in it all would end with the resumed inquest at which he would be expected to give evidence.

He put down the phone and told Tess the news. 'It's as I thought. They're letting Jonathan go on police bail.'

'What does that imply? That they still suspect him of something?'

'Only that they want to keep an eye on him. It means he'll have to report to the police at set intervals and can't leave the country without telling them. But I imagine they'll soon release him from that too unless some new information turns up.'

Halfway through the evening the phone rang. 'I'll get it,' said Tess. 'I expect it'll be Dave or Dawn. Or even Diana. I left a message on her answerphone, she was going to look at some houses for me and send me the details.' She went out to the hall but returned almost at once. 'It's for you,' she informed him, frigidly.

It was Fiona. 'Sorry, was that your wife? She didn't sound very pleased.'

He told her not to worry. She and her friend, Fiona told him, planned to go to the Bristol Old Vic the following evening and wondered if he'd like to come along. Also, she'd be free all day Sunday but was planning to return to Scotland on Monday morning. He told her that he would be going to Stratford for the inquest in the morning, but that he'd be delighted to join them at the theatre in the evening.

'You haven't wasted much time then,' observed Tess, when he came back into the room. 'She sounds Scottish. Is she that woman Jean something you went off to Penzance with and kept going up to Scotland to see?'

Here we go, he thought. 'No, it isn't. And as I told you then and ever since, the only relationship I had with Jean Armstrong was that of an ex-police officer trying to help a woman who thought, quite rightly as it turned out, that her missing husband had been murdered. Since when, so I'm told, she's put it all behind her and is living happily with someone she met while she was doing an IT course. My caller was the widow of that man I also told you about, who set up an ecological website which she now runs, and who happens to be visiting a friend in Bristol. Berry and I met her a couple of times, that's all.'

'And no doubt she was the reason for your important appointment this morning.'

'Oh, give it a rest,' he retorted. 'I'm going down to the pub.'

It was one of those days when it seemed impossible to drive anywhere without encountering traffic problems of one kind or another, as a result of which Latymer reached Stratford only just before the inquest began. It was, as Ross had promised and he had expected, a brief affair. Ross told the coroner how he had been alerted to the discovery of a body and that he had gone to the place in question, a small copse about a quarter of a mile away from Horton Manor, where he had found the body of a man, stabbed through the chest with a billhook with such force that it had entered the ground beneath him.

'Am I to understand the discovery followed a protest against the growing of GM crops which had taken place earlier?' enquired the coroner. Ross agreed that it had. He also confirmed that the investigation was still progressing.

The stand was then taken by Bob Wells who confirmed that he had identified the body as that of his brother-in-law, Lucas Symonds, after which the pathologist who had carried out the post mortem stated that death was caused by the billhook, which had severed the coronary artery, the victim having been stunned first by a blow to the back of the head. The coroner then adjourned the inquest for a fortnight. Latymer waited at the back of the room for Ross, who appeared within a few minutes accompanied by Bob Wells and a woman Latymer assumed must be Mrs Wells. Both looked very strained.

Ross caught sight of Latymer and came over to him. 'Well,

that went off much as we thought,' he said, then, turning to the couple behind him introduced them all, explaining to Bob and Marian Wells that it was Latymer who had contacted him following the discovery of the body. 'I think I told you that the young student, Jonathan Higham, who had stumbled over it, simply didn't know how to cope and called up Mr Latymer, who he knew was in Stratford that night.' They shook hands and Latymer said he was sorry to have been the bearer of such bad news and that it must have been a great shock to them.

'It was,' replied Wells. 'We haven't really come to terms with it even now. It'll be easier once we've been able to hold the funeral.'

'That shouldn't be too long,' Ross informed them. 'It might well be possible to go ahead with it once the inquest resumes in a fortnight if the coroner is happy about it. There's no doubt about the cause of death and we are very confident that by that time we should be able to provide him with a significant amount of further information.'

Marian Wells touched her husband's arm. 'If you don't mind, Bob, I think I'd like to go home.'

He patted her hand. 'Of course. It's all been a bit much for her, Chief Inspector.' He turned to her. 'What about the photographs, dear?'

'Oh yes, of course.' Marian Wells opened her handbag and took out two five-by-eight glossy photographs. 'Our daughter went missing, Mr Latymer, some years ago, since when we've heard nothing. We thought that perhaps with all the publicity there's been about poor Lucas's death, if her picture can be shown again it might just jog someone's memory. Though, of course, she could look very different now.'

'That might not be too much of a problem,' observed Ross. 'They can do great things with computer graphics these days to suggest how people might look a few years on from when the original photograph was taken.' She handed them to him, thanked him again, and left the hall, her husband's arm around her.

Ross looked at the pictures. 'Pretty kid.' He handed them to Latymer. One was the photograph Ross had seen at the Wells' farmhouse of Lucy in her school uniform looking much like any other attractive girl of her age. In the other she was standing in a garden, dressed as a young boy, her hair caught up under a floppy hat. Latymer looked at it closely and frowned, the face seemed familiar. Surely it was the girl who had played Viola to Jonathan Higham's Orsino?

'Anything the matter?' enquired Ross.

Unsure what to reply, Latymer settled for a non-committal grunt, then handed the photographs back. Before he did anything he would have to check and make absolutely certain it was the same girl, though he was in little doubt. He then gave Ross a copy of his Meon Hill research, admitting that it was now probably of little relevance, to which Ross had to agree. 'It looks almost certain Herviser is our man. Everything fits. We're extremely grateful for the help you've given us on this one and I haven't forgotten about your friend identifying his assailant. Two of Herviser's men were brought down yesterday evening and are being questioned. I must get back and see what's happening. Put in an invoice for the work you've done, will you, and even if it didn't work out this time, we might well be able to use your help again sometime if you're willing.'

'Well, if you do find you want me sooner, I'm at home for another week or so,' Latymer told him, 'before I do another tour.' He didn't add that he was now seriously thinking of giving the job up. If he had to change his life so drastically then why not that as well?

'You're telling me *what*?' bellowed Ross at the unfortunate Smith.

'They've both been questioned separately and both say the same thing: that once police reinforcements arrived, Herviser told them to get the hell out of it and they did, except for the one we arrested. They reckon it must have taken about three quarters of an hour before they all got back to the minibus, which for obvious reasons had been moved and parked somewhere else, since they'd run off in different directions. Those who got there first had to wait a while to make sure they'd all made it. All of them, that is, except Herviser. He took longer and they were debating what to do when he finally arrived, walking with difficulty and very out of breath. Then they left for Oxford.

'They say that when they got to Oxford Herviser was obviously far from well but told them it was nothing, he'd be OK and they should go on and leave him in the bus until he'd recovered. He said the sooner they got right out of the area the better and that when they got back to London they should lie low for a bit and avoid contacting him. Which they did. After all they had every reason to do as he said once they'd heard that a policeman had been critically injured. Then came all the publicity about the murder, which is why it wasn't until yesterday that most of them knew Herviser was dead.'

Ross was beginning to feel cold in the pit of his stomach. 'So. Let's get this straight. They reckon it was around three quarters of an hour before they left in the minibus? That would make it about 12.15 a.m. They could be lying of course.'

'I don't think so,' said Smith. 'These two found an all-night caff near the station while they waited to catch a bus or a train back to London. One of them said that he remembered that when they walked through the door the clock on the wall said 1.45 a.m.'

Ross slumped down in his chair. 'My God! If they are telling the truth, then Herviser couldn't possibly have killed Lucas Symonds!'

Fourteen

When Latymer met up that evening with Fiona and her friend Gillian before the evening's performance, he was naturally unaware of this new piece of disturbing information. He recounted the details of the brief inquest to them, pointing out that so far as Ross was concerned the case seemed to be all but done and dusted, before going on to the subject of the Wells' missing daughter. 'It was really weird. Only the day before, Jonathan Higham's mother had shown me a photograph of her son with this very same girl, a girl who I then discover disappeared from home some years ago and has never been heard of since. I was quite thrown. Which begs the question, if she and Jonathan were in the same play together about four years ago, then surely her parents must have known him. I understand that when Ross arrested Jonathan he asked Wells if he knew him and Wells was quite sure he didn't.

'It could be that the only time the Wells came across Jonathan was once and in the play,' observed Fiona, 'and that they simply didn't remember his name. Even if Wells had run in to him somewhere, he'd now be a good deal older and boys in particular change a lot between sixteen and twenty, not to mention the fact that the only time he'd seen him before he would have been wearing costume and make-up. It might be that they'd never even been to a Shakespeare play before and their only reason for going was to see their daughter playing the leading lady and her performance is just about all they recollect of it.'

'I suppose so. Of course, I'll have to check out that it really is the same girl though I'm just about one hundred per cent sure it is. But you have a point. Jonathan's mother genuinely didn't seem to know who she was and said he'd never mentioned her or introduced her to them although they were living near Warwick at the time.'

'It must be awful to lose a child like that,' commented Gillian. 'Just disappear without trace and never be heard of again. Do the police think she was murdered?'

'I asked Ross that and he says not since she left a letter behind saying she was sorry that she was going away and she took money and clothes with her; which doesn't suggest an abduction, though it doesn't rule it out, of course.'

Delighted at the opportunity of spending time with Fiona, Latymer hadn't even asked what play they were to see. In the event *The Revenger's Tragedy* had enough blood, gore and murder to satisfy the most avid palate for crime. Not to mention a villain, or anti-hero, who starts off on his career of serial killing by taking the audience into his confidence, explaining that the evil duke had first seduced, then murdered, his fiancée (cradling her skull as he speaks), and that he intends to get his own back on him. But, of course, it didn't stop there and by the end of the evening he had left behind a trail of corpses including his own.

'Well, they certainly didn't mess about in those days,' Latymer joked to the two women as they left the theatre. 'Retribution followed, of course, but only after he'd despatched half the court.'

Fiona laughed. 'But we tend to forget nowadays that when the plays were written almost everyone believed in a Final Judgement, after which you ended up either in heaven or hell, or, if you were a Catholic, doing time in purgatory, so a story like that would have given the audience a real thrill. Actually, I was rather thinking along those lines when I was reading up all that stuff about the Meon Hill murder and witchcraft. Back in the 1940s the notion obviously added a vicarious thrill to a nasty event and possibly some people genuinely did believe there was something in it but not like they would have done in the sixteenth century.'

'Motives don't change much though,' commented Latymer. 'Sex, jealousy, corruption, money and revenge. Though your average murderer, apart from the serial killers who are nothing like as numerous as the press would have us believe, doesn't leave behind him such a trail of disaster.' He left, after arranging to pick Fiona up in the morning and take her out for the day, the decision as to where to go being left until then.

By the time he got back home it was nearly midnight and Tess was in bed and had left him a scrawled note. 'Your policeman from Warwick rang. Didn't leave a message. Diana called to say the people who are selling the house I wanted have had their sale fall through and are now definitely willing to go ahead with me, so I am going down to Taunton first thing in the morning.' He heaved a sigh of relief, it was hardly enjoyable living as they were. Which reminded him, he'd give the flat owner a call on Monday and see if he could firm up the date when he could move in. As to his job with Becketts Literary Tours, he had now almost definitely made up his mind to pack it in after the next three tours. He had enough money to live on, just about, which would give him time to decide what he was going to do next. Of one thing he was certain: he wouldn't settle for doing nothing.

When he got up the next morning Tess was already finishing her breakfast, her suitcase packed and standing in the hall. The news from her daughter appeared to have put her in a better mood. 'There's nothing to stop everything going through now,' she told him. 'I spoke to the Highams yesterday evening. Very relieved, of course, that Jonathan has been released. He's gone straight back to the university. Of course, he'll have a good deal of explaining to do but he's pretty sure it'll be all right. After all, he didn't do anything except take part in the protest and his friends are prepared to stand by him over that and say they were there too.'

'That's good,' he commented and pondered how best to approach the Highams and ask if he could look at their photograph again. Tricky. The sun was shining when he went over to collect Fiona and he suggested to her they should drive down towards Evesham and follow what was known as the Blossom Trail which would take them on a tour around the orchards of the Evesham valley. The trail did not disappoint them, the masses of pink or white blossom, heaped on the trees like snow, were spectacular. It was a sight to gladden the heart. 'Looks as though they'll have a good fruit harvest,' observed Latymer.

'Stop a minute, will you?' said Fiona as they came up to a particularly beautiful display. 'I must take some pictures, there's nothing like this back home.' He pulled in to the side of the road and she got out with her camera to take the view from a variety of angles. 'I can see why they've made a feature of it. I think I might put this on the website to show what we're likely to lose if we're not very careful.'

'It certainly hardly requires a blood sacrifice to ensure a success this year,' remarked Latymer. 'Whatever it might have been like back in 1945.'

She finished her picture-taking, got back into the car then asked, 'Where's Meon Hill?'

'Not far away. I'll just check, I've got the local map here.' Latymer unfolded it and they both had a look. 'It's the other side of the river, see. When I went over to Lower Horton the first time I crossed the river at Welford, which is there. There's a pub in the village that does good lunches. In fact we could go there today if you like the idea.'

'That sounds nice.' She hesitated. 'Look, would you think me very ghoulish if we went and had a look at it?'

'At Meon Hill, you mean?'

'That is if we can get to it.'

He consulted the map again. 'No problem. You drive to

Upper Quinton and then there's a footpath. The top of the hill is marked Fort; I suppose it must be from the Iron Age.'

'You wouldn't mind?'

'Not at all. I'm quite intrigued myself. Though do you think we should try and buy some garlic to hang round our necks to ward off the black dogs and headless women that infest the place?'

'Why not? Though I suppose we can always nick a couple of knives from the pub to hold up in the shape of a cross!'

They both laughed. He thought how easy it was being with her. It was the first time he had seen her in such an animated mood. Over lunch they discussed a variety of topics including the previous night's play about which Fiona was enthusiastic. 'What was so good was the way the villain was so attractive and had been so badly done by that you were swept along with him, your usual sense of right and wrong on hold, so that for ages you simply accepted what he did. Until you suddenly woke up to just what it was he was doing.'

'A bit like in *Richard III*,' Latymer agreed. 'Both characters, of course, are consummate actors. I don't mean the people playing the parts, though that particular actor was very good, but the characters themselves. So you have an actor in a play, playing an actor . . . Dear God!' He stopped in mid flow.

'What's the matter?'

'Jonathan Higham. An innocent caught up in a murder, a panic-stricken youngster calling me out in the middle of the night . . . Do you know, it's only just occurred to me that he's actually training to *be* an actor! And from what I understand he's very talented, was exceptionally good even when he was at school.'

'Are you saying you might all have been taken in? That all along he's been giving some kind of a performance, ever since you first met up with him by the body?'

Latymer looked across at her. 'Well, you have to admit it's a thought. His story never has really stood up. And as

I told you, the first time we talked he was hinting at some awful thing that had happened to a girl he knew. There's more mystery too. From what I learned from his mother the other day, immediately after Christmas he suddenly told them he had to go down to Plymouth. No explanation, nothing. So what was all that about? Then there's the photographs. Whatever the families may or may not know, Jonathan and the Wells' daughter certainly did know each other, spent a considerable amount of time together; they must have done since they were rehearsing a play.'

'Are you going to say anything to your chief inspector?'

'Not yet. I still don't believe Jonathan's capable of murdering anyone, let alone in so brutal a fashion, not least because I don't think he'd have the strength to drive a billhook right through a body and several inches into the ground. Anyway, Ross has convinced himself that the late Mr Herviser actually did the killing. As to Jonathan's involvement in some other way . . . it's possible, but how? One thing I will say, that if he was acting that night we waited together by Symonds' body, it was one hell of a performance.'

They finished their meal and he drove them over the river to the Quinton villages. Meon Hill looked higher than it was in actual fact, rising as it did out of a relatively flat landscape. They left the car in the lane and took the footpath, which led them through trees to the top and a good view of the surrounding countryside. It was possible to see the racecourse outside Stratford some six or seven miles away, the church spire and part of the town itself in one direction, and over to the Malvern Hills in another.

'I expected it to feel creepier than this,' remarked Fiona. 'You know there are places which really do have an atmosphere. I'm not sure if I'd feel anything particular here if I didn't already know the story, though of course it's a lovely day and the sun's shining. It might be different in the mist or at night. No black dogs or headless women either.'

'Not so far,' Latymer agreed. 'But I'm expecting them any time.'

She looked across the fields again. 'Where's Lower Horton?'

'Down there. After the sharp bend in the road. If you look across in that direction you can see the little hill and the copse where we found Symonds. It's not as prominent as this, though.'

She pointed down towards the road. 'So that must be the church where you saw the flowers on the old grave?'

'That's right. Would you like to see that too?'

'You must think I'm really morbid.'

'Not at all. These places do have an awful fascination. And this story isn't over yet. If you like, we could go on to Hidcote Manor afterwards. The garden there's supposed to be well worth seeing.'

'That would be lovely.' They retraced their steps back down the hill. 'I wonder if I'm right about Charlie Walters and why he was murdered?' she said. 'It would fit.'

'It would. But there could be other hidden reasons we know nothing about either. However, we're unlikely ever to know unless there's a written confession lying hidden somewhere, which I doubt.'

When they reached Lower Horton he turned off to the church, parking the car with some difficulty, as unlike the last time he was there, the small green outside was overflowing with vehicles, and many taking up a substantial part of the roadway. The reason became obvious when they went through the gate just as what was obviously a christening party was leaving the church. It was a large and merry gathering, the baby proudly displayed in a magnificent christening gown which looked like a family heirloom. Outside in the sunshine, the proud parents and relatives chatted to the vicar as friends and relations flashed camcorders and took photographs from every conceivable angle. Not wanting to intrude, Latymer took Fiona round behind the church to avoid getting in the way, then across and over to the old grave. There were no flowers on it now and the weeds were fast growing up over the disturbed earth. No one would have given it a second look or a second thought. Fiona bent down and read the words on the gravestone.

'Jane Hutchens, the vicar, said at the inquest that Elizabeth Bidford had given birth to an illegitimate child, then died in childbirth along with the baby, but that someone must have cared enough to pay for a proper grave and a gravestone,' Latymer told her.

Fiona ran a hand gently over the earth beneath. 'Now here is a mystery. Not only an unwanted child, buried secretly like something out of a Victorian novel, but also, or so you tell me, a box of human ashes on top of it. A relative? Another child? Something else I suppose we'll never know.'

'Well, so far as I'm aware, no one's come forward yet in spite of the publicity.' Latymer looked across at the church. The christening party were now making their way towards the church gate and the cars. 'I think we can decently go there now it's all over.' They began to make their way towards the front of the church. 'While we're here you must have a look at the carvings round the roof, they really are something.'

'You coming on then, Jane?' the baby's father called out to the vicar from the gate. 'The Globe always does a good spread.'

'I'll just tidy up and get changed, then I'll join you,' she called back. 'I wouldn't miss it for anything.' She was about to go back into the church when she saw Latymer and greeted him. 'Haven't we met before? I'm sure I know your face.'

'We met here at the beginning of April,' he replied, 'in what turned out to be rather odd circumstances when I drew your attention to the flowers on that old grave over there. Then I read later that the remains of a baby had been found in it.'

'That's right. A truly sad story. And did you hear that there were also cremated remains as well? We're going to have a little funeral for the baby next week. It'll be buried over there, in the space under the tree and the parish council have agreed to pay for a small stone with the words: "Known Only Unto God – Suffer the Little Children to Come Unto Me".' She sighed. 'Of course, since then, as you must also know, we've had another awful event here. I'm likely to be taking the funeral of Lucas Symonds, the man who was murdered recently, in the near future. And I thought how lucky I was to have such a quiet and peaceful parish where very little untoward occurs.' She looked at her watch. 'Goodness, I must leave you. I've been invited to the christening celebration and I don't want to hold them all up. Now that's how all children should be welcomed into the world. Enjoy the carvings.'

She went back into the church and they continued walking round looking at the absurd, sometimes preposterous figures. They stopped again at the door to look at the carvings each side of it. 'The green man,' Fiona pointed out.

Latymer shivered slightly. The last time he had seen the carving it had seemed merely anarchic, a reminder both of nature and things secular, but the sight of Symonds' body, topped by the grotesque green man mask, was still too close for comfort.

After their visit to Hidcote gardens they drove back to Bristol in companionable silence. 'It's been a lovely day,' Fiona assured him as they reached her friend's house, 'if a bit odd sometimes, but that's down to me. I felt I wanted to see the places I'd read about. I hope it hasn't spoiled what you had in mind.'

'Not in the least.'

'I'd no idea how beautiful this part of the world is, particularly all that blossom. It was wonderful.' She was silent for a moment. 'I've been thinking about that baby.'

'So have I. Possibly on the same lines.'

'It's a bit fanciful, but still. Suppose you're right and the girl in the photograph *is* the same girl, the one whose father owns the land where the crops were being grown and who's gone missing. That, from hardly knowing each other (apart from being in the play together), Jonathan and . . . ?'

'Lucy. I think I recall Ross told me her name was Lucy.'

'Lucy had a love affair, something that seemed to them at the age they both were then to be right out of *Romeo and Juliet.* And that . . .'

Latymer completed the sentence for her. 'And that as a result she found she was pregnant.'

She frowned. 'Though now I've said it, I'm not at all sure. They both come from decent homes, they might well have upset their families, caused dreadful rows, and I doubt they'd have been encouraged to marry, but surely Lucy Wells would have felt able to tell her parents what had happened. Let alone just run off, and when the time came deliver her baby under a hedge somewhere, then dump it in an old grave. If she didn't want to go through with the pregnancy, then given her age she could easily have had an abortion. But if Jonathan had got her pregnant, then in a way it would fit with what he was trying to tell you about this girl who had gone through a dreadful experience and why he couldn't bring himself to tell you about it.'

Latymer agreed. 'He led me to believe that whatever it was happened in the West Country, so I'd assumed it was to a girl he met down there during his gap year. But he could easily have been protecting her. Did she run away to Devon afterwards and he then joined her? But if she had the baby down there without help and it was stillborn or smothered or something, she'd hardly come all the way up here again, right on top of where she lived, to bury it. And why stay away all this time? Jonathan came back at the end of that year and if they were still involved they could have faced the music together. She could almost certainly have got away with not telling them she'd had a child. Then there's this urgent call for him to go to Plymouth after Christmas. Is that where she is now? Whatever the problem, surely to God, whatever the situation, her parents should be told?'

'It doesn't make any sense,' Fiona agreed.

Latymer shook his head. 'Nothing seems to. But it's the

nearest we can get to linking Lucy's disappearance with Jonathan's concern over a girl and a dead baby found in a local churchyard. But none of this explains any possible involvement in Symonds' murder.'

Fiona retrieved her coat and bag from the back seat and opened the car door. 'I must go. I want to get everything packed and ready for the train in the morning and Gillian's having a few friends round for supper. It's been a wonderful break.' Impulsively she leaned across and kissed him on the cheek. 'Perhaps you can see your way to coming up to visit me soon.'

'I'll do my best,' he told her.

'Good. Let me know what happens.'

Fifteen

There were several people with a good deal to think about that Monday morning. His growing realization that Herviser couldn't have murdered Lucas Symonds, since he was either well on the way to Oxford or actually there at the estimated time of the murder, had kept Ross exercised throughout most of a sleepless night. If it wasn't Herviser, then who? One of his followers acting on his behalf? The few questioned so far were adamant that all those who had travelled down on the minibus, also left on it. They could all be lying but unless one of them broke ranks it would be almost impossible to prove. A point he made when Latymer rang him in response to his call.

'It's knocked the whole case for six,' he admitted, 'and just when the specialists had succeeded in retrieving some pretty damning material from his hard disc. He had a good bit of material concerning the Meon Hill murder stored on it along with several maps of the area, on one of which he'd drawn a triangle linking Meon Hill with the fields on which the crops were being grown and the hill where we found Symonds' body. Which suggests a definite connection as well as forethought and planning. Also a lot more deeply unpleasant stuff about blood sacrifice. It's obvious he was thinking along those lines.'

'You don't think his mates are covering up for him?' suggested Latymer. 'You know, they might all have agreed to swear that Herviser was on the minibus back to Oxford with them. It could be that he had a car standing by and that after the murder he got himself driven to where he knew the bus would be dumped so that he'd be found on it which would give him an alibi.'

'Possibly, but from what we've been told by both the men we're holding here, Herviser was obviously ill before they even left Lower Horton. They say he was sweating, breathing heavily and complaining of pains in his chest, though he assured them that he'd suffered such an episode before and that it would pass. Given that he was aware of the state of his health, the obvious thing to do would have been to ask one of them to help him get to a hospital, instead of which he insisted he'd be OK. They'd no idea he'd a heart condition and were shocked when they heard he was dead. Which is another thing. The easiest way for all of them to get off the hook would be to say Herviser did it.' Latymer said nothing. 'You don't believe he did, do you? You never have.'

Latymer was cautious. 'I wouldn't go so far as to say that. Given his beliefs, his track record and desire for self-publicity, then he was an obvious prime suspect. Duplicating a notorious unsolved murder with occult overtones and getting away with it, not to mention all the consequent publicity, would be a real coup and fit in with all we know about him, but . . .'

'But?'

'But I've been thinking about it a lot. First of all, why Symonds? OK, so he had a high profile with regard to GM crops but it was Wells who was growing them. Given Herviser's twisted logic, then surely it should have been Wells, not Symonds, who "paid" the blood sacrifice. Then take the weapons used: an old billhook and a hayfork just like Meon Hill. He could hardly assume he'd find them lying around on a farm somewhere nearby, he'd have had to bring them with him. So how did he get hold of them? Stole them from a bygones museum? I don't even know if you can buy such things any more, but if you can, then surely after all the publicity, someone would have come forward to say that a strange looking person had recently purchased just such a pair of old farm implements from them recently.' This time it was Ross's turn to remain silent.

'And how would he have got Symonds up there?' Latymer continued. 'Symonds was no fool. Surely he wouldn't simply agree to meet some stranger, at what amounts to the blasted oak at midnight, without either taking someone with him or making sure his housekeeper or brother-in-law knew where he was.'

'We know he had a call on his mobile at home later on,' said Ross, 'but it wasn't on him and it's not turned up anywhere. We asked Bob Wells for the number but he didn't have a note of it as apparently Symonds had just changed his phone and his network. Which is why Wells rang him on the house phone when he got back to his farm to say all was well back there. BT have a note of that call.'

'So what now?' enquired Latymer.

'We'll have to go over everything again from the beginning. I'll also organize an ID parade as soon as possible so that your friend can come along and see if he recognizes either of the two we've arrested, though I'm not very hopeful. Also, in view of the collapse of the case against Herviser, I intend keeping an eye on the Higham boy.'

Latymer briefly considered saying something about Lucy Wells, then decided against it for the time being. Anyway, if Fiona's suggestions turned out to be anything like right, the relationship between Lucy and Jonathan had nothing whatsoever to do with Symonds' murder. After giving Ross Berry's phone number, he called his friend himself to tell him about the identity parade and that he'd be hearing from Ross when it had been set up. He then filled him in on the turn of events, adding that something had come up which he could do with talking through with him.

'Suits me,' replied Berry. 'Actually, I want to talk to you, too. Soon as you like.'

'That sounds serious,' commented Latymer.

'It is. I want to make you a proposition – a *business* proposition!'

In the small upstairs back room in the terraced house in a rundown part of Coventry he shared with three other students, Jonathan Higham lay on his bed staring at the ceiling. He was not due in to college until the end of the morning. All in all the college authorities had been rather good about his brush with the police. Officially they did not condone the action of the students joining in a protest to trash GM crops and this was made clear to the students involved, whatever some of them might think privately. Also, there had been both sympathy and understanding for the fact that it was Jonathan who had discovered the body of the murdered man, and at college, at least, his explanation of how he'd spent the time before doing so appeared to have been accepted, and he received a number of offers of assistance should the police seek to question him again.

If only, he thought, if only he could share his awful burden with *someone*. He had tried to bring himself to confide in John Latymer over lunch that day, only to draw back when it actually came to it. He wished with all his heart that he had. If only he'd done so, things might have been so different. Instead it was worse; much, much worse. He could see no way out of the situation in which he found himself without bringing disaster, not only on himself but also on to others. All right, so he'd finally decided to do what he considered to be the right thing, something he should have done a long time go, fully aware that there were likely to be drastic repercussions. But not this. Certainly not this. For the hundredth time he had a flashback to that bare hospital room in that bleak, multi-storey modern hospital Whatever happened now, he'd remember that for the rest of his life.

Later that day Berry rang to tell Latymer that Ross had managed to set up the identity parade for the next day, and also to invite him over for supper that night. Latymer accepted. 'I presume this concerns your proposition?'

'That's right. No time like the present. See you.'

Latymer drove over to Bristol in a thoughtful mood. If the investigation was back at square one, then perhaps it was worth looking through all that Meon Hill stuff again. He'd see what Berry thought.

'Well, there's no point in beating about the bush, I'll put it to you straight,' declared Berry, as he, his wife and Latymer were sitting over a drink before supper. 'I've got the chance to lease larger and better premises in one of the new developments in the docks area. We really are very short of room here now since the second-hand, rare books and book searches sides have proved, happily, to be far more successful than I imagined and I have to have more storage space. It's got to the point where almost every room in the flat is stacked up with stock. Also, though this is definitely an up-and-coming area, we're likely to pick up far more drop-in trade nearer the centre of town. We've been offered what we think is a good deal but have only a limited time in which to make our minds up. Which is where you come in, John.

'You've kept saying you want to give up the tour business and you're about to move nearer. Would you consider coming in with us? I'm not asking you to make a big financial investment, or indeed anything at all at this stage. If the figures are correct, then I think Kate and I can manage it. But it would be really good to have someone else involved and you're the obvious choice. You look surprised.'

Latymer was taken aback. 'I am. I'd no idea you were thinking of moving.'

'We weren't. It's just that it all seems to have come together: increased business, the need for more space and a very good opportunity. I don't expect a definite answer from you now, this minute, but I'll need to know fairly soon so that proper partnership details could be drawn up. Kate and

I intend going ahead anyway, but we could do with bringing in someone else and you'd be ideal.'

'I must admit I've never even thought about getting involved in anything like this,' admitted Latymer, 'though as you know I soon became fed up with early retirement, which is why I took on the dreaded Literary Tours.'

Berry laughed. 'And look what that got you, or rather us, into!'

'And look what it's done to my marriage,' retorted Latymer, grimly. 'As a result, I haven't got one any more. Tess was never sympathetic like Kate.'

'I suppose I always knew Keith had a hankering after the old days,' said Kate. 'And from what he told me, I did feel really sorry for the woman whose husband was murdered. Did you know Fiona Garleston called in again with her friend before she went back to Scotland? She told me some more about what happened and also about her website. It was probably much harder for your wife to accept what you did since she thought you'd given it all up, while I knew Keith would never really give up his police ways.'

Berry smiled and put an arm round his wife. 'Which brings me to my other reason for asking if you'll come in with us, John. With a bigger shop and more book searches and so on, we intend taking on a full-time assistant. Kate will manage the shop and buying-in new books and I'll be responsible for the book fairs, second-hand trade and book searches.'

'So where would I fit in?' enquired Latymer.

'You're good on literature. Obviously, or you wouldn't have your present job. I think you'd enjoy hunting down rare books. However, that's not quite all . . .'

Latymer closed his eyes. 'Go on . . .'

'We've both admitted that our first foray into investigative work got the old adrenalin going again. And in spite of what you said afterwards about it being a one-off, it wasn't, was it? You've been beavering away like anything at this recent case. I'm not suggesting we do anything as obvious as advertising our services as a private detective agency, but we could let it be known, as it were, that we weren't averse on occasion to taking on the odd case.'

'Whoa!' Latymer put down his glass with a thump. 'That really would need some thinking about.'

'But let's face it. Isn't that what we're doing now? It would merely put it on a more formal basis.'

'I suppose. Look, I really will have to think it over. I promise I won't keep you hanging on. I'll come over to Stratford with you tomorrow, then we can talk about it some more.'

Kate got up, went into the kitchen then put her head back round the door. 'Supper's ready. There's one advantage about moving, the flat and the kitchen are bigger. I told him I wouldn't even consider such a move unless I had a better kitchen!'

The two men stood up and went over to the table. 'Now,' said Berry, 'what is it *you* wanted to talk to *me* about?

'So you're convinced that the girl in the photograph Higham's mother showed you is the missing Wells girl?' observed Berry as they set out for Stratford the next day.

'I now know it is. Jonathan's mother obviously thought it a trifle strange when I went round to see her first thing this morning and asked if I could see it again. Fortunately, since we can't stand the sight of each other, her husband had already left for work. Even if there had been any doubt about the picture, she also produced the programme which she'd found after she'd been round to our house that night. It's there in black and white: "Viola – Lucy Wells".'

'Are you going to tell Ross?'

'I'm not sure. My instinct is to hold fire until we have more to go on.'

'There you are, you see!' declared Berry, triumphantly.

'What's that supposed to mean?'

'That you can't leave it alone, can you? Once you get

involved in something like this, you just have to keep on going.'

The identity parade did not prove to be of much use for Berry was quite sure that neither of the men arrested had taken part in the attack on Dee and himself. Apparently the three or four others, currently held in London, would be taking part in other line-ups which Dee would be asked to attend. But no one held out much hope of a result. Everything seemed to have ground to a halt, facing Ross, as he already knew, with the prospect of having to start his investigation all over again.

'But if neither Herviser, nor any of his yobs, then *who*?' he raged at Latymer and Berry. 'Was it, after all, some mad coincidence? That Symonds, for God knows what reason, decided to take a walk up the hill in the middle of the night and came across a raging psychopath who just happened to be in the same place at the same time?'

'Carrying a handy billhook and hayfork with him,' observed Latymer. 'That's more or less what the local police suggested regarding the Meon Hill murder, except that it was a drunk rather than a psychopath whose path crossed with that of the victim. It didn't make much sense then either.'

Ross thanked them for coming over. 'Well, in view of what's happened I'll read through all the material you gave me, Latymer. I can't really see how it can help much but I'm now clutching at straws.'

'Do you have to get back straight away?' Latymer asked Berry as the two men left the police station.

'No. Kate's got a helper in so that she can go through all the paperwork to do with giving up the lease on the shop and sorting out that for the new one.'

'When are you hoping to make the move?'

'We reckon it'll take about two months. I'm not looking forward to shifting all that stock and re-organizing it somewhere else. But as regards today, I'm free. What have you in mind?'

'I thought we might try and contact Jonathan Higham since

he's only down the road. After all, it was he who wanted to talk to me and tell me about this girl he was so concerned about. I thought I might ask him directly about Lucy. I could try and find out from the university where he might be and, if that fails, I do have his mobile number.'

All the university could tell him was that Jonathan should be on campus as rehearsals were in progress for a student production in which he was taking part. Latymer, after explaining that he didn't want to disrupt a rehearsal, asked if Jonathan could be given a message to say that he would be on the campus, outside the Arts Centre (since it was open to the general public) at about one o'clock.

'Are you police?' asked the voice at the end of the phone.

'No, no,' Latymer reassured her. 'Just a friend.'

'I wonder if he'll turn up,' said Berry as they set off for the university. 'If he is hiding something then he's not likely to be very keen to talk to you.'

But when they arrived at the Arts Centre, Jonathan was already outside waiting for them. 'We can go to the cafeteria if you want something to eat,' he suggested, looking at Latymer's companion in some surprise. Latymer explained that Berry was an old friend and ex-colleague and that they'd been over to Warwick for Berry to attend an ID parade. 'But it was a dead loss. Whoever it was attacked Keith in London, it wasn't either of those two.'

After they'd collected sandwiches and soup from the cafeteria counter (at least Jonathan hadn't lost his appetite, Latymer noted), Latymer brought Jonathan up to date on the investigation, or at least as much as he thought it appropriate for him to know. Jonathan was obviously surprised. 'So it couldn't have been this Herviser guy then?'

'It doesn't look like it. It could be that one of his people stayed behind to do the deed and the rest covered up for his absence from the minibus, but that's going to be hard to prove since the police don't know who half of them are.

Ross doesn't think it very likely. In fact he says he'll have to go right back to the beginning and start again.'

Jonathan looked worried. 'Oh God, does this mean they'll be coming down on me again?'

'I wouldn't think so. But I thought you'd best be put in the picture. There is something else, however. Nothing to do with the murder. Do you remember when we first talked, over lunch in Warwick that day and before all this happened, you told me of your concern for some girl you knew who had suffered a dreadful experience. But then you weren't able to tell me any more for fear, as I understood it, of breaking a confidence?' Jonathan looked at him, but didn't reply. 'You see, when you were under arrest, as you probably know, your mother came to see us to ask if I could do anything to help you. She brought along a photograph album to prove, she said, that you weren't the kind of boy who would turn to murder.'

Jonathan screwed his face up. 'Oh God, how embarrassing!'

'Well that's mothers for you. She did it for the best of motives, because she was so anxious. Anyway, among the photographs was one of you in a school production of *Twelfth Night,* standing beside a very pretty girl who I assumed was playing Viola. Who was she?'

Jonathan appeared to give it some thought, then shook his head. 'I really don't remember. It was ages ago.'

'Your mother couldn't either when she showed us the photograph.' Latymer could have sworn that for a fleeting moment the boy looked relieved. 'Well, if you don't,' he continued, 'now comes the difficult bit. At Ross's invitation, I went to the opening of the inquest on Symonds, because I thought it useful as both you and I will be called to give evidence once it resumes. Afterwards I met Bob Wells, the dead man's brother-in-law, and his wife. He'd been called to give evidence of identification. As they were about to leave they produced a photograph of their daughter, Lucy, who went missing some three or four years ago, asking Ross if her disappearance could be publicised again since the family, however reluctantly, was in the news. I had a good look at the picture of Lucy Wells and to my surprise she looked just like the girl with you in your school photograph. I thought I'd better be sure, so I went round and asked your mother if I could take a look at the picture again. In fact I now know it was her, as since her visit to us your mother had found the programme.'

Both men had to admit later that Jonathan took it extremely well, raising again in Latymer's mind the fact that he was dealing with a talented actor. He frowned, shook his head, then exclaimed as if it had suddenly come to him, 'You know, you're right! Of course!'

'Did you know she'd disappeared?'

'No, I didn't. She wasn't at my own school, you see, the girls came in from other local schools. I know we played opposite to each other but I hardly got to know her at all.'

'And you never saw her afterwards?' broke in Berry.

'No. There was no reason to.'

'Then she wasn't the girl you tried to tell me about when we met in Warwick' Latymer persisted, 'the one causing you obvious distress and concern? As indeed you would be if a girl you knew had disappeared without trace, following some traumatic incident.'

'Why are you asking me all this?' demanded Jonathan. 'What right have you to question me in this way? You're not the police. Or are you doing it on their behalf?'

'No, I'm not and I'm sorry if you're upset,' said Latymer. 'I wouldn't have come to you if I hadn't thought Lucy Wells could be the girl in question. I thought you might know why she'd left home and where she went, and that you'd kept quiet about it because she made you promise not to tell anyone.'

'I told you, I met the person I was talking about when I was in Devon during my gap year. Look, I can't stay much longer. I've a lecture to go to.'

Latymer made a final attempt. 'But don't you see? At the very least it's something of a coincidence that this girl you didn't remember is the daughter of the very farmer whose land you trespassed on when you took part in the crops protest? Didn't the name ring any bell?'

'How could it? As you say, I couldn't even remember who she was and I'd no idea who owned the land on which the trials were taking place.'

'There is one more thing. You and your friends attended the inquest on the baby whose remains were found in the Lower Horton graveyard, as you thought it might be a good subject for a play. Well, someone who knew of Lucy Wells' disappearance suggested to me that it might have been her child and that's why she ran away.'

Jonathan stood up. 'I'm sorry, Mr Latymer, but it's beginning to sound like something out of a TV soap opera. How should I know if Lucy Wells got herself pregnant? I've already told you, after the play I never saw her again. Next thing you'll be suggesting it was my baby!' Then he calmed down a little. 'I'm sorry. I'm grateful to you for all you've done. It's just that this whole business has got me down and now you tell me they don't think they got the right man after all. It's going to drag on and on. Now, I really must go.'

'Well, what do you make of that?' enquired Latymer as Jonathan left the café.

'He was lying,' said Berry, 'though he was pretty clever about it.'

'I agree. A very competent actor. The thing is, whether we're right or wrong about his involvement with Lucy Wells, it doesn't help much with Symonds' murder. But it is all very odd. Wells' brother-in-law is found murdered just outside Lower Horton where, a few weeks earlier, the remains of a dead infant have been found in the graveyard. The body is discovered by Jonathan Higham who at the very least knew Wells' daughter, Lucy, who disappeared at about the time the baby's body was buried there. Is it just coincidence? You tell me.'

'So where do we go from here? Tell Ross? See what we can find out ourselves?'

'I think we might risk taking a chance. Jonathan could be telling the truth, that he never saw Lucy Wells again after the end of the play, but I think perhaps the Wells should know that there is a link between the two of them. It might be that she fell for someone else in the play. I can use the excuse that I recognized the picture of Lucy as that of a girl I'd seen in a similar photograph quite recently, and checked it out. That is if you can spare the time.'

'Actually I've been meaning to ask you if we can go over to Tewkesbury after we've finished here, it's hardly out of our way. There's an old bookseller there who's about to give up and I'd like to see what he has in his stock. If that's OK, I'll call him now. How long do you reckon we'll be?'

Latymer looked at his watch. 'It's just on a quarter past two. It'll probably take us half an hour or so to get to Lower Horton, half an hour there say – if Wells will see us. Say about 4.30-ish.'

Berry made his call. 'That's fine. It'll save me making another trip.' They got up to go. 'What if Wells asks why you haven't gone to the police about this?'

'That I thought it might distress them less if we talked to them first.'

'Are you going to say anything about the baby in the churchyard?'

'Not directly. It depends. It might be possible to ask if there was any possibility Lucy was pregnant when she left home. Stop looking at me like that! I still haven't decided what to do about your offer.'

Sixteen

It was starting to rain as Jonathan left the cafeteria. He was still feeling shaken. He found a sheltered corner and made a call on his mobile, only to learn that the person he wanted to speak to was out. Did he want to leave a message? No, he'd call back later. He looked at his watch again. The lecture was due to start within a few minutes. Since there was nothing else he could do for the time being, he hunched himself into his coat and ran towards the lecture room.

By the time Latymer and Berry reached Bob Wells' farm the rain was pouring down. He was obviously surprised to see them but invited them to come in out of the wet. 'I'm beginning to wonder if the rain will ever stop,' he commented as he ushered them into the big farm kitchen. 'The ground's absolutely sodden with what we've had during the winter and early spring, it can't absorb any more. It'll only take a few hours of this and there'll be floods again all over the country.' He turned to Latymer, looking rather puzzled. 'I'm just trying to work out where we've met before Mr . . . ?'

'Latymer. It was at the opening of the inquest into your brother-in-law's murder.'

'Of course. And it was you who called in the police after the body had been found, wasn't it, and your friend . . . ?' He looked enquiringly at Berry.

Latymer introduced him. Rather than going into a lengthy explanation as to why his companion had needed to attend an identity parade in Warwick, Latymer fell back on the excuse that Berry was out on a book-buying expedition in the area and had suggested he came along. 'Which is why I'm here, since he was coming this way. There's something I've come across by chance which I think you ought to know and I thought it might be easier if I called in and told you in person rather than simply contact you on the phone.'

Wells looked considerably taken aback but motioned them to sit down. 'So what is it you wanted to see me about, Mr Latymer?'

'It concerns your daughter.'

Wells stared at him. '*Lucy*?'

'Is your wife here?'

'No, Marian's gone over to see a friend this afternoon. Even if she hadn't, so far as it's possible I try to avoid bringing the subject up, she's been so devastated by Lucy's disappearance. We both have, of course, but Marian's taken it particularly badly. At one time we, that is Lucas and I, were afraid she'd suffer a mental breakdown. But are you saying there's some news of her? If so, why haven't the police contacted us?'

'No news, I'm afraid, I wish there was and I've no wish to raise false hopes. What I've discovered goes back to the time before she disappeared and I don't know if it's of any use, but I thought I'd let you know anyway. It's just that when I saw the photographs of your daughter after the opening of the inquest, I was sure I recognized her, that I'd seen a similar picture somewhere else and recently. I don't know how well up you are on what's been going on, but the young student who found Mr Symonds' body, Jonathan Higham, was arrested, then released on police bail.'

'I did hear something to that effect. I think the chief inspector said it was because he couldn't give a satisfactory account of what he was doing between leaving the protest and finding Lucas, but that they couldn't disprove what he had to say and so had let him go. I told him I felt sorry for the lad, he's been through enough as it is. What about him?'

'After his arrest, his mother came round to see my wife

and I. She was in quite a state, as you might expect, and wanted to know if I could help her son. She brought with her a photograph album to show me, she said, what a decent boy he was and how he couldn't possibly have murdered anyone! Among the photographs was one of Jonathan with your daughter taken when they were in a production of *Twelfth Night* together several years ago. From what I gather it must have been taken not long before she left home.'

'Have you asked him about it?'

'Yes. He said he didn't know your daughter at all well, that they'd never been close friends and that after the production he'd never seen her again. Indeed, he seemed to have trouble at first even remembering her name.'

'So why are you telling me all this?'

'Because I thought you might like to take it up with him yourself. See if you can jog his memory. It might be that she gave some hint to him, or to one of the others, something not recognized at the time, that she was planning to leave home and why.'

Wells nodded. 'I suppose it's worth a try. Though I can't think either Higham or any of the others taking part in the play (supposing we could find them) would remember some vague hint or suggestion so long after the event.'

'It's a strange coincidence that he should now have become so closely linked with your family,' commented Latymer.

'What do you mean?' Wells was becoming irritated.

'That he took part in the protest on your land and discovered the body. Nothing more.'

'What has that to do with anything? Are you here in some capacity for the police? If so, then your time would surely be better spent finding out who killed Lucas since I've now been told they got it wrong.'

'Didn't Ross explain? And by the way we're not here on behalf of the police.'

'Explain what?'

'That Herviser – the man they believed killed Mr Symonds

– almost certainly couldn't have done it. Not only had he been taken ill with the onset of what turned out to be a fatal heart attack, there's ample evidence that he'd left the area before the murder took place. So once again they're looking for a prime suspect.'

Wells stood up, shaking his head in disbelief. 'All I've heard since the inquest is that they're back to square one. We've hardly been kept in the picture at all.' He looked out at the rain. 'So have you told the chief inspector about these photographs?'

'Not yet. I thought you might like to take it further yourself before dragging the police in unnecessarily.'

'I see.' He appeared somewhat mollified. 'Well, that was thoughtful of you and of course I'm interested to know that Jonathan Higham was in a play with my daughter that summer. Have you his phone number and address?'

'He's at the University of Warwick and I don't know the address and phone number of his digs, but I can give you those of his parents in my village.' Latymer drew the conversation to an obvious close. 'That's about it, Mr Wells. I hope we've not taken up too much of your time.'

The farmer looked across at the Aga. 'I'm sorry. I should have offered you a cup of tea or something. Would you like one?' Latymer declined the offer, explaining that they were going on to Tewkesbury. 'Very well, I'll show you out then. If we use the back door you'll be nearer to your car. I take it you're a book dealer,' he commented to Berry as he led the way.

'I have a bookshop in Bristol,' Berry told him, 'new and second-hand books. I've been looking at old stock in Stratford and we're now off to Tewkesbury because someone's selling up there and I thought I'd take a look at what he's got.'

As they reached the back door Wells turned to Latymer. 'Well thank you for telling me about the photograph. I'll ring the chief inspector right away and ask whether he thinks I should contact young Higham directly, or leave it to him. It might be less worrying for the lad if I do it. It'll also give me an excuse to ask Ross why I haven't been told that they still don't know who killed Lucas.' He put his hand on the latch to open the door.

'Your village seems to have been picked out for misfortune recently,' remarked Berry. 'I read somewhere about the remains of a child being found in your local graveyard not long before Mr Symonds' murder.'

'That's right. A sad business. The general opinion round here is that the mother must have been some young teenager who'd got into trouble and didn't dare tell her parents.'

'Presumably your daughter would have told you had she found herself in such a predicament?' prompted Berry, as if the thought had just occurred to him and hoping his question wouldn't produce too angry a response. In the event Wells seemed to take it as a reasonable assumption.

'I'm sure she would have done. She'd hardly have expected us to be pleased and no doubt Marian would have read the riot act, but we'd have supported whatever decision she chose to make. No, we've never considered pregnancy as an explanation for her going missing. To be absolutely honest, unless anything comes of the renewed enquiries, I think however hard it is, we're going to have to face up to the very real possibility that something dreadful has happened to her and that she might well be dead. I can't imagine what other reason there could be for her not to have contacted us, by some means or another, after all this time. Though how Marian would take that . . .' He left the rest unspoken, then made a determined effort as he opened the door. 'By the way, your bookshop, Mr Berry. I rather like browsing round second-hand bookshops myself. Do you specialize in anything?'

Berry smiled. 'Actually I do. I specialize in crime. There seems to be an insatiable appetite for it.'

The rain was still lashing down. 'If I were you, I'd go back into Stratford and take the Alcester Road, at least round

Welford,' Wells advised them. 'The road floods easily there at the best of times.'

They did as he suggested and it was as well they took his advice for when they drove through Evesham on the main road they saw that the Avon had already burst its banks and was beginning to flood across the parkland between the road bridge and the town. It seemed impossible that it could get any worse, but as they approached Tewkesbury the rain was falling so hard the windscreen wipers could hardly cope with it. 'Where are you going to park?' asked Latymer.

'In the car park by Tewkesbury Abbey, it's only five minutes walk from the shop.' But when Berry turned down towards it, the only sign that there had ever been a car park was the top of a notice sticking out of an expanse of flood water. In the end they parked in the street on the assumption that there would be few traffic wardens or police touring the streets issuing parking tickets.

There wasn't a great deal of stock of interest to Berry, but he bought and paid for what there was. 'Bring your car round the back,' said the bookseller, 'turn into the road opposite the abbey and you'll see a narrow road on your left, about twenty yards down. You can drive out the other end. In the meantime I'll try and find some bits of plastic to cover the tops of the boxes.' He turned to Berry. 'It's just occurred to me that I know where you might find some other stock that might be of interest to you. I've the address and telephone number here somewhere.'

'I'll go and fetch the car then while you look,' said Latymer. He got wet through just crossing the road to the car. He reversed it, put the heater on and turned into the road opposite the abbey as instructed; then braked, with a jolt. In front of him, under an overcast sky, a great expanse of water stretched away into the far horizon. It was as if the town stood at the head of an enormous lake or coastal inlet. My God, he thought, it's Noah's Flood! He found the left turn, drove up behind the shop and helped the other two put the boxes into the boot. 'I've never seen anything like it,' he said to the bookseller, wiping the water from his face. 'Are you worried you might be flooded out?'

'We never have been so far,' the bookseller replied, 'and I've had the shop for thirty years. But there's always a first time.'

It was the end of the afternoon before Jonathan was able to speak to the person he'd been so desperately trying to contact, and when he did, the subsequent conversation was anything but reassuring. If it was left to him, he would now finally give up and at the very least confess to Latymer, if not to the police, but as he wasn't the only one involved that wasn't an option. He wondered how much longer he could keep up the pretence without starting to crack; he was rapidly reaching the end of his tether.

The idea of going back to his noisy student digs or spending the evening in the union bar had precious little appeal. Neither did driving through the awful weather to spend the night with his parents. There was, however, one other possibility. When the Highams moved from Warwick to Gloucestershire, his father had bought a rather smart caravan on what was described as a 'luxury' site near Stratford. The idea was that he'd use it as a base for fishing, then his favourite recreation, and also for Jonathan and his sister who at the time were keen on canoeing. Higham had been warned by some of the locals of the possibility of flooding, and that another site closer to the river had been closed down because of it, but he'd been assured by the site's owners that the possibility had been thoroughly looked into and that he would be quite safe where he was, and so far this had indeed proved to be the case.

But as time passed Higham had taken up other interests, both children were away from home a good deal of the time, and he'd decided he'd sell it, but as yet hadn't got round to doing so. Jonathan knew his parents had been out to the caravan to check it out and spent a couple of nights in it over Easter, so it must be in good order and he still had a key. Very well, he'd go back to his digs, pick up a few things, get himself a takeaway meal, milk and bread (no doubt there'd be coffee and tea left there from Easter), and spend the night in peace and quiet even if it was raining hard. Hopefully, a night or so on his own might clear his head and finally help him decide what he ought to do.

He drove over to Coventry and was relieved to find the house empty, so collected some bedding, a battery radio and a torch, in case of emergencies, and left a note to say he would be away overnight. The rain had been bad enough going to Coventry but by the time he skirted Warwick on the way to Stratford, it was appalling and after stopping off to pick up basic supplies and a pizza he began to think for the first time that holing up in a caravan for the night might not be the best of ideas. It was unlikely he'd be able to drive up as far as the site, so he parked his car just inside the gateway, hidden behind some bushes out of the way, he hoped, from any opportunist thief. Then, very laden and doing his best to avoid the bedding getting wet, he made his way in pitch darkness to the site. It was managed by a couple who lived in a house nearby but there was no light in the windows, no sign of life at all, and since their car wasn't outside they must be out at least for the evening. None of the lights along the path to the site were on either, hardly surprising as it was extremely unlikely anyone else would be so foolhardy as to visit their caravan at such a time and in such weather.

He walked cautiously down the path and squelched across the sodden grass to the caravan. The traffic from the main road a couple of hundred yards behind him threw up a lurid glow, highlighting as it did so the muddy, swirling water of the Avon. But the water was still a good few yards from the site and surely, some time soon, the rain would stop and the floods recede. He fumbled for the key, almost dropping everything in the process, and opened the door. Inside it smelled damp and musty. He dumped his stuff on the floor and switched on his torch, searching for the device which switched on the bottle gas that supplied the lights, oven and a small heater. He finally found it and, after struggling for a while with damp matches, succeeded in lighting the lamps. It was several years since he'd visited the caravan but nothing had changed. There was a separate bedroom and a sitting room large enough to take a double bed folded into a couch, a small kitchen and a shower room. For what it was it was nicely furnished and well equipped. He lit the heater, then took his damp bedding into the bedroom, leaving the door open to let the warm air in.

His mother had covered up much of the furniture with sheets and he removed them, and stood close to the heater, realizing that while it did at least offer some warmth, it also seemed to add to the condensation. He shivered. What he needed was some warm food and drink. He found coffee in a jar and put the kettle on, put the pizza in the small oven, then peered out through the window. He hoped it was his imagination that made it look as if the flood waters had crept nearer even in the short time he'd been in the caravan.

Now he was alone, with time to think, he felt desolate. It probably hadn't been a good idea. The lack of outside lights, the dark house (perhaps the managers were actually away), the rain hammering on the metal roof and the growing sense of isolation were only making him feel worse. Well, now he was here he'd stick it out until the morning. He had some lines to learn and he'd brought the script along with him. He'd work at that, then turn in early. He needed the sleep but sleep no longer came easily. He shut his eyes briefly and saw again the summer garden of the fine Elizabethan mansion where he and Lucy had played Orsino and Viola. A sudden squall lashed against the window and he thought of the opening of the play, when Viola stumbles out of the storm and asks 'What country, friends, is this?' To which the captain of the shipwrecked vessel replies: 'It is Illyria, lady.' And Illyria it had been for them all that lost summer. It was all he had to hang on to, to help blot out that hospital room in Plymouth.

'No,' returned Ross, mystified. He had rung Latymer to tell him that Dee had identified one of his assailants from the London line-up and that the man had been charged. 'No, I've not had any telephone call from Bob Wells. What was it about?'

'Well, when I left him yesterday afternoon he was going to ring you straight away. Presumably you were out.'

'No. I was in the office all day. And why on earth should you call on Bob Wells anyway and why was he going to contact me?"

'Because something has come up, by chance, which I thought might possibly be of interest to him and since Keith Berry and I were already in the area, I called in to tell him about it. I left him to decide whether or not he wanted to bother you with it. As it turned out, he said he would, that he'd ring you straight away after we'd gone. He also wanted to ask you why you hadn't told him about Herviser.'

'I was fully intending to tell him the position myself, once I had a spare moment.' It was clear Ross was far from pleased. 'You didn't have to do it for me. So what is it you say has come up? *By chance*,' he added, sarcastically.

Latymer told him about the photographs and how Lucy and Jonathan Higham had acted together in a play shortly before she disappeared from home. 'So they must have known each other during the period shortly before she disappeared. As I say, I've no idea if it's of any significance, most likely not. But it's something of a coincidence, given that Jonathan also took part in the protest on Wells' land. But I'd rather Wells'd told you himself. Perhaps, on second thoughts, he decided it wasn't worth pursuing and might simply upset his wife unnecessarily.'

'I don't really have the time for all this speculation,' snapped Ross. 'I'll be in touch again *if* I need you. In the meantime, I suggest you leave the investigation to us.' He was still angry when he walked into the main control room. 'I'd like to bring that boy in again,' he barked at Sergeant Wilkins, then passed on what Latymer had told him. 'Go down to the university with a constable and bring him back with you. Tell him it's not an arrest. I don't intend arresting him again – yet. Just say something's cropped up I need to question him about. There's no need to say any more.'

The sergeant got up from his desk. 'I'll be off straight away then, but we're pretty short-handed, sir. We've men out diverting traffic all over the place and there's been a couple of nasty accidents, quite a big one on the by-pass, which will mean going round through Kenilworth and there's floods there. It could take quite a time.'

It did. In fact it was an hour and a half before he returned and he was empty-handed. 'Apparently Higham wasn't in college today, sir,' he told an increasingly exasperated Ross, 'and was away from his digs all night.'

'Does anyone know where?'

'No, he just left a note to say he'd be out. His tutor was surprised he wasn't there today as he had an essay which had to be in this morning and also a rehearsal for a play in which he has a big part. He thought Higham must have got himself cut off by floods somewhere.'

'Oh, very well,' returned Ross, irritably. 'Tell the college to call us if and when he does come in. In the meantime I'll see what Wells has to say.' But Wells was out, his wife informed him, helping to shift stock to higher and dryer ground and was unlikely to be back for some considerable time. As a last resort Ross rang the Highams to see if by any chance Jonathan had stayed with them the previous evening, only to draw another blank.

'No, he's not here,' Dawn Higham told him, sounding alarmed. 'We've not heard from him since you let him go. Surely you aren't going to tell me you still suspect him of being involved in that murder?'

'This is to do with a different matter,' Ross informed her.

Dawn became tearful. 'You're determined to get him for something, aren't you? Just because you can't prove he did anything wrong, except for taking part in the crops protest. If you intend arresting him again his father will want to know at once – *at once* – so that he can tell his solicitor.'

'I trust it won't come to that, Mrs Higham. But please let us know if your son does turn up or if you discover where he is.'

Latymer too was on edge. He felt in some way that he'd let Jonathan down as he'd been fully convinced that Wells would do as he said and ring Ross himself. Now it looked as if he would probably end up having offended everybody: Ross, Jonathan, the Highams and Bob Wells. He rang the landlord of his new flat and sorted out a date to move in. It could just about be fitted in the gap between the next two literary tours. Then, almost as soon as he'd put the phone down, he had a call from James Stevens, the senior executive at Becketts Literary Tours, who didn't sound particularly happy. 'We were beginning to think you'd disappeared, Latymer,' he'd told him. 'The office say they've rung you several times and you always seem to be out. I trust you haven't forgotten that you collect your next tour from Heathrow next Saturday?'

'Of course I haven't,' objected Latymer. 'I don't know when people are supposed to have rung me, but I've been here a lot of the time and I've answered any messages left on the phone for me and answered all the emails. It's not as if these are new tours which need research and upfront discussions.'

'It's not only the lack of communication,' Stevens continued. 'I think all of us at head office have sensed a distinct lack of enthusiasm. And that just won't do. It won't do at all. You know as well as I do all the problems we've encountered since September 11th. We need all the business we can get. *You* need all the business you can get.'

Why, oh why, mused Latymer, do these people think they have to say everything twice to get their point across?

'As I recollect,' his caller droned on, 'we had to send someone down to bring your last tour back to London because you had domestic problems of some kind. I trust these are now sorted out?' There didn't seem much point in going into long explanations about the break-up of his marriage and his moving house, so he merely made placatory noises. 'So,' continued Stevens, relentlessly, 'I want you up here for a meeting immediately after your next tour. My secretary will call you with the details.'

It really was going to be make-your-mind-up time, thought Latymer. Saturday not only marked the start of the first of the three tours to which he'd committed himself, it was also the date by which he'd promised to give the Berrys their answer. He put on the lunchtime television news which led with stories of floods. His local station showed graphic pictures of the floodwater surrounding Tewkesbury and Worcester and water washing around the theatre in Stratford. Well, there was no point in going out. He returned to his study and dug out the Meon Hill material yet again. He'd go through it just one more time. Outside the rain continued to fall.

Seventeen

The downpour continued throughout most of the night and the morning news bulletins were full of it. 'What's it like then down your way?' enquired John Dee when he rang Berry in the middle of the morning.

'Wet! And we've discovered a bit of a leak in the roof, but we haven't been flooded out. I'm wondering how the poor sod we visited yesterday in Tewkesbury's getting on. The town's almost surrounded by water. He said he thought he'd be OK as his bookshop hasn't been flooded in thirty years, but this really is exceptional.'

'Glad to hear you haven't had to build an ark then,' joked Dee. 'Just thought I'd bring you up to date on what's been happening up here. You probably know I did pick out one of the yobs who assaulted us and he's been charged, but so far as I can gather (and they don't tell you much), it's not possible to prove he was ever at the protest, let alone killed someone, either by proxy for Herviser or off his own bat. It seems Herviser, or Shrieve – I still think of him as Shrieve – was also mixed up in some kind of far-right set-up as well. It was probably thugs from both of his groups that he encouraged down to Warwickshire. Anyway, I understand you'll be needed as a witness when this guy comes up for trial so I thought I'd warn you that the police up here will be contacting you for a statement.'

'That's OK. Thanks for letting me know.'

'I thought I might take a trip down your way sometime soon. I'd be interested to see your shop.'

'Do that. Actually we're intending to move nearer the centre of town shortly, but one way or another we'll be contactable. I'd like to keep in touch.'

'Who was that? asked Kate as Berry came off the phone.

'John Dee, the lecturer who got done over by the bully boys with me. He's managed to identify one of them. I must find out if John knows.'

'Do you think John will come in with us? He hasn't said anything more to you about it, has he?'

'No, not even yesterday when he had ample opportunity. But he must have a lot on his mind just now: his break-up with Tess, having to move out of his house, and his tour job. Not to mention the fact that he can't leave this murder inquiry alone, which is why I've a hunch that he will join us. Anyway, he's promised to let us know by the end of the week and I'm sure he'll keep his word.'

Meanwhile, the object of their discussion was pacing up and down, going over and over in his mind a possibility that had come to him in the early hours of the morning. Knowing that he'd find it difficult to sleep if he went to bed at his usual time, he'd finally sat down with a large sheet of paper (rather than using his computer) and written down on it all the salient points. First, the Meon Hill murder, then its sequel at Lower Horton. Under the heading over the first, he briefly noted Fiona's suggested motive for the earlier murder, setting it against those of witchcraft or robbery which were obtained at the time. Next, he listed the bare facts of the discovery of the dead baby in the graveyard and of the casket of ashes buried above it. In another column he put down what he knew of the relationship between Jonathan Higham and Lucy Wells, and Lucy Wells' disappearance. Lastly, he wrote a brief account of the GM crops protest reminding himself, from the limited information he had, of who was there, its outcome and the discovery of Lucas Symonds' body.

Out of it all there had finally emerged, albeit with gaps

and a good deal of surmise, a possible scenario and at least one potential suspect. He wondered what Fiona would make of it, finally deciding that there was only one way to find out and that was to tell her. Only to discover, when he'd nerved himself to voice his theory, that she was out. There was, of course, email and it might even sort things out better in his own mind if he set out briefly the conclusions he'd come to. It took him a good hour to edit the amorphous mass of material circulating in his head down to a manageable and coherent storyline, but in the end he felt reasonable satisfied.

'So, I now have a potential motive for that particular victim, but I'm still not at all sure who actually did do it. It requires quite a leap of imagination, and, as you'll see, there are still big gaps that need to be filled in. But if I am on the right lines, then the whole premise of the investigation has been wrong right from the start. Call me, if you can. I'm not at all sure what I should do next.'

Reluctantly and with a sinking heart, he then dug out the paperwork for the next tour in the knowledge that after it was over he'd be facing his meeting with Stevens at Becketts' Canterbury headquarters. The senior executive was right, of course. He had lost his enthusiasm, added to which the prospect of regularly going away on tour with a bunch of strangers then returning when it was over to a cold and unlived-in flat, was deeply depressing. At least if he went in with the Berrys, he'd be working with friends and when he took his turn in the shop it would bring him into contact with the customers, without his having to spend all evening with them as well. He also rather liked the idea of going out and buying books, though he'd have to swot up on fictional crime. As to the other string, the other suggestion, that required far more thought.

Halfway through the afternoon, Tess arrived back without warning, grumbling at having had to follow a roundabout route in an attempt to avoid the floods. 'After all this coming and going it must have crossed your mind by now that you might just as well have stayed here, rather than tearing everything apart to move about forty miles down the road,' Latymer observed.

She ignored this. Her house purchase, she told him, was now going through without a hitch and she'd come back solely to make sure there were no problems with their own sale. 'I don't know when I'll be able to get up here again. Although Diana's baby isn't officially due for a month, they think it might be earlier. Her blood pressure's up a bit too and they've told her if it stays that way she might have to have a caesarean. So, I don't want to leave her now until it's born. I can sign anything else necessary by post.' Latymer resisted the temptation to suggest that a frenetic mother clucking round all the time would be enough to send anyone's blood pressure up.

'So when I've got my breath back, I'll go round to the Highams and ask Dawn if Dave can pull out all the stops to get our sale through as fast as possible. Perhaps he could call in tonight after work, if he isn't too tired, so we can discuss it with him.'

'Considering the fee he's going to get from us for doing more or less damn-all, I imagine he'll just about find the strength to totter round here,' commented Latymer, 'even if he is tired.'

'You would say that, wouldn't you? Why do you always have to be so disparaging? Actually,' she continued, 'I'd have thought *you* would have known where everything was at since you're here all day with nothing to do. When do you next go away?'

'Saturday,' he told her, 'but only for a week. Then I have just under a week off, followed by two more tours, a few days apart.'

'And after that . . . ?'

'I don't know. I think I'm going to resign.'

'Resign? Why?'

'I'm fed up with Becketts Tours. I've had enough.'

'And do what?' She was obviously disconcerted.

'Something different. I haven't yet quite made up my mind.'

A few minutes later she went out to see Dawn Higham. He expected her to return almost at once but in the event it was some time before she returned, and when she did she was looking worried. 'Is there a problem about the house sale?' he asked her, seeing the expression on her face.

'No. It's not that. It's nothing to do with us. It's Jonathan again. Apparently the police rang Dawn yesterday to ask if she knew where he was as he hadn't been into college and he wasn't in his digs, though he'd left a note to say he'd be out that night. Dawn wanted to know why they were looking for him and the policeman, I think she said he was a chief inspector, told her it was because they wanted to ask him a few questions. They wouldn't tell her what it was about, only that it was to do with a different matter. Naturally she was upset. Then, yesterday evening, she'd a call from some farmer near Stratford, also looking for Jonathan. It turned out it was his land the crops protest took place on. He wouldn't tell her what he wanted to talk to Jonathan about either, except that it had something to do with a photograph of his daughter.

'Then, this morning, she'd another call from the police. Jonathan still hasn't been seen or heard of and Dawn's now really worried. She's rung Dave and he's coming home as soon as he can, given the state of the roads. Do you know what it's all about?'

Latymer avoided a direct reply. 'It needn't be anything for them to worry about. From what I've seen of him, Ross doesn't enjoy being kept hanging about, he likes everything done yesterday, so he'll be irritated that he can't talk to Jonathan straight away. No doubt he's frustrated, too, since he isn't getting far with his murder inquiry.'

Tess nodded. 'I suppose so. Well, since I am here, I'll do some more packing. At least I can sort all my clothes out and decide what I'm keeping and what I can throw out and give to the charity shops. Have you finally decided what you're taking with you?'

Latymer went into his study and looked around, daunted at the prospect of packing all his books and papers. At least the book cases were free-standing and could go with the books, but they'd all have to be parcelled up or boxed and it would take forever to get them all into proper order again. He switched on his computer and checked his email to discover, to his disappointment, that there was only one and that was from Becketts. 'Since you and your tour will arrive back in London on the Saturday night,' wrote Stevens' secretary, 'and you will be going to Heathrow with them on Sunday morning, I've fixed the first possible appointment after this for your meeting with Mr Stevens. We will, therefore, be expecting you at the office on 10.30 a.m. Monday morning. In the circumstances no doubt it will be easier for you either to stay in London overnight Sunday or here in Canterbury, therefore Becketts are prepared to cover any necessary expenses.' So that was that. He rang Fiona again but there was still no reply.

So once again he found himself sharing a supper table with his soon-to-be ex-wife, since on this occasion the weather offered little alternative. The rain had eased off during the afternoon, but now it had begun again and when he looked out of the back door at about seven o'clock the sky was so dark it was like an evening in mid-winter rather than early May. They were just finishing eating when the doorbell rang. He went and answered it. In almost a re-run of the last occasion, Dawn Higham again stood on the step, but this time she'd brought her husband with her. It was clear he hadn't come to discuss their house sale.

'What the bloody hell have you done *now*?' he yelled at Latymer. Dawn looked acutely embarrassed.

'I've no idea what you're talking about, for God's sake calm down.'

'The police are looking for Jonathan again, that's all. And it's all down to you. I've just heard it myself from the chief inspector. It's not enough that he was arrested as a possible murder suspect, now it's to do with some girl he knew who's gone missing. No doubt they think he murdered her, too. So go on, Sherlock Holmes, what's it all about?'

Latymer sighed. 'It's not what you think. The other night your wife showed us a photograph of Jonathan in a school production, standing next to a pretty young girl. When I attended the opening of the inquest a few days ago on the man whose body Jonathan found near Lower Horton, Bob Wells – the farmer who owned the land and, incidentally, that on which the crop trials were taking place – had brought in a photograph of his daughter, Lucy. It seems she disappeared from home some years ago and hasn't been heard of since. Wells and his wife asked the police if they could renew their enquiries since the family was now splashed across the local papers whether they like it or not, and someone, somewhere might remember something. When I saw the photograph I recognized it as a picture of the same girl I'd seen in the photo shown to me by your wife. I merely mentioned the fact, that's all.'

Higham refused to be placated. 'Why? What had it got to do with you? Or Jonathan? The picture was taken years ago and neither Dawn nor I have ever even heard of the girl. You didn't have to poke your nose in and say anything. All it's done is make more trouble.'

Latymer tried again. 'Look, sit down and let's discuss this sensibly. I'm sorry you feel like that and I know how worried you've both been about Jonathan, but so have the Wells family; they've lost their daughter. So far as I'm aware, all Ross wanted to know was whether or not Jonathan might remember, even after all this time, something she'd said, or hinted at, when they were in the play together, about trouble at home, being unhappy or even going away for a bit. It might not even mean much if she did, since she didn't disappear from home for another two or three months. But in such circumstances anything's worth following up.'

'Just think, Dave,' broke in Dawn, 'how worried those poor people must be. Imagine not hearing from their daughter for years, not even knowing if she's alive or dead. You can't blame John for telling the police about the picture.'

Higham suddenly deflated. 'I suppose so. But for heaven's sake, Latymer, if you feel you have to tell the police anything else about Jonathan, bloody well tell me first!'

'Drinks?' suggested Tess, anxious to restore calm.

Higham hesitated for a minute, then finally sat down. 'Why not.'

'I'll see what we've got,' said Latymer, 'there's some scotch and some gin over there and I'll see if there's anything else out in the kitchen. I don't think we've got any ice though.'

Without Tess's orderly presence the kitchen had become somewhat cluttered and he was no longer sure where anything was. He rooted around until, at the bottom of a cupboard, he found a bottle of indifferent red wine and several cans of beer. He picked them up and was about to return to the lounge when Dawn came in, ostensibly offering to help, but it was obvious she had something to say to him.

'Do you have any idea where Jonathan is?' he asked her, quietly. 'If so, and you can contact him, urge him to come home. Staying away won't help anything.'

'I know where he might be,' she whispered. 'We have a caravan on a site called The Willows, near the river outside Stratford. Just off the Warwick Road. I've been wondering if he's there.'

'I imagine it'd be pretty dodgy in this weather,' said Latymer. 'I'd have thought it was certain to be flooded by now.'

'It never has been before, even when the weather's been really bad. It's the only thing I can think of. I've been ringing his mobile all day but he's either not taken it with him or he isn't answering it.'

'What's taking you so long?' Tess was standing in the doorway, looking from one to the other.

'Dawn fancied a glass of wine. I've been trying to find if there's anything else here, this stuff isn't up to much.'

'Well, Dave will be happy with a scotch and I'll have a gin and tonic, even if we haven't got any ice.' Tess was obviously waiting for them to make a move.

Dawn gave a weak smile. 'The wine looks fine to me,' she said. 'All we need now is a corkscrew.'

By the time they left, Higham had simmered down to the point where he was able to discuss their house sale sensibly. He had decided not to tell their purchasers that there might be a delay, so all was still well in hand. 'So long as your people get a move on in Taunton, Tess, then I'd say you'd be out of here in six weeks, tops.'

Before going to bed, Latymer checked his emails yet again but there was still nothing from Fiona. Possibly she was trying to work out whether or not he might be right. He was on his way to bed when his mobile rang. The voice at the end of the phone was indistinct and there was a great deal of interference. 'Who's that? he enquired. 'Who's calling me?' There was more noise. The voice sounded even fainter. 'Speak up,' urged Latymer. 'Shout, if necessary.'

'Jonathan. It's Jonathan. The battery's going. Oh God, I'm desperate!' There was more noise. 'I must tell someone . . . Help. I need help.'

Latymer could hardly make out what he was saying. 'Where are you? Tell me where you are.' There was another burst of noise and the line went dead. He punched in recall but nothing happened. He tried again and after a brief silence a message appeared telling him the call had failed. He looked at the clock. It was half past eleven. What now? Did he tell the Highams? But surely if Jonathan had wanted to contact his parents, he would have done so. Could Dawn Higham be right, was Jonathan hiding out in a caravan near Stratford? Perhaps he was cut off by flood water and that was why he'd sounded so desperate, but surely if he'd hardly any battery left, he'd have used what power there was to call the emergency services out to rescue him?

It was reluctantly becoming borne upon him that his only course was to go and find out for himself. Tess had gone to bed before him and presumably was asleep. He found an old pair of rubber boots, took his heavy duty anorak off its hook, found a large torch and picked up his phone. His own battery wasn't too healthy but there was no time to recharge it now. He hadn't put his car in the garage and he hoped Tess hadn't parked behind him, as he didn't relish the prospect of trying to find her keys or waking her up and asking her to move it. He opened the back door and went quietly out, at least it didn't seem to be raining quite so hard now. He went round to the front of the house and was thankful to see that Tess had parked beside him. With a heart like lead he got into his car and set off for Stratford.

It was nearly three o'clock in the morning before he reached the outskirts of the town, after a nightmare journey. It had taken three attempts simply to get from the village on to the main road which would take him to Gloucester, but before he'd gone more than a couple of miles he was stopped by police putting in place diversion signs. 'Where are you trying to get to?' asked a constable, rain streaming down his yellow waterproof jacket. Latymer told him Stratford-upon-Avon. The constable shook his head. 'Well, you won't do it this way, mate. Even if you could get through here, you'd hit floods this side of Gloucester. Your best bet is to turn round, go back up to the old Severn crossing and then on to the M5, though what you'll find when you come off it at the other end is anyone's guess. Unless it's a matter of life and death, mate, I'd leave it 'til the morning.'

Latymer turned the car round and set off back the way he had come. The policeman was right, of course. It would be sensible to leave it until morning and it was light. But there was no doubt Jonathan Higham sounded genuinely desperate and he was sure that this time he wasn't acting. 'A matter of life and death,' the copper had said. Suppose he did leave it until morning only to discover when he finally got out to him, that the lad had done something stupid. Bad memories of overdose victims whose cries for help had been ignored and who had been found too late, returned in force. Grimly, he'd pressed on, driving through pools of water so deep he was scared the car would stall. Finally, he wound his way through the deserted streets of the town and on to the Warwick road. He drove slowly, his lights on full beam, searching for a sign which might lead him to the caravan site. There were a couple of bed-and-breakfast notices, followed by a dark gateway, but when he got out to have a look he could see it led only to a farm. However, about half a mile further on he saw a more substantial sign by the roadside and stopped. His lights picked out the words: 'The Willows Luxury Caravan Site. Managed by B. and J. Wood.' Underneath a smaller notice had been added: 'Office closed owing to illness.'

He turned his car into the drive and drove cautiously towards a building he assumed must be the managers' house and office, then parked the car. The rain, thank God, had stopped. He changed into his boots, put on his anorak and set off along a path which he presumed must lead to the site itself. It was rapidly becoming wetter and wetter until he was faced with water stretching away in every direction. Ahead of him loomed the dim shapes of caravans. It suddenly struck him that he'd no idea which one belonged to the Highams and he could be wading round freezing water all night. Then, he saw a faint glimmer. Yes, there was definitely a light in one of them. Surely it had to be Jonathan Higham.

He set off towards it, the water soon reaching his knees, then filling his boots. He began to wonder just how deep it would get. Up to his waist? He kept on going. I must be mad, he thought, I *am* mad. Finally he reached the caravan. The whole site was on a slight incline and the owners had built a substantial wall between it and the river, but even so the water reached almost to the top step. With great difficulty he clambered up the steps, worried that he'd slip, and banged on the door. There was a faint rustle from inside, then silence. He knocked again. 'Jonathan,' he said, urgently. 'Jonathan! It's me. John Latymer.' The door opened a few inches and the boy's face, sheet white in the torchlight, looked down at him. 'Go on then. Let me in, for God's sake! The water's over my knees.'

Jonathan opened the door wider and he went in. 'I see you've a heater there. Light it, will you, while I get these boots off. Hell's teeth, my socks are soaked too and my trousers.'

'There's some old fishing trousers belonging to Dad in the bedroom,' said Jonathan. 'I think they'd fit, but they might be a bit damp.'

'Then get them, will you? At least they won't be soaking wet.' Jonathan fetched them and Latymer struggled out of his own and put them on. Then he turned to him. 'So, now I'm here, what's really the truth of the matter, what's driven you to this?'

Jonathan sank into a chair and put his head in his hands, racked now with sobs. 'I don't know how much you know, or have guessed. But I can't cope with it any more. I give up. The police were right. I am directly responsible for Lucas Symonds' death.'

Eighteen

'Before we discuss anything, said Latymer, 'put the kettle on and make us a hot drink.'

Jonathan swallowed, then pulled himself together. 'Of course. You must be very cold. There's half a bottle of scotch too that Dad must have left behind at Easter.'

'Then some of that as well.'

He went over to the stove and lit the gas. 'How on earth did you know I was here? The battery ran out before I could tell you.'

'It was your mother's suggestion.'

'What about Dad? Does he know you've come? And the police?'

'The way your mother told me led me to believe she didn't want to say anything to anyone else, at least not last night, though I imagine she might well do so in the morning' – he consulted his watch – 'or rather later this morning. At present no one knows I'm here. Now get a move on with that tea.'

The familiar task eased the tension between them. There was still an overwhelming smell of damp and the condensation from the heater was steaming up the windows. Latymer wiped one clear and looked out. It felt quite eerie, as if the two of them were marooned on a boat at a mooring. The rain was still holding off but a slight wind had blown up, rippling the water into small waves which lapped against the steps of the caravan. The situation was beginning to take on the surreal atmosphere of a dream.

The kettle boiled and Jonathan made them two mugs of

tea. 'Right,' said Latymer, 'now let's start from the very beginning. I take it I'm correct in assuming that you were involved with Lucy Wells? And that this relationship has a bearing on the death of Lucas Symonds?'

Jonathan gulped down his tea. 'It's so complicated. I don't know if I'll be able to make you understand.'

'Try me. As I said, begin at the beginning then go on, so far as is possible, to the end.'

As he had guessed, Jonathan and Lucy had become involved with each other during the rehearsals for *Twelfth Night*. 'I was eighteen and I'd had a couple of girlfriends before, but nothing special. She was very pretty, beautiful in fact, as you must have seen from the photographs, and I was knocked out. We had plenty of time to get to know each other since we had quite a long rehearsal period, about seven weeks in all. At weekends, when the weather was fine, we rehearsed in the garden of the house where we were going to put the play on, which meant us all spending a good deal of time together, sitting around chatting and fooling about.

'I asked her out early on but at first she was hesitant. She said her parents were quite strict and didn't want her getting involved with serious boyfriends, and as she was only fifteen, she'd gone along with their wishes. That really shook me. I knew she must be younger than me, but not that much and certainly not that she was under age. She was so confident, so assured. But after a week or two she changed her mind and we started seeing each other on the quiet, neither of us telling our parents. Well, one thing led to another . . . inevitably, I suppose. It was then I first began to think she wasn't telling me the whole truth for it was . . . well . . . obvious that she must have had a previous boyfriend, and one who knew what he was about for she was far more experienced than I was. The best I'd managed up until then was a few bonks in the back of a car and a couple of pretty unsatisfactory afternoons at a girlfriend's house when her parents were away. With Lucy it was quite different.'

The love affair had progressed until the end of the play and continued for a few weeks after the end of the summer term, Jonathan having left school once his exams were over. From then on it became more and more difficult for them to meet. Lucy was still insisting on keeping the relationship under wraps, still citing her age, and there was always the chance that they'd be seen by someone somewhere. He had done his best to make her change her mind and to introduce him to her parents. 'I couldn't understand it. She would be sixteen in October and anyway they didn't have to know how far it had gone. We'd been very careful right from the start and she'd assured me she was on the pill; another lie, as it turned out. But after all, we were both from decent families, had caring parents – even if Dad does drive me mad. There was no good reason why we shouldn't see each other.'

But he couldn't move her and shortly afterwards she began to draw away from him without any explanation, increasingly unwilling to make love, then refusing him all together. 'I realize now it was because she knew she was pregnant. But it didn't show, or at least I didn't notice it, even when we . . . well. And during the rehearsals all the girls were wearing long, full, practice skirts and when she was dressed as a boy, as Viola, she wore a kind of tunic thing over her tights. When I thought about it later, though, I did remember that when we met up after the play she was usually wearing a loose sweater or something like it.'

'Presumably her family hadn't guessed?'

'No. I'll tell you about that later.' He stopped. 'It wasn't my baby, you know. Truly it wasn't. She was already pregnant before I even met her.'

'I believe you. Go on.'

Then one day she told him that they must never see each other again. He'd been devastated. 'We had a terrible quarrel, we both ended up in tears. But she was quite, quite adamant.' For several weeks afterwards he'd tried to call her on her mobile phone but she never responded either in person or to his messages, and his letters were returned unopened. He had been accepted for a place at Warwick, dependent on his examination results, and when they came he found he had achieved the necessary grades. But the break-up and consequent depression had made him restless and he decided, to the fury of his father and the concern of his mother, to defer taking up his place until the following year.

He'd debated then what to do with his year off; should he try and do voluntary service overseas, see if he could get some kind of menial work in a theatre, find what might pay best and do that so that he had some money in the bank for when he did start at university? In the end, he'd got himself a temporary job at the Arts Centre in the converted tobacco factory in Bristol which offered the prospect that it might last until the following summer. Then in November, out of the blue, he received a letter from Lucy, postmarked Newquay, in which she told him she'd run away from home. Something awful had happened, she told him, she was feeling suicidal and was there any chance that he could get down to see her? She was working as a waitress at The Queens, one of the big hotels in the town.

'I left a message on her phone, told the people I was working for that a relative had been taken seriously ill in Cornwall and that I had to go down there with my parents at once, and told Mum and Dad that I'd heard from a friend in Cornwall who was having some kind of a crisis and wanted to see me; which was near enough the truth. I packed a bag that day and got a coach down to Newquay.'

He'd found the hotel easily enough and asked if he could see her but she was on duty and sent him a message asking him to meet her outside when she'd finished work. He stopped and shook his head. 'When she came out of the door, I hardly recognized her. She seemed to have aged five years. She'd cut her hair and dyed it a funny colour and she looked, well, lifeless. She told me she was off now until the following morning and that she'd a room in a bedsit somewhere which wasn't up to much but at least I could camp out there with her for a few days. I'd desperately wanted to see her again but she'd changed so much, I hardly knew what to say to her.' She'd taken him back to her room, 'which was pretty awful but at least it was clean and had a lock on the door.' He'd left his bag there and then they'd gone out again and started walking along the beach together in an uneasy silence.

'I didn't know what to do. She was behaving so oddly, she hardly looked at me, just stared straight ahead like a zombie. I thought she must be on something and I could see us walking round for ever without saying anything that mattered, yet I was only there because she'd asked me to come and made it sound so urgent. I began to get really cold, it wasn't a very good day and there was a chilly wind blowing in from the sea.' Finally, as they passed a beach café which was still open after the end of the season, he finally persuaded her inside and sat her down. He fetched them some coffee then asked her outright why she'd left home. 'I told her I hadn't wanted to come away, I was working with people I really liked and felt lousy about letting them down and now felt like going straight back home. So what the hell was wrong?'

'Everything,' she'd told him, her eyes full of tears. 'It's been a nightmare. I wrote to you because I had to talk to someone, I thought you might understand.' Jonathan had felt at a loss. Why him, he asked her, after she'd made it so clear she didn't want to see him again, that it was all over. Why couldn't she have talked to her parents, whatever her problem was? Surely it would have been preferable to doing something as drastic as running away. And what about her brother? Couldn't she have confided in him?

She'd just shaken her head and said she couldn't tell anyone, anyone at all. 'After it . . . what I did, I *had* to run away.' It was then she told him that she'd realized she was pregnant that summer and he'd naturally assumed the child was his. 'I reminded her that she'd told me several times that she was on the pill, but if that wasn't true or there'd been some kind of slip-up, surely she should have told me straight away, as soon as she'd found out for sure? If she had then there would have been ample time to do something about it, to have a termination if that was what she wanted. After all, she was awfully young to take on bringing up a child. But if she'd wanted to keep it, then I'd have married her as soon as she was sixteen, scrapped going to college and got a job, any job. And whatever choice she made I'd have gone with her to see her parents and taken full responsibility for my part in the situation in which she found herself. But it defeated me why she'd run away since she must either have had an abortion or lost the baby as she would still have been pregnant.'

It was then she told him that the child hadn't been his, that she was already pregnant when they first met. If not mine, then whose, he'd demanded, but she'd just become even more tearful and shaken her head, telling him she couldn't say, she couldn't ever say, not to him, not to anyone. So what had happened to it? he'd insisted. Was it being fostered somewhere? Adopted? 'She just looked at me then and in said in a voice without any expression, "I killed it."

'It all seemed quite unreal, like we were acting out a scene in a play. We were sitting in a quiet corner of the café, but all around there was the clatter of cups and general noise. I remember a party of school kids came in, shouting and yelling, squashing round the tables together to eat plates of chips, some of them showing off and smoking.' He stopped and shivered. 'I was so shaken, I said I didn't understand, that I must have got it wrong. Was she saying that she'd somehow managed to conceal the birth of the child and it had died as a result and that she'd left home without her parents ever realizing that she'd been pregnant? So what happened?'

It seems they hadn't realized, she'd concealed it so well. The school term had started again which made it easier since she was out of the house all day though she said she wasn't really herself, she was so scared and worried.

'Dad got pretty irritable with me,' she'd told him, 'but

Mum just said it was nothing, all girls of my age were moody and emotional. I didn't know how far on I was, I thought about six or seven months, but I still hardly showed at all. At school I was now in the sixth form so didn't have to do any sport or anything and we could wear our own clothes which made it easier.'

But how much longer had she thought she could possibly keep the deception up, he'd asked her in exasperation. However furious they might have been, her parents would hardly have thrown her out into the street like something from a Victorian melodrama. She'd started making plans, she told him. An old school friend had moved to Cornwall and she thought she'd tell her parents that she'd been invited down for a long weekend. Then, when she got there, she'd see if her friend could put her up until the baby was born, after which she'd make arrangements for its adoption. 'It would have still meant me staying away from home for a few weeks and missing school, but I'd have gone back afterwards and made some excuse and said how sorry I was. Really, I would.'

Then towards the middle of September her parents, the harvest now safely in, had gone off to spend a long weekend with friends in the Lake District. She was on her own on the Sunday, Lizzie who came in to help during the week having the day off, when she felt the first twinges of pain and realized that she was about to have the baby much earlier than she'd guessed.

'I still can't get my head round it,' Jonathan told Latymer. 'I said surely now it had come to it, she could have asked for help. There were women neighbours nearby, even her uncle, for God's sake, who, as you know, was just down the road. Any one of them would have taken her to a hospital. She didn't answer. I asked her what the hell was the real reason? Simply upsetting her parents wasn't enough. Was she trying to protect the father in some way? Because she was frightened he'd get into trouble because she was under age? Had *he* realised she was under age? So what else could it be? That he was not only older but a married man? But even if he was, so what? He'd got her pregnant and if it messed up his marriage, then tough!' But still she said nothing.

Then, after what seemed like an endless silence, she'd told him the rest. When things got really bad she'd gone out into one of the big barns, taking with her some old sheets, a piece of blanket and a pair of scissors. She then sat in the hay with her back against a wall and waited. It didn't take long. Because it was premature the child had been born quite quickly. Afterwards she'd cut the cord with the scissors. 'It was alive,' she'd told him. 'It was very small, but it was alive.' She'd tried to force herself to pick it up but was overcome with revulsion. Appalled and panic-stricken, she'd snatched up a bunch of hay and pushed it down on its face. Once she had the courage to remove it, the child was still, quite still. She'd then cleaned up as best she could and wrapped the child in the blanket.

'It was like I was on automatic pilot,' she'd told Jonathan. At first she thought she'd bury it somewhere on the farm but was frightened someone would see her or that it might be dug up by a fox or one of the dogs; and anyway it didn't seem right. So, after she'd rested for a while she decided on what she would do: she would leave the child in the churchyard, close to the church door, where it would be found and given a decent burial, but making sure there was nothing to link it with her. She waited until the middle of the night then she crossed the fields, then the road, and made her way to the churchyard, then as she went inside she saw a spade leaning against the wall and changed her mind.

'She said she'd been fascinated by one of the old graves, that of a young mother and child. In spite of the state she was in, she managed to dig a hole deep enough to put the baby in, then she covered it with earth again, trampled it down and pulled the brambles back which had been growing across it. Somehow she managed to get home, put her clothes and the old sheets into the washing machine, and fall in to bed.

When Lizzie came in the following morning she stayed in bed, telling her she was feeling rough and must have 'flu or something.

Her parents returned the next night. Her mother was concerned at how pale and tired she looked and told her she intended making an appointment to take her in to see the doctor. She said she couldn't face it. The doctor was bound to discover what had happened and she would have had to say where the baby was and what had happened to it. The night before the appointment she left the house in the small hours, hitched a lift to Cheltenham and from there took a coach to Newquay, only to discover her friend was no longer living at the address she had given her. She and her husband had split up, a neighbour told her, and she'd no idea where either of them had gone. Not knowing what to do next, she saw a notice in a shop window advertising for a waitress at The Queens and had applied for the job.

'So,' said Latymer, 'Lucy Wells *was* the girl you tried to tell me about? You were right, what a dreadful experience!'

Jonathan got up and stared out of the window at the water outside. 'You don't know the half of it,' he said.

'I think I can guess,' said Latymer. 'Symonds' murder had nothing to do with the GM crops protest or green men, did it? The reason was much closer to home.'

Tess came down in the morning and was surprised to discover that Latymer wasn't up as he had always been an early riser. She made coffee and some toast and then called up the stairs to him. There was no reply. After a few minutes she called again then, as there was still no sign of life, went upstairs and knocked on his door. But when even this didn't provoke a response she went in to discover that the bed hadn't been slept in.

She came back downstairs and looked round to see if he'd left her a note of some kind, but couldn't find anything. Then she noticed that his heavy weather anorak was no longer on the peg by the back door and that the big torch, kept by the fuse box, was also missing. He must have gone out, therefore, in the middle of the night, in that awful weather. But what on earth for? So far as she was aware, he hadn't had taken any phone calls after the Highams left the previous evening. It was a complete mystery. She felt more annoyance than concern. Now she'd satisfied herself that the house sale was going through there was no reason for her to stay on and she wanted to get back to Diana as soon as possible. It was typical of John to do this to her. Typical. Since they'd been separated she could see more clearly why the marriage had come to grief. When they'd met they'd seemed to have so much in common, both having recently left their professions, were on their own and were looking for a change of scene and a new start. At first it really had worked out very well, as they settled into the new house and new lives, with the added luxury of having the time to do all those things one had been prevented from doing before.

Except that for John unlimited time to himself had soon proved to be a burden rather than a luxury. During the early days of their relationship he'd told her relatively little of his previous career, as if he wanted to put it all behind him. She'd understood and sympathized with his reasons for taking early retirement: policing had altered out of all recognition since his early days in the force, and he was fed up with drowning in seas of paperwork. She was glad she'd met him after he'd left the force as she knew she would never have made a good policeman's wife, faced with the irregular hours and rarely being able to plan ahead, let alone the possible dangers involved and some of the gruesome work that would have come his way. He'd been quite frank about the fact that his unpredictable lifestyle had been one of the main causes of the break-up of his first marriage.

That being so, it had never occurred to her that he might start hankering after it again. Realizing that too much leisure didn't suit him, she'd been quite happy when he took on the work for Becketts Tours if it stopped him being so restless, but then came that strange business in Scotland and his taking up again with his old colleague, Keith Berry, who'd actually *encouraged* him in his unofficial investigation. She'd met the Berrys several times afterwards but felt she had little in common with them. As little as John did, she told herself sourly, with the friends she'd made in the village like the Highams, or in the various societies she'd joined. Well, it was sad the way things had turned out but it would all soon be over.

As time went on and he still didn't come home, she rang him on his mobile to say she was planning to return to Taunton towards the end of the afternoon and was he likely to be home before she did so. But there was no reply and she had to leave a message. Was it something the Highams had said that had set him off? she wondered. Perhaps she'd better find out. Feeling decidedly irritated, she walked round to their house, relieved to discover that at least the rain had finally stopped. Dave had gone into his office, Dawn told her, as he had a sale about to go through, leaving her on her own to worry about Jonathan from whom they'd heard not a word. He was still not answering his phone and every time their phone rang she was frightened it was going to be the police again.

Tess told her about Laymer's unexplained disappearance. 'You know what he's like. I wondered if you'd said something to him that might have caused him to hare off in the middle of the night.'

Dawn frowned. 'Well I did tell him that the only place I could think of where Jonathan might be is our caravan near Stratford, the one Dave uses when he goes fishing. Except that he prefers golf to fishing now and has decided to get rid of it,' she added, inconsequentially. 'But I didn't ask him to go out and look for Jonathan or anything.'

'You wouldn't need to,' Tess observed sourly.

'What do you think I should do then?' Dawn asked her.

'Tell your husband what you've told me and see what he says. But surely if you thought you knew where Jonathan might be, you should have told the police. Last night.'

'It's easy for you to say,' retorted Dawn. 'It's not your son whose got himself into so much trouble. I'll give Dave a call.' She went out to the phone returning a few minutes later to say that her husband was on his way back. 'He thinks we should go down there ourselves straight away and see if Jonathan is in the caravan. I can't understand it. Did your John just take it into his head and go? Or did Jonathan contact him? But surely he'd have phoned us first; he must realize by now how worried we'll be and . . .' She stopped in mid flow. 'Tess, will you come with us?'

Tess was taken aback. They'd got to know each other quite well during the relatively short time the Highams had been in the village, but Dawn hardly counted as a close friend. It was a bit much. She hesitated. 'I don't know. I'm not sure. How long is it likely to take? I promised my daughter I'd try and get back home by this evening. She's not looking too well and the baby's due quite soon now.'

'Please, Tess! I'd be so very grateful to have a woman along. God only knows what we'll find.'

There seemed no way out. 'Very well then,' she replied, with real reluctance. 'But whatever the situation is when we get to Stratford and whatever happens, I need to be back here by the end of the afternoon. I suppose I'd better call my daughter and tell her I won't be back until later.'

Half an hour later she was sitting in the back of the Highams' large car on the way to Stratford. Diana had sounded perfectly all right and had assured her mother she was fine. 'It's not as if I'm due this week,' she said. 'You wait, I'll probably go past the date and you'll be sitting round waiting for a good month!'

As with Latymer the previous evening, the journey took them a considerable time due to the various diversions caused by the floods, and it was nearly two o'clock before they finally arrived at the entrance to The Willows car park. Higham pulled over and peered at the sign. 'Closed due to illness,' he read out. 'That's a bit much. Fancy them going off at this time of year and in this weather. The managers who were here before would never have done such a thing,' he explained to Tess. 'These two haven't been here very long.' He turned the car in through the gate and drove cautiously along the drive through the deep puddles.

'Wait!' Dawn called out suddenly. 'Stop! Look there, behind those bushes. Isn't that Jonathan's car?' Higham stopped. 'It is,' she assured. 'So, he is here. I was right.' They continued on up to the house, daunted by what they saw. Behind it there was nothing but water lapping round the half a dozen caravans. To their surprise, as they pulled up outside the extension marked 'Office', the door opened and the manager came out, followed by his wife.

'After reading the notice, we didn't think we'd find you here,' Higham told them.

The manager smiled broadly. 'Ah, Mr Higham, isn't it? Yes, we've been away, I presume you saw the notice. We had to go down to Manchester three days ago, the wife's father had a coronary and they thought he'd had it. But he's pulled through, he's a tough old stick. Once we knew he was going to be OK, we set off back in the small hours to avoid the traffic round Birmingham and were back here about seven o'clock. Just as well we did come back today, given all the excitement. But what brings you here? The floods, I suppose,' he continued, answering his own question. 'You can see the state of the site, I can assure you we'd no idea what was likely to happen when we left for the north, everything was in good order. But from what I've seen so far, the water hasn't actually got into any of the vans and it's now dropping, so . . .'

'We can talk about all that some other time,' snapped Higham. 'I'm here looking for my son, Jonathan. We thought he might be in our caravan.' He paused suddenly, taking in the import of what the manager had just said. '*What* excitement?'

The manager's wife pushed herself forward. 'Oh, so it must have been your son we saw this morning. I didn't recognize him but then I don't think he's been here since we took over, has he? He was with another man. I didn't recognize him either.'

'What do I have to do to get you to tell us what's been happening?' roared Higham.

'You don't need to speak to us like that,' retorted the manager. 'I don't like your attitude.' Then, pausing to ensure the maximum effect, he continued, 'Now, before the police came—'

'*What*!' Higham looked as if he was about to burst a blood vessel.

'Well, I'd better go back to the start. As I said, we got back about seven o'clock. There was a fairly large car parked near the house, which surprised us, and I was going to look into it once I'd had something to eat as I couldn't think what it was doing there. Jean was just getting us a bit of breakfast when I looked out of the kitchen window and saw your son and this other man, wading through the water. It was still pretty deep, almost up to their knees. I tapped on the window to attract their attention and the older man waved at me, so I opened the door. I said they were up early and he said they'd been checking the caravan was all right, which was fair enough. Then they got into his car and drove off. Didn't think any more of it until—'

'The police came,' his wife interrupted. 'That was, oh, about half past twelve at a guess. They asked us if anyone had stayed on the caravan site overnight as they'd had a report of a light being seen in one of the vans. I said I didn't know, since we hadn't been here, but that two men had been on the site earlier to see if the floods had done any damage and quite possibly that was when the light was seen. Then they told us that as well as checking on the light, they were also looking for a man who needed to be brought in for questioning and asked if we had keys to the caravans so they could search them. Also if we'd any outbuildings in which someone could hide out without being seen. It made me come over all goose pimples to think that some criminal might have been lurking out there all night.'

But when they saw how deep the water was, the police had told them they'd better find out what they should do. They'd certainly need boots, possibly a rubber dinghy. 'So one of them, a sergeant I think he was,' said the manager, taking up the story, 'called in to his boss and I actually heard the voice over the radio telling them not to bother and that they might as well come back. Whoever it was said, "It's OK. We've got him here. He's been charged."'

Dawn went white. 'Oh my God! Jonathan!'

'Come on,' said her husband. 'We'd better go to Warwick.' He turned to Tess. 'Sorry about this, Tess. But we have to know.'

Nineteen

As a grey dawn broke over the watery landscape Jonathan had needed little persuasion to go to the police and tell them all he knew, even though he felt sad and guilty that by so doing he would be betraying someone else. As Latymer wearily drove them towards Warwick he went over Jonathan's story again in his mind, one which would haunt him for a long time to come.

Jonathan had stayed in Newquay with Lucy until the New Year, although he'd realized almost at once that it was impossible to pick up the pieces of their earlier relationship. He managed to earn enough to get by, saddened by the fact that he'd been unable to return to the work he'd enjoyed in Bristol, 'but I felt I couldn't just leave her,' he told Latymer. 'She never mentioned suicide again, but I felt she'd given up on everything. It's become a bit of a cliché but she seemed to have lost any sense of self-worth. I could understand how traumatic the childbirth had been, not to mention its outcome, but all along I had this sense that there was something else, something she hadn't told me. I tried to get her to go for counselling, even if it meant confiding to someone what had happened to her, but she refused point-blank.'

Then one morning he'd woken up to find her missing. In a note propped up by the kettle she told him that she was going away and that she didn't want him to look for her. She thanked him for coming down to her when she so badly needed a friend, and for his support since, but it was best they part. 'There's no longer any future for us, is there? I don't think there ever was. But for a few weeks last summer I managed to persuade myself that there might be.'

He rang his family to let them know he was all right and the Arts Centre to learn, as he'd expected, that they'd had to find someone else to take his place. For a few days he didn't know whether to stay in Cornwall or go back home, but seeing an advertisement for workers at the Eden Project he applied and for six months worked hard, banked as much of his money as he could, and did his best to put the whole experience out of his mind. By the time he returned home at the end of August he considered he was over it, looking forward to starting his college course, full of enthusiasm and quite himself again.

He had more than enough to occupy him during his first year at college. He'd heard nothing more from Lucy and as time past she faded from his mind. 'I was having a great time, had made a lot of friends and was able to stand back and see how I'd felt about her quite objectively. Everything had combined to encourage romantic young love: the play itself and the roles we played; the beautiful gardens of the old house where we put it on; high summer; and the fact that from the first there was something mysterious about her. I'd idealized her. For a few weeks I felt like Orsino, Romeo and Troilus all rolled into one. In reality, as it turned out she was my Cressida, not my Juliet!'

It was at the end of the first term of his second year that he finally had news of her and what he learned was highly disturbing. 'I was in a pub in Warwick one night when a guy came up to me who I vaguely recognized. His name was Tom Carter and it turned out he'd been in the sixth form when I first started at the grammar school and he was now some kind of a finance specialist. He bought me a drink and we chatted of this and that and what we'd both been doing since we left school. Then, he said, "You used to know Lucy Wells, didn't you?" I must have looked surprised because he laughed at me.

"Don't look so gobsmacked! You used to see her on the

quiet, didn't you?" I asked him how he knew and he said he'd seen us mooning around once or twice, that he'd always been the sort that noticed such things. "A couple of kids coming out of a copse somewhere, hand in hand and pink in the face, are unlikely to have been bird watching! I don't blame you, I fancied her myself but she gave me the brush off, told me some tale of her parents being super-strict. I thought, good luck to you Dear God, you wouldn't fancy her now."

'I asked him what he meant and he said that the previous week he'd been down in Plymouth. He was between girl-friends, stuck in an anonymous kind of hotel, he didn't know anyone, it was raining and, to put it bluntly, he wanted sex. It wasn't difficult to discover where he could get it and he'd been on his way to one of the dubious clubs in the red light district when this girl walked off the pavement almost into the wheels of his car. He said she was wearing one of those flimsy little tops that leave the midriff bare and a miniskirt, no coat or anything and she was soaked to the skin. He told her to get in the car and she sat in the passenger seat, her teeth chattering with cold. He said she was so thin he thought she must be ill. At first he'd thought she was only about fourteen or fifteen, which alarmed him, but when he saw her face close up she looked a lot older and she told him she was nearly nineteen.

'"She looked so pathetic," he said. "She recited what she had to offer in a dreary voice like she was ticking off a shopping list for Tesco's. I was certain she was whoring to support a habit. We were sitting in the car and I was wondering what to do when she suddenly turned to me and said, 'You're Tom Carter, aren't you?' I just stared at her. She said she wasn't surprised I didn't recognize her and that she was Lucy Wells from Lower Horton. Then I could just about see it. She'd had such smashing long, dark, curly hair and now it was all spiky and dyed a kind of puce, and the lamplight made her face look greenish, like she'd been drowned. She used to have a lovely figure too. But it was definitely her."

'He said he was totally turned off by this time, so he gave her twenty quid and told her to go and get herself something to eat. He said he hadn't told anyone else back home but when he saw me he thought I might want to know.'

The story had haunted Jonathan all through Christmas, which he'd spent with his parents, then, a few days into January, he'd received the phone call. The woman on the other end of the line told him she was calling from the big district hospital in Plymouth and that she had some bad news for him. 'I guessed before she told me that it was about Lucy.' They'd had a young girl brought in the previous night, the woman told him. She'd taken an overdose of Paracetemol washed down with alcohol and was still conscious but the amount of the drug, coupled with her general condition, made it unlikely that she would survive. 'We've asked her for the names of her next of kin but she's refused to tell us. We can't make her, of course. But she's asked us to contact you. She says will you come this one last time?'

He'd gone, of course, straight away. They'd been very kind to him at the hospital, busy as they were. Her liver was damaged beyond repair, they told him, and there was no hope, but she wasn't in any pain. He found her four storeys up in a bleak little room, attached to a drip and oxygen. When she saw him she managed a feeble smile. He'd sat down beside her, taken her hand and asked her why she'd done it. 'Do you need to ask?' she'd replied. 'If I hadn't done it this way, then I'd probably have ended up overdosed on something else or murdered by a punter.' He'd asked her if there was anything he could do, anyone he should tell, but she shook her head. 'It's better they never know,' she'd told him. There was a packet in the locker next to the bed containing enough money 'to see to everything. I didn't take the pills until I knew I had enough.' There was also a letter which he was not to read until later.

When he tried to remonstrate with her she reminded him that she was nineteen, therefore of age, and was in her right mind. In a separate note on the top of the locker, addressed directly to him, she'd written down that she wanted to be cremated. 'I want you to put my ashes in the grave where I put my baby. The stone says "Elizabeth Bidford and child". Now it will be Lucy Wells and child, too.'

None of it seemed real, he told Latymer. 'It was like she was consciously acting out a role.' He'd sat there for hours while she drifted in and out of consciousness. Then, not long before she died, she opened her eyes and said, 'I always loved Lucas, Jonathan. I still do. I knew it was wrong when it started, but it didn't feel wrong for either of us. He loves me too. It wasn't like you read in the papers, it was wonderful. If it was anyone's fault, it must have been mine.' Less than an hour later she was dead. 'The name meant nothing to me – then. I assumed I'd been right, the child was the result of a secret affair with a married man.'

After she died he'd made the necessary arrangements and then returned to Warwick taking the little casket with him. As she'd requested, he'd taken it to the Lower Horton churchyard one night, found the grave and buried it, 'though I was frightened I'd disturb what else was there.' A couple of months later, knowing he would be passing through the village, he'd bought some spring flowers and left them on the grave.

It was some time before he was able to bring himself to read her letter and only then did the meaning of what she'd said sink in, along with the exact nature of her relationship with Lucas. 'For weeks I simply didn't know what to do. I kept going over and over it in my mind until it was making me ill. My friends kept asking me what was wrong but I couldn't bring myself to tell them. Or you, when we met in Warwick that day, though I wish to God I had, it would have saved a good man being tried for murder.'

'I'll try and give Ross the bare bones of the first part of the story,' Latymer told him, as they drove into the police station car park. 'But in view of your own part in what happened at

Lower Horton you'll have to make a full official statement to the police and this time it has to be the truth. No more prevaricating.'

Jonathan made a conscious effort to get himself together. 'I did my best to warn him. I suppose he'll be arrested now. 'And what do you think will happen to me?'

'From what you've told me, I imagine you'll be charged with being an accessory. You can ask for a solicitor to be present before you say anything, of course. As to the sentence, that will be up to the judge.'

When they arrived at the police station Latymer asked at once for Ross, explaining that he had Jonathan Higham with him. Whatever Ross might have felt when he saw the two of them together he made little comment, merely asking a constable to put Jonathan in an interview room. 'Before you question him,' said Latymer, 'I'd like you to read this. It's a photocopy of a letter Lucy Wells left with him just before she died. Her father now has the original. It explains a lot.'

Ross took it from him and sighed. 'I won't even ask you yet how come you turn up here with someone we've been scouring Warwickshire to find for the last forty-eight hours. No doubt you'll have an explanation. Are you planning on staying for a while?'

'I could sleep over a rope, but I'd like to see how he gets on. Perhaps someone could tell his parents he's here, I know they've been very worried about him.' He yawned. 'And his solicitor.'

Ross nodded. 'I'll get that done straight away.' He paused. 'So the boy did play a part in Symonds' death.'

'A relatively small one,' Latymer agreed, 'and I imagine a jury, when they've heard all the facts, will have a great deal of sympathy for him. Read the letter.'

'He'll still have to be charged.'

'He realizes that.'

Telling the story of what took place at Horton Manor on

the night of 23rd April, and the lead up to it a second time, enabled Jonathan to be more coherent then when he'd first limped it out to Latymer as they sat in the caravan in the midst of the flood. There had been no reply from his parents' house, he was told, but the police had managed to track down the solicitor who was now on his way. Fifteen minutes later, Jonathan, the solicitor, Ross and a constable were sitting together in the interview room, with the tape recorder switched on.

It was when he'd gone over to Lower Horton, Jonathan told Ross in answer to his first question, 'to suss out where the GM crops trials were', that he'd realized they were growing on land belonging to Bob Wells. Afterwards, he'd driven back to Warwick and agonized yet again over what he should do about Lucy's letter, before finally making up his mind. He'd returned to the farm the day before the protest and asked to speak to the farmer.

'Fortunately Lucy's mother was out or I don't know whether I'd have been able to go through with it. It was difficult enough as it was.' He started off by explaining to Bob Wells, as briefly as possible, his own relationship with Lucy nearly three years earlier, how she'd contacted him after she'd run away and then told him about her pregnancy.

'I thought he was going to throw me out when I told him about the baby. At first he simply wouldn't believe it. Then, when I described what happened to it, he went mad. On the one hand he accused me of trying to blacken his daughter in his eyes to get myself out of trouble for getting her pregnant, and on the other of making it all up. I swore I was telling the truth and that it was the remains of Lucy's baby, his own grandchild, that had been found in the grave in the village churchyard.

'I was still debating whether or not to give him Lucy's letter when he began to accuse me of everything from having had sex with an underage girl, to conniving at infanticide. Then he asked me if I'd come looking for some kind of payoff to stop me telling anyone else that Lucy had killed her child. That decided me and I handed over Lucy's letter. I felt I'd no choice and I'd made a copy of it. At least he didn't accuse me of forging it, he recognized her writing.'

'Wells read it through, then stared at me and said, "Lucas? *Lucas*!" Then he got up and started walking up and down. "God in heaven! Lucas! I'll kill him."

'I suggested that it could be that it wasn't true. That it wasn't unknown for young girls to fantasize relationships with older men they had a crush on, or even convinced themselves they'd fallen in love with. That it might have been someone else who'd got her pregnant, though I must admit I didn't think this was the case. But he just shook his head. He said that looking back on it, it all made sense, that many things now fell into place.' He wanted to know everything, he told Jonathan, every last thing.

'I did my best. I didn't tell him she'd turned to prostitution in the end, I just couldn't face that, instead I told him she'd ended up living rough on the streets. I told him how I'd gone down to Cornwall after she'd run away and begged her to go back home and that she'd run away again. And about the overdose and how she'd sent for me because she thought it would be too painful for her parents to bear and how I'd carried out her wishes to the letter and that it was her ashes that were in the box found in the same grave as the baby. He kept shaking his head and saying, "And to think it was going on under our noses all that time. From when she was eleven years old. My brother-in-law, Marian's own brother! Abusing Lucy when she was still a child. Telling us how he thought the world of her, taking her for days out, having her over there at the manor for hours on end. We used to joke he was like a second father to her, the daughter he'd never had, and all time the sick pervert . . .".'

'So after all, you did manage to convince him,' observed Ross.

'You've seen Lucy's letter. It's quite explicit. I also pointed out that if he did have any doubts that Symonds was the father of Lucy's baby, it should be possible to prove it from DNA taken from him and the remains of the child. He asked if Symonds had known Lucy was pregnant and I said I didn't think she'd told him, after all, she concealed it from the rest of us brilliantly. But in spite of what I said to Mr Wells, about young girls and fantasies, I didn't really believe it. The most awful thing to me, Chief Inspector, is that from first to last Lucy never saw it as child abuse. What a terrible misuse of his authority, and the love Lucy felt for him, on Symonds' part. And she really, genuinely loved him. I'd been fooling myself when I thought she was in love with me. She could never have shaken off what she felt for him.'

After that Wells had been quiet again for a while, then he'd turned to Jonathan and made him promise that he wouldn't say anything to anyone yet, and he'd agreed. 'Then he said he wanted me to help him punish Symonds. He didn't want to tackle him head on, hear any of his excuses, take him to the police, he wanted to sort it out himself.'

'That was when you should have said you'd have nothing to do with it,' said Ross, 'told him that wasn't the answer. That there was sufficient evidence to put his brother-in-law behind bars, his reputation in ruins, and that was the path down which to go.'

'I did, but he wouldn't listen. I told him he ought to go to you, taking the letter with him and explain what had happened to Lucy.' He hesitated briefly. 'I suppose I should have come to you myself, but although he'd said he wanted to kill Lucas, I didn't think he actually intended to do it and I felt so sorry for him. I thought he was just going to teach Symonds a lesson of some kind after what he'd done to Lucy.'

As he listened to Jonathan's account of what had actually happened, Ross could only marvel at the complexity of the theories that had been put forward to explain Lucas Symonds' murder, theories that'd had them running round in circles. Compared to Shrieve and his ritual blood sacrifices, ancient witchcraft rituals as at Meon Hill, the ultimate protest against GM crops, the reality seemed almost straightforward. At the end of the day it was an old-fashioned 'domestic', with overtones of incest and child abuse.

Far from happy, Jonathan had finally agreed to help. Wells told him he'd call him when he'd decided how best to proceed. 'And I thought that perhaps after he'd had time to think about it, he'd have changed his mind. But he didn't.' The next morning, that of the protest, Wells rang him and gave him his instructions. He was to turn up with his friends as arranged to take part in it and as soon as it was under way, make himself scarce. It was impossible at that stage to know how it would all turn out, Wells told him, but one thing was certain, that there would be a good many protestors on his farmland uprooting his crops and causing a disturbance. It would be a perfect cover for what he had in mind for his brother-in-law.

'I rather thought he'd take a shotgun to him,' said Jonathan, 'it seemed the kind of thing a farmer would do. Threaten him with it, make him confess (with me as a witness), then possibly beat him up before sending for the police. Anyway, he said all he wanted me to do was to go up to the top of the hill while the protest was going on and wait. Your policewoman had told him and Symonds that you'd all be there in force so he knew there'd be plenty of action, though of course none of us expected it to get as violent as it did. In a funny way those green men actually helped. The plan was that after it was all over and he and Symonds had both gone back to their homes, Mr Wells would ring him to say he'd just had a tip-off that there were people up on the hill and they'd better go and investigate. All I had to do when I saw their torches was to run down with some story of people hiding out in the copse, keep Symonds talking when we got back up there and leave the rest to him. I know I should have dipped out then and told you, but I kept thinking of Lucy having her baby in the barn, dying in that hospital room in Plymouth . . .

'So I did as I was told. Of course it all went on much longer than we'd expected and I was getting colder and colder, waiting up there in the copse not knowing what was happening. Eventually I rang him on his mobile and he told me to stick it out, everything was still going to plan. He'd be bringing Symonds up there just as soon as it was possible and the police had gone and that when I saw them coming, then I knew what I had to do. I said surely after what had happened Symonds would expect him to contact the police and he said he didn't think so, that he'd agree that they'd be able to deal with a few yobs and teach them a lesson without bringing half the Warwickshire police force out again, and one they wouldn't forget in a hurry.'

Everything had gone according to plan and Jonathan had duly run down with a rambling tale of having seen lights at the top of the hill and that he was sure some of the green men had gone up there when they ran off and could be up to anything. Wells was indeed carrying a shotgun and, once they'd reached the copse he'd dropped behind as if searching the bushes, as Jonathan kept Symonds talking. Then, in the dark, he'd come up behind his brother-in-law and hit him hard on the back of the head with the barrel of the gun and Symonds had fallen down without a sound. Wells then told Jonathan to go and wait for him at the bottom of the hill, while he sorted things out in his own way.'

'And what did you think he meant by that?' asked Ross.

'I didn't know. I suppose I didn't want to know. I left it for about ten minutes, then when he didn't come down to me I went back.' His voice wavered. 'I couldn't believe what I saw. Symonds was there lying on his back like he'd been crucified, with some kind of long pointed thing through his chest and the prongs of a hayfork each side of his neck. Wells must have put the tools up there ready earlier in the day. I just stared at him.

'Wells was quite calm. He said it was the way people would have punished such a crime in times past. It was the old way. That it had been done once before in recent years, on Meon Hill at the end of the war. Then they'd called it witchcraft, he said, but it was retribution. Retribution for the sins of incest, the ravishing of a child, and was a way of ensuring the dead didn't walk. Witches, murderers and suicides used to be buried at crossroads with stakes through their heart for the same reason. Then he pulled one of those green masks out of his pocket and put it over Symonds' face, saying it would look like it had been done by one of them. He said he'd trust me not to tell anyone, since I was part of it all, and that I should give him time to get back home then call the police, saying that I'd run away from the protest in a panic and stumbled over the body. In the end I didn't ring the police, I rang Mr Latymer. The rest you know.'

'I think it's time my client had a rest,' said the solicitor. 'Not only is he under great strain, but he's been up all night.'

Ross agreed then turned to the constable. 'See to it that he gets something to eat and a cup of tea. I'll take Sergeant Wilkins over to Lower Horton with me and we'll bring Wells in.'

Bob Wells showed no surprise when the police car drew up at the farm door. 'I've been expecting you,' he told them. 'It's a relief, really. I don't think I could have lived with it much longer. If you'll allow me a few minutes, I'll tell Marian where I'm going. How she's going to cope when it all comes out, I can't bear to think.'

The Highams and Tess arrived to be told that Jonathan was being interviewed by the police, was to make a statement, that it was taking some time and yes, his solicitor was with him. The desk sergeant suggested that it might be a good idea if they went for a walk or went to a hotel or a pub for an hour or so. Reluctantly, they left the police station in stony silence, Tess furious that she'd ever agreed to accompany the

Highams to Stratford. She tried ringing Diana, but there was no reply; presumably they were out shopping. Meanwhile Wells had been brought in and since he'd not only confessed but agreed to assist the police in any way he could, was formally charged with the murder of Lucas Symonds.

After hanging about over tea in a dismal café, the Highams and Tess returned to the station to be informed that Jonathan had been charged with being an accessory to murder and would be kept in custody over night. Both he and Wells would be brought before the magistrates the following morning, after which it was more than likely they could take him home subject to bail conditions being met.

It was then that Latymer appeared with Ross from out of the depths of the station. The Highams made no response when Ross told them they should be grateful that Mr Latymer had encouraged their son to tell the truth and that hopefully this would stand him in good stead when the matter came to court, a statement which reduced Dawn to tears. Latymer was amazed to see Tess. She looked at him with a face like thunder when he asked her why she was there. 'Because Dawn asked me, because she wanted a friend with her as she was so worried,' she informed him, icily. 'If I'd been sure we'd find you here, I would never have come. I suppose it was too much to have expected you to let us know.

'I presume you'll be able to take Tess back home, Latymer?' enquired Higham, finally forcing himself to speak. 'I think we'll book into a hotel and stay over until the morning to see what happens.' He looked at Latymer and shrugged. 'I don't know whether we should thank you or not.'

'Neither do I,' replied Latymer, honestly. 'But I don't think your son could have kept it all to himself any longer. Things shouldn't work out too badly for him, he's done the right thing. Very well then, Tess, we'd better go.'

They said little to each other on the long drive home. It was now nearly six o'clock and the rain had started again. Given the conditions, it would be well into the evening before they reached home. Latymer tried to apologize, to be met with the response that had he only minded his own business she would have been safely back in Somerset with Diana. She supposed there was nothing for it now but to leave it until first thing in the morning. When they finally arrived at the house she went straight to the telephone to find there were two messages. From the other side of the door Latymer heard what sounded like a woman's voice leaving a message, resulting in an exasperated exclamation from Tess. The second voice was obviously that of a man and was followed by Tess's frantic dialling. As her call was answered, he heard her voice rise in obvious distress.

Five minutes later she reappeared from the hall wearing her coat and scarf, stalked across the room and picked up the two packed suitcases she'd left there that morning. 'What's the matter?' enquired Latymer. 'Where are you going?'

'To Diana,' she snapped.

'But you said you weren't going to go until tomorrow morning.'

'Diana's in the maternity hospital. She was taken in this afternoon. She's had a caesarean section and the baby's in the special care unit. And thanks to you I wasn't there!'

There was no point in trying to argue with her. 'So how are they?'

'Diana's well enough, if shocked. The baby is small and will need special care for several days.' She picked up the cases and motioned him away when he offered to help her out to the car. 'I don't know when I'll see you again. At least both the house sale and the divorce look as if they should go through without any more problems. Oh, and by the way, there was a call from one of your lady friends in Scotland.' He opened the front door and she went out to her car without looking back. As she drove away he realized he hadn't even asked her whether her new grandchild was a boy or a girl.

Twenty

As soon as Tess had gone, Latymer rang Fiona and explained, as briefly as possible, what had happened. 'It was you who made me look again both at the original Meon Hill murder and the recent one. Once we'd decided that the first had become overlaid with all the witchcraft stuff and might possibly have been something more domestic, then I started thinking about that at Lower Horton similarly. Suppose the discovery of the remains of the baby found in the local churchyard was connected with Symonds' murder in some way. After all, Lucy Wells, a girl who fitted the profile of a desperate teenage mother, had disappeared without any explanation. That naturally led to possibilities of child abuse though I was inclined to look to the brother or the father, even though it was the uncle who'd been killed. I admit I hadn't made my mind up when Jonathan spelled it out for me, then it all seemed quite obvious.'

He heard her sigh. 'I feel sorry for that poor young man. He's obviously deeply caring or he wouldn't have kept going back to her like that when she wanted him to, even though his feelings for her had changed. And he was in an almost impossible position once he'd told the girl's father.'

Latymer agreed. 'And I believe him when he says that whatever Wells might have threatened, he didn't actually believe he had murder in mind. If only he'd confided in me that day in Warwick it might have been preventable. Not to mention all the time wasted by everyone, just as at Meon Hill, chasing up ritual sacrifice, witchcraft and green men. I doubt Ross will want to be reminded of that in the future.'

'Yet, from what you say, ritual was involved in the killing. It could be the farmer was right, that it was the way such things were dealt with centuries back as a lesson to others. Memories of old customs and superstitions linger on and often aren't talked about. I know that from living up here.'

'Possibly. But I don't think that's a path I particularly want to go down again,' replied Latymer, grimly. 'The researches dug up some pretty unpleasant and perverted stuff.'

'What do you think will happen to them,' she asked, 'to Jonathan and Wells?'

'A lot depends on the jury and the judge. Since Jonathan not only went to the police voluntarily, but gave them a full and frank statement of his own involvement in the affair, it should help him, especially if they believe him when he says he really didn't know he was going to be involved in murder. So he can rightly plead not guilty. He's young, doing well at college and with a good career in front of him. He might even get off with a suspended sentence. As to Wells, there'll be a whole lot of sympathy for him, especially given today's climate regarding child abuse. I imagine the tabloids will have a field day. But you can't just take the law into your own hands and turn to murder. We'll have to wait and see.'

'We'd better talk some other time,' said Fiona. 'This call must be costing you a fortune.'

'It's worth it. Oh, by the way, I might well be able to come and see you in a month or so?'

'Do you have work up here then?'

'No. I'm packing in my job!'

Following submissions made by his solicitor, Jonathan was remanded on bail as also, after a great deal of discussion, was Wells since the police did not oppose it and strict bail conditions were enforced. Both were to attend court again in two weeks' time. Special arrangements were to be made for a funeral service to be held in Lower Horton church for Lucy and her baby, followed by the re-interment of their remains in the churchyard.

Latymer went to the hearing and considered the result as satisfactory as possible in the circumstances. Outside the court he saw the Highams, both of whom looked as if they'd spent a sleepless night. In spite of his parents' remonstrating with him, Jonathan came over to Latymer. 'I can't thank you enough,' he said. 'You've helped me as no one else could. I just keep thinking over and over, if only I'd told you all about it earlier.'

'So do I,' admitted Latymer. 'But then, hindsight's a wonderful thing.' He held out his hand and Jonathan took it. 'Good luck. I'll be keeping an eye on how you get on.'

He went to his car and set off at once for Bristol, thankful that at last the floods were receding. He would be leaving home at the crack of dawn in the morning to ensure he was at Heathrow to meet his tour group, and he'd promised the Berrys to tell them of his decision before he left. He'd arranged to meet them at the new premises but before doing so he called in to see his new landlord, paid his deposit, signed his lease and arranged to move in as soon as the first tour was over. The prospect of sitting around in his house waiting for it to be sold, faced with the possibility, in spite of what she'd said, of further hostile visits from Tess, was too much.

Finding his way to the new shop through the middle of Bristol held him up briefly, its one-way road system apparently devised for mathematical geniuses with expertise in cryptic crossword clues, but he made it successfully in the end. After talking to Fiona, he'd rung Berry and given him the bare bones of the story, promising to fill them both in properly over lunch. They greeted him warmly then showed him over the premises, enthusiastically pointing out its merits: a bigger shop front, more storage space and a room at the back which could be made into a proper office. When they'd finished extolling its virtues to him they bore him off to a rather smart restaurant for lunch, neither side voicing the matter exercising all three of them.

They sat down and finally Kate, unable to contain herself any longer, leaned across the table to Latymer and said, 'Well?'

'Well what?' he replied, with a grin.

'You know very well what.'

Latymer assumed a thoughtful expression, then frowned and drummed his fingers on the table. 'I don't know . . .' he began. Then seeing their faces laughed out loud. 'Then yes. The answer's yes. I will come in with you. I'll give my notice in to Becketts on the Monday after this tour. I'll obviously have to do the other two, but after that I'm free.'

'Er . . . and what about the other string?'

'The other string? Remind me.'

Berry threw his serviette across the table at Latymer, watched spellbound by the party at the next table.

'Well, possibly that too.'

'This,' said Berry, 'calls for a really decent bottle of wine!'

In a small room over a pub not far from his flat, Mark Ransom, James Weaver, Penny, and a handful of others met to wind up the Sustainable Agriculture Forum. It proved to be a short and acrimonious meeting. Almost all those who had taken part in the protest now knew that Friends of the Earth had specifically advised Mark Ransom against it, yet not only had he gone ahead, he'd allowed it to be hijacked, as one of them put it, 'by a bunch of thugs in green masks which had done their cause no good at all'. Not only that, the whole event had been linked to a particularly revolting murder, even if the local farmer on whose land the demo had taken place had now been charged with it. The SAF now had no standing of any kind with the people that mattered, rather the reverse. That being the case, the forum was officially wound up, what small funds were left in the kitty to go to Friends of the Earth.

Before he and Penny left, James enquired what, if anything, Mark was proposing to do with himself now. He'd hardly be welcomed with open arms by people like Greenpeace. 'I rather think I'll try and take a degree,' he told them, airily. 'There's a really interesting course at the University of Scunthorpe on the origins of Wicca, the history of witchcraft, that kind of thing.'

James gazed at him and shook his head. 'Wouldn't it be better to put your mind to something better than a Mickey Mouse degree like that? You could end up like Shrieve.'

'You always think you're so clever, don't you?' Mark responded and stalked out of the room in a huff.

'What makes me furious,' observed James when he and Penny had joined the others for a drink in the bar downstairs, 'is that protesting against growing this stuff is desperately important. The number of people who don't want GM foods at any price, or the rest of it polluted by cross-pollination, is growing all the time and the government is only paying lip service to "consultation", in spite of all the evidence we now have of cross-pollination miles away from the sites. Now nobody will remember what the reason was for our going to Lower Horton, only that there was mayhem and violence, followed by a murder which, whatever the truth of the matter, will sink into the collective consciousness as being part of it. They'll tar us all with the same brush. I could cheerfully have strangled Mark when I got back.'

There was general agreement. There was to be a major Friends of the Earth protest near Norwich in a couple of weeks' time and several of those present were taking part. 'See you there then, James?' said one of them, as he got up to leave.

'Not this time, mate,' he replied. 'Penny and I are getting married the week after next. With a bit of luck we'll be in Greece.'

* * *

In their house on the outskirts of Taunton a few days later, Diana and Peter were sitting next to each other on the sofa glowing with pride at the sight of their son, having finally been allowed to bring him home from hospital. Tess had seen to it that everything was immaculate and there were flowers in every room. The discussion now concerned the grand christening to be held the next month to which Tess's father and his wife had also been invited. Peter had thought Latymer should be asked along too, but this had been met so frostily by Tess and Diana that he had swiftly dropped the idea. The baby was to be christened Brian, after Peter's father, and George, because it was a name both Diana and Peter liked.

'With any luck, I could be in my own house by then,' Tess told them. 'I had a call from Dave Higham, the agent, this morning and the sale's going through without any trouble at all.'

'He's the one whose son's been in such trouble, isn't he?' commented Diana.

'That's right. He's out on bail. They say it shouldn't be too long before it comes up in Crown Court since the man who did the murder is pleading guilty, with extenuating circumstances.'

'Personally I don't think he should be punished at all,' said Peter. 'What kind of sick pervert sleeps with his own sister's kid? I reckon the father deserves a medal for what he did.'

Tess agreed. 'Though that's not what John thinks. I said that to him when he was driving me home and he said that it doesn't matter how justified you might feel, and this was a dreadful case, you can't put yourself above the law. But it doesn't bear thinking about. That farmer's lost a daughter, a grandchild and heaven only knows what it will do to his marriage.' The mention of Latymer resulted in an uncomfortable silence, finally broken by Tess. 'Right, I'll make some tea. Of course,' she said, putting her head back round the door, 'even when the sale does go through and I can move into my own house, I could always stay on for a while if you needed me.'

They assured her it wouldn't be necessary and as soon as she finally disappeared into the kitchen exchanged a speaking look. 'Thanks but no thanks,' commented Peter, *sotto voce*. 'I can't wait to have the house to ourselves again. Don't get me wrong,' he assured his wife, 'but your mother sort of fills it up!'

His tour over and the members of the party seen safely to Heathrow, Latymer stayed overnight in London then went down to Becketts' head office for his meeting with Stevens. The firm must be doing pretty well, he thought as he looked round Stevens' office, with its limed wood walls and steel and glass furniture. Stevens was in pompous mode.

'Well, I won't beat about the bush,' he boomed, after motioning him to sit down in an uncomfortable steel chair. 'Your recent work hasn't been up to scratch.'

'Have the tour parties been complaining then?' enquired Latymer.

'No, I can't say they have. It's as I told you, it's your whole attitude. What appears to be a growing lack of interest. It won't do. Therefore—'

'Before you say any more,' Latymer interrupted, 'I'd like to give you this.' He handed him an envelope. 'It's my resignation. As from the end of this series of tours.'

It was obvious Stevens hadn't been expecting it. He looked distinctly taken aback. 'I see . . . Well, I don't know what to say. I'd merely been going to suggest you worked up here for a while to get back in the swing of things, had a few chats with our marketing and human resources people. Are you sure you know what you're doing?'

Latymer smiled. 'Quite sure.'

'Have you another job in mind then?'

'Crime,' said Latymer. 'Selling it and investigating it.'